"I can't believe what I'm about to do."

Camilla carried her cat into the bedroom, brooding as she rested her chin on his head. She'd been worrying about her safety ever since the beginning of the school term when Jon Campbell had turned up in her classroom and scared her half to death.

But despite her fear, she was taking more and more risks—edging farther out onto thin ice with every day that passed.

"I *really* can't believe I'm doing this, Elton. I'm falling in love with his kids, and now I've actually agreed to go to his ranch this weekend. What on earth is wrong with me?"

She tossed the cat onto the bed, where he curled up and watched with interest as she opened her closet door.

"I don't have the slightest idea what to pack." She hauled down a couple of leather duffel bags from an upper shelf. "What exactly do you wear for a weekend jaunt with a man who terrifies you?"

ABOUT THE AUTHOR

Memories of You, Margot Dalton's seventeenth Superromance novel, is set in Calgary, Alberta, Canada, where she and her husband have recently decided to spend their winters. For Margot, it's like coming home. She was born in Alberta, and despite the cold temperatures, she takes pleasure in the clear, crisp, sunny days.

In addition to her Superromance novels, this bestselling author has also written seven books in Harlequin's popular Crystal Creek series. She has an upcoming title in the new Delta Justice series, and has contributed novellas to two anthologies. As well, she writes mainstream novels for MIRA Books.

Books by Margot Dalton

HARLEQUIN SUPERROMANCE

622—KIM & THE COWBOY
638—THE SECRET YEARS
664—MAN OF MY DREAMS
693—THE HIDING PLACE
714—A FAMILY LIKENESS

MIRA BOOKS

TANGLED LIVES (February 1996)
FIRST IMPRESSION (April 1997)
SECOND THOUGHTS (March 1998)

Don't miss any of our special offers. Write to us at the following address for information on our newest releases.

Harlequin Reader Service
U.S.: 3010 Walden Ave., P.O. Box 1325, Buffalo, NY 14269
Canadian: P.O. Box 609, Fort Erie, Ont. L2A 5X3

MEMORIES OF YOU
Margot Dalton

Harlequin Books

TORONTO • NEW YORK • LONDON
AMSTERDAM • PARIS • SYDNEY • HAMBURG
STOCKHOLM • ATHENS • TOKYO • MILAN
MADRID • WARSAW • BUDAPEST • AUCKLAND

ISBN 0-373-70749-5

MEMORIES OF YOU

MEMORIES OF YOU

PROLOGUE

June 1977

TODAY WAS MY seventeenth birthday; nobody remembered but me.

The rain is coming in the window again where some of the glass has broken away. Last week I nailed a scrap of tar paper across the opening, but it keeps coming loose. The rain blows in and falls onto my face and shoulders. I'm so cold.

I can hear them outside my room, so I turn my face to the wall and try to concentrate on the rain. It rattles on the metal body of the trailer like gunshots, and the whole thing shakes in every gust of wind.

They're both drunk, but my mother is worse. She's been screaming and throwing things. Now she's starting to cry, so it won't be long till she passes out. That's the way it always happens.

I wonder what shape the man is in. This is a new one, a guy she picked up last week at the bar. I don't know him yet, so I'm afraid. They're all like wild animals, you have to learn their habits so you can feel safe around them. This one looks at me sometimes, but he's never made a move.

He's so ugly. It makes my stomach heave, thinking

about him. I'm not sure my mother even realizes anymore how ugly they are. He's got a big roll around his middle and a spotty little beard, and his breath stinks. One of his front teeth is missing, too.

A bug scurries over my blankets, and I flick it away and hope it's gone. God knows what else is living in here. It's always so dirty. I try to clean things up but it's impossible because every night my mother brings some filthy man home to drink with her. They drop food and knock things over, then pass out on the floor or on her bed. They spill liquor, too, and it makes sticky pools that draw the bugs.

I can't hear my mother's voice anymore. She must be asleep. The man's singing some kind of drunken song. I remember how he looked at me earlier and I wonder if he's going to try to come in here tonight.

If he does, I intend to kill him. I have a hunting knife under the pillow and I'm not afraid to use it. I'm not.

Today is my seventeenth birthday.

CHAPTER ONE

Twenty years later

JON CAMPBELL WATCHED in surprise as the beautiful woman at the back of the classroom stared at him across the row of desks. It was just a few seconds, but it seemed like an eternity that their eyes locked, and the colour drained from her face.

Could she be startled because he was so much older than the rest of the class? Somehow her reaction seemed disproportionate.

He certainly wasn't the only middle-aged man who'd ever gone back to college to finish a degree. Even Jon had been surprised by the number of people his age he'd encountered on this first day of classes.

In fact, Jon wasn't the oddity he'd feared he might be. And the campus was big enough that he wouldn't be an embarrassment to his children, especially his son Steven who was a freshman at the same college.

While he was puzzling over the professor's reaction, the woman turned abruptly and made her way to the front of the room.

"Good morning," she said, moving away from her desk to stand in the middle of the room. "My name is Dr. Camilla Pritchard, and this class is intended to develop your creative-writing skills as well as to examine the work of some well-known authors. There is an extensive reading list that I will distribute at the conclusion of today's session. You will need to read every book promptly in order to be prepared for assignments and class discussions.''

Her voice was crisp, but her hands, gripping a notebook, trembled slightly. Again Jon wondered at her nervousness. Did she feel threatened by one of her students?

They all looked so young. This was a senior class, but the participants still seemed like babies, fresh-faced and anxious. A couple of them were chewing gum, while the thin boy sitting across the aisle from Jon appeared to be asleep.

''The workload is quite heavy,'' the professor went on. ''And, as you may have heard, I'm not tolerant of slackers.''

Jon grinned privately, amused by the contrast between her face and manner.

Oh, I'll bet you're not nearly as tough as you pretend, he told her silently.

She glanced at him almost as if he'd spoken aloud, and her cheeks turned faintly pink. She looked away quickly.

''There will be a daily writing assignment in addition to research papers and regular class work. If you feel this may be too much for you, I encourage you to drop the course immediately while you're still in time to transfer to a different class. Otherwise, you run a very real risk of being assigned a failing grade or an incomplete rating.''

No wonder some of the students complained about Dr. Camilla Pritchard, Jon thought. He'd overheard a group of young men earlier in the day, loudly discussing this English professor.

A ''dragon,'' one of them had called her. And then, practically in the same breath, a ''real babe.''

Now that Jon had seen her, he could certainly understand the boy's conflicting reaction. Camilla Pritchard was tall and graceful. Her face was finely carved, with high cheekbones and deep blue eyes, and she had an elegant straight nose.

But her beauty went beyond these physical attributes. There was something in the depths of that face, those remarkable eyes, that hinted at a person hidden in a complex private world.

Jon shifted awkwardly in the little desk as she began to discuss the process of creative writing, putting a few terms on the blackboard like ''stream of consciousness'' and ''constructionism.'' Jon tried to pay attention, but the sun from the adjacent window was warm on his back, and the room was so quiet, and he was not accustomed to this complete lack of physical activity.

Eventually his mind began to wander down sunlit paths of its own. He found himself wondering idly what the blond professor would look like in a bikini—or completely naked.

He shifted in his desk, aware suddenly of an uncomfortable stirring in his groin.

At that moment, the professor caught his eye. She'd moved nearer to ask a question of a student in the next row. Jon looked down hastily.

What a fool, he thought. Like a kid in seventh grade with a crush on the teacher, getting aroused by his daydreams. Next she'd ask him to go to the blackboard and he'd have to figure out some way to save himself from real embarrassment.

But the professor seemed reluctant to have anything to do with him. She directed rapid-fire questions at most of the others, but none at her oldest student.

Again Jon thought about that strange moment when their eyes had first met. She'd been so shaken.

Could they have met somewhere?

There *was* something about her that was vaguely familiar, but he couldn't get close to the memory. It was as elusive as the disappearing image of a half-forgotten dream. Maybe he was simply experiencing déjà vu.

After all, if he'd actually met somebody like her, he wouldn't be likely to forget her. Because she, without a doubt, was one of the most beautiful, desirable women he'd ever seen.

She moved toward the back of the room and stopped by the desk of the sleeping young man, who gave a start and looked up in alarm.

"Your name?" she asked.

The boy swallowed hard and cleared his throat. He was pale and obviously scared. He looked even younger than his classmates.

Probably no more than nineteen, Jon thought. Awfully young to be in a senior-level English class.

"Enrique," he whispered at last. "My name is Enrique Valeros."

"Do you intend to sleep through every class, Mr. Valeros?"

The boy had a shock of black hair, expressive dark eyes and clothes that were shabby but well tended. His voice was softly accented with the musical cadences of Spanish, and his thin hands trembled on the wooden surface of the desk. Jon couldn't tell if the tremor was because of fear, or fatigue.

"I'm very sorry, ma'am," he muttered. "It won't happen again."

Something about the boy tugged at Jon's heart. He wondered why Enrique Valeros was so tired, or what he was afraid of. A quick glance at the professor's blue eyes convinced Jon she shared these feelings of sympathy, though she was trying to remain stern and expressionless.

"I really hope it doesn't happen again, Mr. Valeros," she said.

She moved to the front of the room and picked up one of the books on her desk, a thick volume on grammar, punctuation and usage.

"This will be our only formal textbook," she told the class. "I expect you to obtain a copy and use it as your guide. Failure to comply will result in immediate deductions from your grade on all written assignments. Are there any questions?"

A sullen-looking young woman near the front of

the class asked for more details about the daily written assignment and the reading list. Dr. Pritchard clarified her expectations. Without another word, the girl picked up her books and left the classroom.

The professor surveyed the group. "Anybody else?" she asked. "Let me repeat that it's much better to leave now if you feel incapable of handling the work. In two or three weeks, dropping the course will no longer be an option."

The students listened silently.

"Mr. Valeros," she said, moving partway down the aisle, though she was still careful to keep a row of desks between herself and Jon, "have you had occasion to read *Silas Marner?*

"Yes, ma'am," the boy whispered. "I have read it."

"And what can you tell us about Eliot's narrative style in that book?"

"It... The book is much more..." Enrique struggled for words while the teacher watched him in silence. "It is more gentle and poetic than *Adam Bede,* or *Middlemarch,* he said at last. "It shows George Eliot's...it shows her quiet, mystical side."

The professor's eyebrows rose in surprise and approval. "Very good, Mr. Valeros. I'm pleased to see you've already done some of the required reading."

Enrique relaxed visibly under her praise. "I got the list a couple of weeks ago, ma'am," he said in a shy, almost inaudible voice.

"Well, that's excellent. Now, if you can find a way to stay awake in class, we'll get along just fine."

But her voice belied the sharpness of her words, and she gave the young man a brief, teasing smile before she turned away.

When Jon saw that glow on her face, he was totally undone. The woman's smile was like a ray of sunlight in a darkened room, illuminating all kinds of treasures. For a fleeting moment her face was light and sparkling, young and sweet.

Young...

Again that elusive image tugged at his memory. Something to do with warmth and youth, a distant place and time...

He shook his head in frustration and watched as she moved around the room, probing first one student and then another with her skillful questioning, trying to gauge their knowledge and understanding.

"Hey, Enrique," Jon whispered, leaning across the aisle.

"Yes?" the boy asked.

"You did good, son. I think you really impressed the professor."

His words were rewarded by another shy smile. The poor kid might be dead on his feet, but he was still courteous and friendly.

Jon glanced at the boy's frayed shirt cuffs, the worn-out shoes and patched jeans, the thin body and shaking hands and general air of fatigue.

He wondered how he could learn a little more about Enrique Valeros.

The class continued with a discussion of plotting techniques. The professor never asked him a question or directed a comment at him. Jon found himself both relieved and annoyed by the omission.

When the class ended and the students began to disperse, Jon approached her desk.

Dr. Pritchard's head was bent over her work. She had dark blond hair with a few streaks of sunny highlights, cut short and combed back in a simple, elegant style. Her hands were ringless, with the nails neatly trimmed and free of polish.

"I like that perfume," he said as he drew near.

She looked up, and her eyes widened in alarm. He could sense that she had to force herself to meet his eyes, though her gaze was calm and steady.

"Thank you," she said.

"What is it?"

"What?"

"The perfume."

Her cheeks turned faintly pink. "I doubt that it's any concern of yours, Mr...."

"Campbell. Jonathan Campbell. People usually call me Jon."

"I see." She gave him a wintry smile and returned to her work, clearly dismissing him.

Jon watched her for a moment, fighting the unsettling urge to reach out and stroke her shining hair or touch her bare arm.

"Is there something else. Mr. Campbell?" she asked without looking up.

"I was just wondering why you never called on me during the session. Do you think I'm not capable of answering questions?"

"The fact is, I didn't really think about you at all."

"I believe that's not altogether true," Jon said quietly. "When you first noticed me sitting over there, you acted like you recognized me."

"You must be imagining things." She got to her feet, gathered the pile of books on her desk and moved toward the door.

"Have we met somewhere?" he asked, following her. "Because I can't believe I'd ever forget a woman like you." She looked back at him, and this time he caught a trace of genuine panic in her eyes, a fear that was urgent and almost childlike. But her voice was cool when she answered.

"I really don't think so, Mr. Campbell. Please excuse me."

Then she was gone, vanishing down the crowded hallway until all he could glimpse of the woman was the distant gleam of overhead lights on her smooth blond head.

THE CALGARY UNIVERSITY sprawled over many acres of prairie in the northwest section of the city. A number of apartment buildings were located on campus but most faculty members chose to live elsewhere, preferring to leave their jobs behind when they went home at night.

Camilla Pritchard, however, lived on the university grounds. Her apartment was just a few steps from the building where she taught most of her classes.

She hurried down the leafy paths of the campus, heading home for lunch on the first day of school, anxious to reach her apartment. She could hardly wait to be safely inside the door, out of sight of everybody.

Camilla had suffered for years from intense shyness, and a personal reserve that gave her an air of detachment bordering on rudeness. Except when she was in her own home—a bright and comfortable place, filled with whimsical ornaments, bright woven afghans and wall hangings, nature prints, Aztec pottery and throw rugs. And masses of plants, crowded on every available windowsill.

She also had two cats, both illegal according to the rules of the buildings but tactfully overlooked by the apartment supervisor, who liked Camilla and found her a perfect tenant except for her pets.

In return for the super's indulgence, Camilla kept the cats out of sight. They were sleek gray tabbies called Madonna and Elton. Madonna had a boisterous, exhibitionist nature, while Elton, the smaller of the two, was timid and affectionate, named for the heavy black markings around both eyes that resembled the frames of the glasses worn by the famous pop star.

Today Elton was waiting when she came through the door. He promptly lay upside down on the rug in a golden ray of sunshine, his paws waving lazily.

"Okay Elly, I'll scratch your tummy for a second," she said. "But I have too much to do to stay here all day and play with you."

She sighed and dropped an armful of books onto the table, feeling a deep anxiety on this first day of classes. Normally she enjoyed the prospect of a new term, a horde of fresh faces, another fall and winter.

But not this year. Not after seeing one face in particular at the back of her classroom... She sighed again as she bent to rub Elton's tummy.

Madonna appeared in the kitchen entryway and arched her tail, rubbing herself sensuously against the door frame.

"I know it's him," Camilla stood up and addressed Madonna. "He's sitting right there in my English class, and I haven't got the slightest idea what to do about it."

Madonna licked one of her paws and rubbed it across her whiskers, then advanced with exaggerated stealth toward Elton, who still lay in the sunshine with his eyes closed. The cat pounced stiff-legged onto her unsuspecting partner. Elton yowled and scurried for cover beneath the couch, where his black-framed eyes could be seen peeping out fearfully from the darkness.

"Oh, sweetie." Camilla knelt on the carpet and peered under the couch. "Come out, Elly. Madonna didn't mean to scare you, she was just playing. Come, let's sit in the armchair and cuddle."

Elton whimpered and edged forward a couple of inches.

"Come on," she coaxed, reaching under the couch to stroke his furry paw. "Come out and sit with me. Madonna won't hurt you."

He crept toward her. Finally Camilla was able to grip his body gently and drag him out. She sat in an armchair and cuddled the shivering cat, resting her chin on the top of his head.

As she stroked the cat with rhythmic, soothing strokes, her mind kept going back to that shocking moment in class when she'd first seen Jon Campbell.

Even though he'd been seated, she could tell he was tall and well built. His square face was tanned and pleasantly masculine, his eyes clear and direct. He had thick brown hair dusted with gray, and his hands were hard and callused.

After that first horrifying moment of recognition, Camilla had kept hoping maybe he wasn't the man she remembered. But when he'd turned away to glance over at Enrique and she saw the hard line of his cheek, the aquiline profile, she knew it was true.

She clutched Elton tightly in her arms, trying to battle rising surges of memory. But the images were too insistent.

A boy, a motorcycle on a deserted road, a hot weekend in summertime...

Once more she tried to tell herself it couldn't possibly be the same person.

That all happened twenty years ago, and far away from here. This was a different world.

But Camilla knew beyond a shadow of a doubt that Jon Campbell was the man she remembered. Somehow he'd managed to find her again. And his presence here on this campus spelled terrible danger. It could mean an end to the whole careful life she'd struggled for twenty years to build.

CHAPTER TWO

CAMILLA FINALLY LEFT her cats and her apartment, feeling a little comforted but still worried and tense. She locked the door, hurried down the hall and entered the elevator. Three other people stood inside the little enclosure, a couple of graduate assistants and a young janitor with a mop and pail. Camilla greeted him with a smile.

The elevator doors opened as they reached the lobby. Camilla walked down a shady path to one of the buildings in the English department, then made her way through a maze of corridors to a suite of cramped, book-filled offices where she shared a secretary with three other professors.

"Hi, Camilla." The secretary looked up from her computer keyboard with a bright smile. "Did you have a nice summer?"

"Very nice, Joyce." Camilla took a bundle of files from one of the compartments. "How about you?"

Joyce shrugged. "I'm glad to be back at work. My kids were really driving me crazy."

"Didn't you manage to get away for that vacation in Banff? I remember how much you were all looking forward to it."

"Oh, that was fun, all right, but it only lasted two weeks. The kids always get so bored by the end of August."

"How old are they now?" Camilla paused, then shook her head. "My goodness, Jamie must be ten already. I can hardly believe it."

"He sure is. And Susan's eight. Little monsters," Joyce said darkly, but her smile was fond.

Camilla tried to imagine what it would be like to spend a whole summer with children that age.

Most of her experience with younger children involved the primary-school study group at the university. This class was made up of about fifteen gifted children aged six to ten years. The children came from all the western provinces to receive an accelerated education. They were also tested and observed by some of the senior professors who were doing research into intelligence.

"So, did you go home for the summer?" Joyce was asking.

"No," Camilla said after a brief hesitation. "I had a couple of papers to get ready for publication, so I stayed here and worked."

"What a pity. It must be beautiful in New England at this time of year," the secretary said wistfully.

"New England?" Camilla asked.

"Barry says your people have a summer home out there, near the Kennedy compound."

Camilla shifted the stack of books to her other arm, putting the files on top. "Well, I haven't been to New England in a long time," she said.

"Okay." Joyce gave her a conspiratorial wink. "Whatever you say."

Camilla hesitated for a moment, wondering what to say, then nodded and let herself into her little office. She dumped the books and files onto her desk, troubled by the secretary's words.

These rumors about Camilla's family had started circulating around campus a few years ago, and grew more outlandish all the time. By now, her half-hearted denials only served to make people more convinced that she came from a lavishly privileged, aristocratic background and chose for some reason to keep her private life a secret.

Although Camilla was sometimes dismayed by the exaggerated stories, she was grateful that they served to keep her colleagues a little intimidated. People seldom invited her to functions like staff parties and backyard barbecues, assuming that she wouldn't want to attend. As a result, she wasn't forced to get close to people, or form any relationships that required an uncomfortable level of disclosure about her personal life.

She was almost always lonely, but she was safe at home with her plants and books, her cats and her research work. And safety was more important to Camilla Pritchard than anything else.

Much more important...

She crossed the room and stood for a moment looking out the window at the throngs of students, wondering what her colleagues would think if they ever discovered the truth.

But, of course, none of these people could possibly learn the truth about Camilla Pritchard. As long as she kept everybody at arm's length, there was no danger.

She pushed aside the fears, sat down at her desk and began to work.

A knock sounded at the door. "Come in," she called.

The door opened and Gwen Klassen appeared, looking brisk and cheerful. She was one of the professors who shared their suite of offices and taught the class of gifted primary children in their bright, toy-filled study center down the hall.

"Hi, Camilla," she said, coming into the room. "I need to borrow a couple of your books on cognitive processes. Are you all ready for the new term?"

Camilla moved some papers so her colleague could sit on the corner of the desk. "Actually, I'm even less ready than usual."

"You?" Gwen asked. "Go on. You're so superorganized, I thought you always prepared about three years ahead," she said as she perched on the desk, swinging her feet in their white running shoes.

Gwen was about fifty, with a slim figure, a shock of gray hair and a manner so sunny and engaging that even Camilla's shyness and reserve tended to melt under its warmth. A born teacher, Gwen Klassen treated her scholarly colleagues exactly the way she did her little students, with a humorous, gentle indulgence that endeared her to everybody.

Camilla examined the file on her desk, containing

class lists and an outline of her teaching schedule for the fall term. "I mean, I'm not emotionally prepared. I feel less ready every term," she said in a rare display of her personal feelings. "I love teaching, but I keep thinking maybe I'm missing something. Like there should be...I don't know." She moved books around restlessly on her desk, trying to smile. "Maybe I'm just getting old."

Gwen looked down at her with surprise and sympathy. "It sounds more like you're getting burned out, honey. Why don't you consider applying for a sabbatical? You know they'd give it to you in a minute, because there's nobody on staff who deserves it more. You could spend a whole year doing research and writing, and come back feeling like a brand-new woman."

"I don't know what I'd do with myself if I took a sabbatical," Camilla said. "A year off from teaching would be too long. I just need...some kind of change, I guess."

"Like what?"

Camilla shrugged and leafed through some papers, embarrassed at having revealed so much of herself.

"Why don't you come over to my place on Friday night?" Gwen said casually. "Dan and I are having a few people over. Barry and his wife, and Gail and Joe from the administration office, and one of the new professors who's a whiz on the electric guitar. It should be a good time."

"I don't think so, thanks." Camilla smiled regretfully at the other woman. "It sounds like fun, but I have...I have a prior commitment."

To Camilla's relief, Gwen didn't ask about the commitment. Instead, she changed the subject with her usual tact.

"Did you go away at all?"

"Not really. I pretty much stayed home and looked after my cats, and did a lot of writing."

"That's not what Barry's been telling people," Gwen said with a brief grin.

Camilla sighed.

Barry Bellamy was another of their office-mates. He taught modern drama. He was a terrible gossip, and seemed fascinated by all the myths about Camilla's background. In some perverse way, he enjoyed retelling and embroidering these far-fetched stories, as if contact with such an imposing personage somehow gave him additional status.

Camilla found it all embarrassing, but she didn't know how to stop the man from gossiping and meddling in her life without revealing the dreadful truth about herself.

"Barry's too much," she said. "I don't know where he comes up with all the stories he keeps telling people."

Gwen gave her a keen, thoughtful glance. "So, have you looked over your class lists?" she asked after a moment.

"Briefly. The freshman class is pretty huge, but at least my senior-level creative-writing courses still look to be a decent size. I guess the full impact of the budget cuts hasn't reached us yet.''

Gwen smiled happily. ''Well, I've got a nice little group this year. You'll love them, Camilla. Your first session with my kids is scheduled for tomorrow afternoon, isn't it?''

Camilla checked her calendar. ''That's right,'' she said. ''Two o'clock. I'm planning to do a study with some of them on the relationship between symbol recognition and the early development of reading skills. I've been collecting the research materials all summer.''

''We've got the cutest pair of twins this year,'' Gwen said. ''Seven years old, named Aaron and Amelia. Just darlings, both of them.''

''Twins?'' Camilla said with interest. ''I don't believe we've ever had twins before.''

''I know. Even though they're fraternal twins, a boy and a girl, they look almost identical. Wait till you see them, Camilla. They've got the sweetest smiles, and IQ's so high we haven't even been able to measure them properly. But they're both quite reserved. I'm having a hard time getting close to them.''

''Where did they come from?''

''Out in western Saskatchewan. They were living on their family's cattle ranch, attending first grade at an elementary school so far away they had to spend almost two hours on the bus every day.''

''Are they boarding at the university?'' Camilla asked.

Gwen shook her head. ''Their father bought a property on the edge of the city. He's divorced—I'm not sure where the mother lives. But he moved out here with them so they could attend the study group.''

"What about the ranch? Did he have to sell it?"

"Apparently, money is no problem for this guy. He turned over the ranch to a foreman and flies his own plane back to Saskatchewan every weekend to oversee the ranching operation.''

"All this," Camilla asked, "just to get his kids into an accelerated program for a few years?''

"Not entirely. He also has a couple of other children who'll benefit from the better schooling opportunities in the city. In fact, one of them's a freshman here on campus. And guess what?''

"What?" Camilla asked.

"The man ... Jonathan Campbell, that's his name...he's actually taking a full load of courses himself. He says it's a good way to fill his time since he has to spend the winter in the city, and—'' Gwen stopped midsentence. "Camilla," she said in alarm. "You're as white as a sheet. Is something wrong?"

Camilla began to gather books and papers. "No, I'm fine. This man," she said with forced casualness, "the twins' father...how old is he?"

"Oh, probably about forty, I'd guess. Quite a handsome fellow in a rugged, Clint Eastwood kind of way. Apparently, he had a couple of years of college when he was young but never finished his degree, so now he's decided to go back to school along with his kids.''

Camilla got to her feet and lifted the pile of books.

"Well, I'm looking forward to meeting these brilliant little twins of yours," she said. "Help yourself to whatever books you need, Gwen. I'll see you later this afternoon, okay?"

She hurried out of the office and down the hall, trying to calm herself as she walked.

After all, she wasn't in any danger, Camilla reminded herself. Now that she was a fully tenured professor, her academic position here and her life were both utterly secure.

Being granted tenure had been, for many years, the most important concern in her life. She'd passionately wanted the security of that position.

Once she managed to acquire tenure, she was guaranteed a future that nobody could ever take away, no matter what happened.

She'd achieved this coveted status almost three years ago, and had hoped that, for the first time in her life, maybe she'd begin to feel safe.

But it hadn't worked that way. The fears remained, stirred by feelings of anxiety whenever people began to speculate about her personal background.

And now that Jonathan Campbell had inexplicably popped up once more in the middle of her life, she was more afraid than ever.

THE SUN WAS still hanging above the mountains when Jon finally bought the last of his textbooks, checked some materials out of the library and left the campus. He drove through the city of Calgary and headed west toward his new property, a sprawling acreage in the foothills of the Rockies.

He parked the car in the garage, walked past the aluminum hangar where his six-seater airplane was kept and strolled toward the house, which seemed unnaturally quiet in the early-autumn afternoon.

He glanced at his watch and realized it was almost time for supper. The kids liked to eat early, leaving plenty of time for their various activities in the evening. In fact, they might already be waiting for him. Margaret always had them wait for their father if there was any chance he might be home in time for dinner.

Jon quickened his steps, still looking at the big house. It was a modern split-level made of pale fieldstone, with a brown-tiled roof and banks of high, sharply angled windows.

A lot different from the comfortable old clapboard mansion at the ranch, with its shady veranda and white picket fences.

Again he reminded himself that this move was necessary. Besides, it was only temporary. In a few years when the twins were older the bus ride wouldn't be so hard on them. Then they'd all be able to go back to the ranch full-time.

He walked up a path at the side of the house and let himself inside, pausing to wash his hands and hang up his hat and jacket. Then he entered the kitchen where a storm was brewing.

"You little *animal*," Vanessa shouted, gripping the telephone receiver in one hand as she glared across the room at her seven-year-old brother. "You absolute *beast.* Ari, give me that before I kill you!"

Aaron smiled up at her with maddening calm. He stood in the doorway holding a book in his hands. Amelia hovered just behind him, eyeing their sister with a cautious, frightened expression.

The twins were beautiful children with curly dark hair clipped short around their heads, and slim, straight bodies. Amelia had green eyes while Ari's were gray, and she was a little smaller than her brother. Apart from these slight differences, they were very similar in appearance.

During their early years, the twins had hardly spoken to anyone but each other, and they still inhabited a private world that few adults were allowed to enter. Ari was usually the instigator, impulsive and creative. Amelia acted as his partner and support, always ready to help him carry out his schemes.

While Vanessa watched in speechless outrage, Ari opened the book and pretended to read from it. "I just love Jason Weatherly," he said in a loud, exaggerated voice. "When he smiles at me across the room in math class, I go all—"

Vanessa screamed, dropped the receiver and lunged at her little brother.

Ari dodged away from her and ran around the kitchen, still reading. "I go all shivery inside, and then I feel..."

The teenager continued to scream. Steven, Jon's elder son, watched idly from the adjoining family room where he lounged on a couch, watching television. None of the children seemed to be aware of Jon's arrival on the scene.

Vanessa tripped on the kitchen tiles and fell sprawling to her knees. She crouched on the floor, glaring furiously, long dark hair falling messily around her face.

When Jon strode into the middle of the room, an abrupt silence fell. He crossed the kitchen, lifted the telephone and said, "Vanessa will call you back."

Then he hung up and turned to face his children.

"Where's Margaret?"

Nobody answered. The only sounds were Vanessa's heavy breathing and the roar of gunfire on the television.

Jon looked from one young face to another. "Where's Margaret?" he repeated.

"In the garden," Steven said at last. "She went out to pick some tomatoes for the salad."

"I see." Jon turned to his younger son, who stood near the archway leading to the family room. "What's that book, Ari?"

"Van's diary," Ari said reluctantly.

"What are you doing with your sister's diary?" Jon asked. "You know better than to go into somebody else's bedroom."

"It wasn't in her room," Ari said.

Amy stood close behind him, lending support with her presence. She nodded earnestly.

"Where was it?" Jon asked.

"Under the couch." Ari gestured toward Steven in the family room. "She left it right over there in plain sight. We found it when Margaret made us clean up our Lego.''

"You horrible little monsters,'' Vanessa muttered, getting to her feet. "*Do* something, Daddy,'' she added bitterly. "You always let them get away with everything.''

Jon looked at his elder daughter with a familiar mixture of sympathy and exasperation. At sixteen, Vanessa was a beautiful girl, and bright enough that she was already in her final year of high school. But her looks and personality were so similar to her mother's that he often worried about her.

Jon and Shelley Campbell had suffered through a dozen years of a stormy, unhappy marriage, complicated by the fact that they shared almost nothing in the way of tastes, dreams or attitudes. In fact, they shared nothing at all except their children, and Shelley's interest in her offspring had always been so limited that even this tie was tenuous at best.

Jon had met her when he she was nineteen and he was twenty-two. It had been immediately after the most distressing experience of his life, a painful time that he still remembered with frustrated sorrow.

Lonely and desolate, Jon had been an easy target. He'd mistaken Shelley's sexuality for warmth, her frenetic gaiety for intelligence, her possessiveness for loyalty. By the time he discovered his mistake, it was too late. She was pregnant with Steven, and both Jon and Shelley came from families where getting married was the only possible course of action.

After Steven's birth, Jon couldn't bring himself to

leave, for fear of losing his child, though the marriage was increasingly miserable. By the time Vanessa was born, less than two years later, Shelley had interests of her own and was seldom home.

The twins had been the unexpected result of a final attempt at a reconciliation. Shelley was appalled when she discovered her third pregnancy. She demanded an abortion.

Jon had talked her into carrying the twins to term, but it was the last straw for their marriage. Soon after the birth, angry and bitter, claiming that the kids were all he'd ever cared about, Shelley dumped all four children with him and left for good.

At the moment she was living in Switzerland, using her lavish divorce settlement to support the young ski instructor who was her current lover. She barely managed a couple of trips a year back to the States to see her brood of growing children, and when she did fly in for visits, all of them were invariably hurt and disappointed by her flippant, erratic manner.

Still, she was a beautiful woman, Jon thought ruefully. Even at forty, Shelley looked a lot like her older daughter, with the same violet-blue eyes, delicate complexion and slim figure. But Vanessa at least had an excuse for her selfish behaviour, since she was caught in the miserable throes of adolescence. Jon had hopes that his daughter might yet develop into a mature and caring person. Shelley, on the other hand, simply refused to grow up.

Jon turned from Vanessa to look at Ari. "Just because Van left her diary out here doesn't give you the right to read it," he said. "Everybody's entitled to privacy and respect for their belongings, Ari. Give me the book."

Ari moved forward silently and handed the diary to his father.

Behind him, Amy's green eyes filled with tears. Jon knew his children well enough to understand a little of what was going on with the twins.

They'd never known the security of a mother who loved and cared about them. Over the years Jon had tried hard to make up for their loss, but he knew they were as hurt and confused as the older children by their mother's carelessness. As a result, they tended to cling fiercely to familiar and comforting things.

Now they'd been uprooted from the isolated ranch home they both loved. Their security was further disrupted by this move to a strange new environment, a different kind of school and a modern, unwelcoming house.

Their loneliness and homesickness tore at Jon's heart. He knelt on the kitchen floor and took Amy's little body in his arms, reaching for her brother. "Come here, Ari," he said.

Ari hesitated, then pressed against him.

"Tell Van you're sorry," Jon whispered. "Tell her you'll never do it again."

Ari gulped, swallowed hard and turned to Vanessa. "We're sorry," he mumbled.

"We won't touch any of your stuff ever again," Amy added.

"Daddy, for God's *sake*," Vanessa began furiously. "Don't let them get away with this! You should make them…"

But Jon was holding the twins again, cuddling them tenderly. "How would you both like to come with me to the ranch this weekend?" he murmured against their dark curls.

Ari's gray eyes shone. "Really, Daddy?" he whispered huskily.

"Really. But you have to be super-good between now and then." Jon kissed Amy's cheek and wiped her tears. "Now run and wash your face, sweetheart," he said gently. "Let's eat our supper."

While the twins ran out of the kitchen, he got up and seated himself at a big oak table that was neatly set for seven.

When the twins came back, all four children joined him silently. A side door opened, and Margaret came in from the garden, carrying a basket of ripe tomatoes.

The housekeeper was a big, friendly young woman with a mop of red hair and plump freckled arms. She had a boyfriend who worked on the oil rigs north of Edmonton, and who came home infrequently to visit his sweetheart. This erratic courtship seemed to suit both of them well enough, much to Jon's relief. Margaret was the only housekeeper he'd ever found who was able to deal patiently and lovingly with all the children, and he dreaded the thought of losing her.

She greeted Jon with a smile and carried the tomatoes to the sink.

"What's all this?" she asked when she saw Amy's reddened cheeks.

"They've been reading my diary," Vanessa said sullenly. "But Daddy refuses to punish them, as usual. Little monsters," she muttered, glowering at Amy, whose eyes began to glisten with tears again.

"Poor little chicks." Margaret ruffled Amy's dark curls. "That's all right, love. You know, Ari, you shouldn't have touched that book," she said, turning to the other twin. "Did you apologize to your sister? Poor Vanessa, she has to put with an awful lot from the pair of you. Steven Campbell, don't you dare start eating till your daddy has a chance to dish up the food."

The tension left the room with her cheerful arrival and evenhanded approach. All the children watched as Margaret served bowls of salad and sliced tomatoes along with a macaroni casserole.

Jon sat at the head of the table, looking around at the young faces that were so dear to him.

The twins had obviously been comforted by their promised trip to the ranch. Even Vanessa appeared somewhat mollified. Only Steven was quiet, his handsome face looking bored.

Steven resembled his father more than any of the other children, but nowadays he lacked any trace of Jon's casual air or easy smile.

Jon felt increasingly troubled about the boy.

When Steve was a child, they'd had a warm, open relationship. Father and son had spent long hours together on their windswept prairie ranch as they fished, rode horses and tramped through the coulees. These days, though, Steve was slipping further away from the entire family, wrapped up in some mysterious world that Jon could no longer enter.

"How are your classes, Steve?" he asked.

The boy shrugged. "Okay, I guess."

Jon glanced at his elder son again, but didn't press. Instead, he turned and addressed the twins. "Tom called me last night. He says the calves are just about ready to sell."

"What else did he say?" Ari asked.

Tom Beatch was the foreman at the ranch, a grizzled old cowboy who was a great favorite with the twins.

Jon told the children the news from Tom and the other cowboys, including the latest in Tom's sporadic courtship of Caroline, who ran a lunch counter in a Saskatchewan border town.

"Those two will never get together," Margaret said placidly from the sink. "Tom Beatch doesn't want to get married any more than my Eddie does."

"When's Eddie coming back?" Jon asked the housekeeper.

"Next month," Margaret said, beaming. "He'll be home for a whole week at least, then off north to look for work again."

Jon looked at the twins, whose animation at the mention of Tom seemed to have disappeared. They were picking at their food, looking disconsolate. Apparently, their homesickness was as deep as ever. He sighed and cut up a tomato, searching for something else to say.

"Tom's getting real worried about me," he told

the children finally. "He wonders what I'm going to do with myself for a whole winter here in the city."

Steven gazed out the window at the trees bordering the front driveway, clearly lost in his own thoughts. The twins exchanged an unhappy glance and continued to move bits of macaroni around on their plates while Margaret watched them.

Only Vanessa, who seemed to have recovered from her sulks, was interested in what her father was saying. "I know what I'd do," she told him. "I'd spend the whole day shopping. I'd buy every single thing I ever wanted, and spend all day trying clothes on."

Jon watched her pretty face, wondering whether her preoccupation with material things was just a teenage phase—something she would outgrow. "Well, Van, I know what I'm going to do, too," he said calmly. "I've got it all planned. In fact, I started today."

"What's that, Mr. C.?" Margaret got up and began to load the dishwasher.

"I'm going back to school." Jon helped himself to more casserole while the others watched in astonishment. "I had my first two classes today."

Vanessa's jaw dropped. "Back to *school?*" she said at last. "Like, to college, you mean?"

Jon smiled at his elder daughter. "Don't look so amazed," he said. "I took two years of college when I was young, then had to quit before I graduated. I thought this would be a good opportunity for me to finish my degree."

Vanessa gripped her fork and continued to stare at her father, aghast. "You're going to *university?*" she asked. "On the same campus with Steven? The same place I'll be going next year?"

"The very same," Jon told her solemnly.

She dropped her fork, speechless with horror. Privately, Jon was a little amused by her reaction, but took care not to show it. In fact, he often tried deliberately to ruffle Vanessa's feathers to keep her from getting as self-absorbed as her mother.

But this time, judging from her look of white-lipped shock, it seemed Jon might have pushed his daughter too far.

"It's a big campus, Van," he told her gently. "Thousands and thousands of students. Nobody's going to notice me."

"But what if you're in one of my *classes* next year?" she wailed. "God, I'd just *die*."

Steven's lip twisted. "Oh, shut up, Van," he muttered. "Why do you always have to be such an idiot?"

Jon frowned at him and turned back to Vanessa. "I won't be in any of your classes, You'll be a freshman. I'll be taking fourth-year courses next term."

"But having my *father* on the same campus..." Her face twisted with distress. "This is the worst thing that's ever happened to me," she said tragically. "The totally, absolute worst." She pushed her chair back, got up and ran from the room.

There was a brief silence in the kitchen.

"She'll get over it, Mr. C.," Margaret said comfortably. "She gets upset about a dozen times a day, and every time it's the very worst thing that's ever happened to her.''

Jon looked at the doorway where his daughter had vanished. "I'll talk to her later," he said. "She won't be so upset once she realizes that our paths are never likely to cross on that big campus."

Steven's brief spurt of animation had vanished. He ate macaroni in gloomy silence.

"How about you, son?" Jon asked. "Will it bother you, having me on campus?"

Steven shrugged. "Why should I care?"

"You don't seem to care about much of anything these days," Jon said, trying to keep his voice casual. "What's the matter, son?"

Steven looked at him with a brief flash of emotion, and Jon held his breath, hoping the boy was about to say something meaningful. But the moment passed and they all returned to their meal, eating in silence while Margaret continued to load the dishwasher.

A COUPLE OF HOURS LATER, on a hill near the house, Ari lay on his stomach in the slanted rays of evening sunlight. He drummed his feet on the ground as he chewed a spear of grass.

"Churks," he muttered. "Fizzlespit."

Amy looked at her brother with tense sympathy. These words were part of their private language, seldom used and shockingly profane. The fact that Ari was saying them now showed how sad and lonely he was.

"We get to fly to the ranch this weekend," she

said, watching a dark green beetle as it lumbered through the tangle of grass. "Daddy promised. It'll be fun to see Tom and ride our ponies, won't it?"

But Ari wasn't ready to be comforted. "I wish Daddy would get married." He plucked another blade of grass. "We need a mother."

Amy turned to him in confusion. "We already have a mother."

"I mean, we need one who lives in our house. If Daddy got married, we'd all move back to the ranch and live together and be like a family."

"Do you think so?" she asked wistfully.

"If Daddy was married, he wouldn't worry so much what school we went to. When Mummy was home, Daddy and Van and Steve all lived on the ranch together. I hate being in this place."

"It's not so bad here," Amy said loyally. "Daddy wants us to go to school without having to ride so far on the bus, and Mrs. Klassen is really nice. I like the aquarium at school," she added. "And the model of the hydrogen molecule. Don't you?"

Ari scowled. "I want to go back to the ranch. We need to find a lady for Daddy to marry."

"Maybe he could marry Margaret."

"You're so *dumb*," Ari said. "Daddy could never marry Margaret."

"Why not? She's nice to us all the time, and she cooks and cleans and everything."

"I don't know," he admitted after a few moments of deep concentration. "But it can't be Margaret. It needs to be somebody different."

"Like who?"

"I don't *know*," Ari repeated. "But I'll think of somebody."

The twins lay quietly for a while. Then, like birds or fish moving in response to an invisible signal, they got up at the same moment and began to run, swooping down the grassy hill with their arms spread wide and their legs flying.

They ran until they were exhausted, then climbed another hill, heading for one of their favorite places on the new farm. It was the oldest building on the property, a big stone barn nestled at the foot of the hill and surrounded by trees.

The previous owner had used the barn to house a couple of vintage automobiles, and several improvements had been added to protect the valuable cars. All the windows were stoutly boarded, and a metal overheard door that was operated from outside by pressing a button had been installed. The control button was inside a panel that could be secured with a padlock.

Although the lock had been removed along with the contents of the barn, the control button remained functional. Ari loved to press it and watch the big door slowly open and close, sliding as if by magic.

When Vanessa reported on the existence of the automatic door, Margaret had immediately forbade the twins to play anywhere near the barn because they might get locked inside, a suggestion that made Ari scoff privately in derision.

"How could we get locked inside?" he asked Amy

when they were alone. "You have to be *outside* to push the button. Margaret doesn't know anything."

So they ignored the housekeeper's order and continued to frequent the barn. Amy was a little anxious about their disobedience, but her loyalty to Ari always outweighed her caution.

Now she followed him down the hill and crept along behind him as he edged toward the old building. The door was open which meant that somebody was inside.

Ari glanced over his shoulder and nodded. Amy understood at once, following him to the base of one of the trees beside the barn. The twins climbed silently into the middle branches, then moved out of the tree onto the shingled roof and crept up toward the row of air vents.

These vents were about two feet square and situated near the peak of the roof. Each twin stopped at the edge of an open vent. They clung to the rough shingles and slithered forward until they could peer down into the shadowy depths of the barn.

Steven's yellow sports car was parked in the shadows, and Steven himself sat with three other boys on some baled hay as they passed a skinny cigarette back and forth.

The twins exchanged a wide-eyed, startled glance, then edged forward for a better look.

They'd never seen these boys, who must have slipped onto the property through a back road. They were a tough-looking group, hard-faced and scary, not at all like the happy neighboring kids who used to be Steven's friends on the ranch.

The twins watched the four boys for a moment, then withdrew from the vents and looked at each other in alarm.

They slid back down the roof, melted into the tree branches and considered their next move.

"We should tell Daddy," Amy said in a hushed voice. "Let's bring him over here. They're not supposed to be smoking."

Ari shook his head.

"Why not?" Amy whispered. "The hay might catch on fire. Then the barn would be wrecked."

"It can't burn," Ari muttered. "It's made of stones."

"But we should—"

He waved a hand to silence her. She settled more comfortably on the branch and swung her foot, liking the feeling of being up in the sky, hidden like a bird among the rustling green leaves.

But she didn't like the boys who were down in the barn with Steven. They looked mean and threatening, like bad dogs who might bite you for no reason.

"We could push the button and close the door," Ari said at last. "If we do, they can't get out. They'll be trapped."

Amy shivered. "No, Ari. It's so dark and scary in there."

"Serves them right," Ari said. "They're bad, and Steve shouldn't be with them. Dad would be mad if he knew what they were doing."

"But it's really mean to lock them inside the barn. You know it is."

He avoided her eyes, looking down at a long scratch on his ankle.

"Besides," Amy went on, "if we close the door and trap them, Daddy will lock up the button so we can't open the door by ourselves anymore. He was going to do it last week but he forgot. Let's just go away and leave them alone."

Ari was on the point of climbing down from the tree. He scowled and hesitated.

Amy pressed her advantage. "It's so much fun to play in there, Ari. If Daddy locks the barn, we won't be able to get inside."

"We could get a rope and swing down from the air vents like mountain climbers."

Amy thought about the peak of the barn, almost as tall as the tree they were sitting in. "It's too high. Besides, how would we get back up?"

"We could climb the rope," he argued, but Amy could tell that he was weakening.

With relief, she turned and began to climb down the tree, slipping rapidly through the leaves and branches until she dropped to her feet on the hillside.

Ari joined her, and they ran back up the hill toward the flaring colors of the sunset, their small bodies lost in the vastness of the prairie sky.

CHAPTER THREE

SOMEHOW, CAMILLA MANAGED to get through the remainder of the first day in a blur of classes, meetings and seminars. By the time she finished her office work and sent her reading lists to the library to be posted, it was twilight.

The campus was peaceful in the slanting rays of light, with small groups of students strolling and talking quietly. Thunderheads were beginning to mass beyond the snowcapped mountains and the sky was vivid with sunset colors—streaks of orange and dusty pink and violet.

Though it was still early in September, the air already carried a hint of frost, and some of the trees were beginning to wither. A few leaves drifted to the sidewalk in front of her, crunching underfoot as she walked toward her apartment.

Camilla looked down at the fallen leaves, lost in a deepening melancholy.

Madonna and Elton were both at the door when she entered her apartment. They welcomed her with enthusiasm, mewing and rubbing frantically against her legs, which only happened when they wanted something. Camilla soon determined that Elton was hungry, while Madonna was eager to go outside.

Camilla opened the glass balcony door to let Madonna escape into the branches of the adjacent poplar, then set her pile of books on the kitchen table and filled Elton's bowl with dry cat food.

While he was eating, Camilla went into the bathroom and ran the tub, adding a liberal dash of scented bubbles. She stood at the counter to take out her contact lenses, then stored them in their little plastic case. She rubbed her eyes with relief as she looked at herself in the mirror.

The change was always so dramatic, because her eyes weren't blue at all. They were actually a clear, pale gray, like the sky on a cloudy day.

She'd chosen the tinted lenses mostly for practical reasons, because they were easier to find if she dropped or misplaced one of them. But tonight she was gratified to see again how much the lenses altered her appearance.

When Jon Campbell had seen her all those years ago, she'd had gray eyes....

Camilla touched the bridge of her nose, then picked up a hand mirror to study her profile critically. The plastic surgeon had repaired the cartilage in her nose skillfully. But back in that long-ago summer, her nose had been freshly broken and wasn't healing properly. It had been noticeably crooked, and somewhat thicker at the bridge.

And her hair, too, had darkened a lot over the last two decades. Twenty years ago, her long braid had been pale blond, almost silver, hanging all the way to her waist.

Camilla put the mirror aside, stripped off her clothes, turned off the faucet and stepped into the tub, settling with a weary sigh among the fragrant mounds of bubbles.

Perhaps the man wasn't lying, after all. It seemed quite possible that he didn't recognize her, and he'd only arrived in her classroom by some kind of ghastly coincidence.

When their eyes first met, he'd looked puzzled by her own shocked reaction. There'd been no answering spark of recognition from him, no meaningful smirk or veiled threat. Just a look of good humour, masculine admiration and a readiness to smile and respond if she gave him any encouragement.

Jon Campbell seemed too blunt and forthright to carry off some kind of sinister deception. Still, she could hardly dare to hope that the man truly had forgotten what happened between them twenty years ago in that dirty motel room.

Camilla lowered herself among the bubbles so the water came to her chin. She lifted a slim foot and touched the faucet with her toe, idly tracing the outlines of the gleaming brass.

Maybe, for once in her life, she was going to be lucky. Perhaps the tinted contact lenses, her nose surgery, darkened hair and a few more inches of height were going to be enough to disguise her real identity from Jon Campbell.

Briefly she wondered what the man was like, how he'd turned out after all these years.

He seemed similar in some ways to the boy she

remembered, but there were subtle differences, as well. Jonathan Campbell now had a look of wealth and power, despite the casual air. He was obviously a man with a privileged background and enough money to do anything he wanted—even go back to college full-time if he chose.

In fact, he seemed to be everything the campus myths claimed *her* to be. Camilla smiled grimly at the irony, then sobered and reached out to run more hot water into the tub.

Regardless of what he'd become, he was a threat to Camilla, and she knew she had to get the man out of her life quickly to preserve her own safety.

Elton wandered into the room, licking his whiskered chops with satisfaction. He stood erect, with his front paws resting on the edge of the tub, and stared at her solemnly. Camilla blew a couple of soap bubbles into his face, making him blink.

She smiled sadly. "Too bad a professor can't just walk out of a class the way her students do. Should I drop that creative-writing class, Elton?"

The cat watched her with his usual inscrutable expression.

"Oh, I know. You're right, of course," Camilla said. "Dr. Pritchard can hardly drop a class simply because…"

Because the professor happens to share some unpleasant and embarrassing sexual history with one of her students.

Camilla's throat tightened with anxiety. Of course,

she had the power to remove a student from her class, but in order to do that she'd need a good reason.

Maybe if the work was hard enough, the man would quit of his own accord. After all, he'd probably been away from college for more than twenty years, presumably doing a lot of rugged, outdoor work, if his callused hands were any indication. No doubt he was going to find it difficult to adjust to the daily grind of classes and homework.

Camilla's spirits lifted a bit.

Maybe she could give out the individual research assignments a couple of weeks early, and find some way to make Campbell work harder than anybody else. But she'd have to do it soon—before he had a lot more opportunities to sit at the back of that room and study every detail of her face and body.

Camilla climbed from the tub, dried herself on a big green towel and slipped into a terry-cloth robe and slippers, then made her way to the kitchen with Elton at her heels. She brewed a pot of herbal tea, put a small frozen entrée into the microwave and spread her books out on the glass-topped table.

What assignment could she give Jon Campbell? It had to be something tedious enough to convince the poor man that he wasn't really interested in completing a senior writing class.

Camilla put on her reading glasses and began to work. After a few minutes, the microwave beeped and she got up, carried the tray to the table, picked up a fork and ate without tasting the food.

A short while later Camilla returned to her problem.

Maybe an analysis of character development in Chaucer?

How about a comparison of editorial styles of seven major newspapers, or a definitive look at the American novel from Hawthorne to Updike...

The pages blurred in front of her eyes. Camilla took off her glasses and dropped her head into her hands, rubbing her temples wearily.

It was beginning to rain. She could hear the heavy drops flowing down the windowpanes, pattering on the floor of the balcony. The sound was seductive, almost mesmerizing, carrying her back through the years.

Back to 1977, and the terrible events of that early summer...

July 1977

IT'S RAINING AGAIN, but I'm so cold and dirty that I don't care anymore. It's weird how people are always so afraid of being caught in the rain, as if getting wet is the worst thing that can happen to them. I've spent the last three nights out in the rain, sitting in the ditch by the highway with a jacket over my head. My clothes are filthy, my hair's all stringy and I haven't eaten since...I can't remember the last time I had anything to eat.

It's been a couple of days at least, but the hunger pangs have mostly passed. I'm dizzy a lot of the time and I still feel like throwing up whenever I remember what happened.

My knife didn't help me a bit when he finally came to my room. He just laughed and snatched it from me like it was some kind of toy. When I tried to fight back, he hit me so hard that I could feel my nose breaking. The taste of blood in my throat sickened me almost as much as the things he was doing to me.

I can't bear to think about the things he did. I won't think about it. I won't...

After he was finished, he rolled over and fell asleep. I got up, found the knife on the floor and jammed it as far as I could into his chest. He shouted and thrashed around, clutching at the knife handle. I don't know if I killed him, but I hope so. I didn't stay long enough to find out, I just grabbed some clothes and money and ran away.

My mother was passed out in the living room when I left. She never even knew what happened.

I'm not sure what I'm going to do next. After what he did to me, nothing matters anymore. It doesn't matter what I do.

But I have to eat if I want to stay alive, so I'll probably get to the city and start selling myself on the street. I'll have to find some way to get cleaned up first, though. Nobody would pay to have sex with a girl who looks the way I do right now. It's been two weeks since I ran away, and I haven't seen a mirror for a long time so I don't know if my nose has started to heal. It doesn't hurt quite so much anymore, but I think it's still pretty swollen.

I'm kind of scared at the thought of being a prostitute. Until he did what he did, I'd never even... nobody had ever touched me before. But now it doesn't matter. Nothing matters. I just have to find some way to get a little money. I have to clean myself up and wash my hair, and find some clothes somewhere.

The sky is starting to lighten, and the sun will be rising soon. Meadowlarks are singing on the prairie all around me. They sound almost crazed with happiness. It's amazing how the dawn can still be so clean and beautiful when it shines down on a world as ugly as this.

I'm sitting on a piece of cardboard in a wide, grassy ditch, and I'm stiff and cold, sore all over. I'd give anything to have a hot meal and a bath. A hot bath would be the most wonderful thing in the world.

Maybe I can flag down one of the semitrailers that keep passing on the highway, and get to the city that way. But people are such busybodies. The driver will want to know where I came from. He'll take me to the police and they'll either put me in jail for murder or send me back home.

Home.

God, what a laugh. I'll die before I go back there. But I don't know what else to do, and I'm so scared. I'm really scared. The mist is clearing and I can see for a little way down the ditch. There's a man over there by the intersection. He must have stopped sometime during the night. He's got his motorcycle pulled off the highway, and he's been camping in a little tent. Now he's up and moving around. He's got a portable stove set up on some rocks. I can smell bacon frying.

Oh, Lord, it smells so good! I think he's brewing coffee, too. Maybe a guy on a motorcycle won't be so likely to call the cops.

Before I can lose my nerve, I get up and begin walking down the ditch toward him. It's funny, I'm putting one foot in front of the other but I'm not sure if I'm still upright. The world is spinning, and all of a sudden there's sky where the ground is supposed to be.

I feel somebody kneeling beside me, lifting me. Now I can see a face. It's not really a man at all, just a boy not much older than me. He's got blue eyes and thick brown hair, and he looks so nice....

SHE LOOKED BLANKLY at the streaming window. Tears spilled down her cheeks. She wiped at them with the back of her hand, then fumbled in her pocket for a wad of tissues.

Finally, she pushed the books aside, stumbled into her living room and curled on the couch, hugging her knees. She switched on the television and let waves of brightly coloured images wash over her, drowning the painful memories in gusts of canned laughter.

NEXT MORNING, Camilla crossed the campus and went into the arts building. She bypassed her office and headed straight for the large theater where she taught freshman English.

Ninety-six students were registered this term, practically an impossible number. She sighed when she looked up at the tiered rows of seats filled with anxious young people.

While they stared down at her in hushed stillness, she moved across the front of the room, set her books on the desk and found the class list.

"Good morning. My name is Dr. Pritchard."

There was a nervous murmur of greeting.

"When I read your name," Camilla went on, "please indicate your presence with the word *here* and a raised hand so I'm able to check you off on the list. Regular attendance in class is vital because we'll be moving rather quickly through a very large body of material. Anybody who skips more than two sessions without a valid excuse will receive a grade of incomplete on the term. Is that understood?"

The students nodded.

Camilla looked down at her alphabetized class list. "Aaronson?"

"Here."

"Anders?"

"Here."

"Appleby?"

"Yo, Doc!"

Camilla glanced up sharply. Appleby, who wore a bandanna and a couple of earrings, gave her a cherubic smile and waved. Camilla ignored him and went on reading names.

The sixth name was Campbell, and Camilla looked up at the speaker.

My God, it's Jon! she thought in confusion. But how can it possibly…that was twenty years ago, and I saw the man yesterday in my…

She struggled to get her thoughts under control while the students watched her curiously.

Of course. This had to be Jon Campbell's son.

He was no more than eighteen or nineteen, but he looked exactly like Jon as a young man. This boy had the same clean-cut good looks and direct blue eyes, the thick brown hair highlighted by streaks of gold after long days in the summer sun…

Camilla took herself firmly in hand and continued to call off the students' names, stealing a couple of glances at Steven Campbell as she read.

Despite the physical resemblance, he certainly didn't have the same open, pleasant look that Jon used to have. This boy seemed sullen and morose, coldly withdrawn.

Still, the unexpected appearance of him in her class was unnerving. And yet, deep down, there was a warm and unsettling feeling of excitement, too, when she looked up at the boy and remembered…

Twenty years ago, she told herself. Long ago, lost in the past.

Not even Jon Campbell remembered.

She shoved the thoughts out of her mind and finished taking attendance, then spoke to the students.

"Open your notebooks and write me a two-page essay about your goals in life," she said amid a chorus of groans.

"What if I don't have any?" Appleby inquired, grinning around at his fellow students.

Camilla gave the boy a thoughtful glance. "Goals don't necessarily have to be personal, Mr. Appleby. If you have no goals for yourself, perhaps you have some for the human race, or for the planet. At any rate, I want a two-page essay on goals, and I want it to be accompanied by your full name, and your class and student number so I can begin to get to know each of you."

Steven Campbell glared into the distance for a while, concentrating, then began to write. Although she was still badly shaken by the boy's presence, Camilla found herself looking forward to reading his essay.

She moved around the room, up and down the tiers of seats while her students worked, and passed the time answering questions, offering advice on punctuation and style.

She paused briefly by Steven Campbell's desk, looking down at his thick, gold-streaked hair and his broad shoulders. Even his hands were shaped like Jon's, lean and strong, with square fingernails.

Camilla remembered those hands...

"Is your father by any chance a student here on campus, Mr. Campbell?" she murmured, wanting to hear his voice.

The boy gave her a noncommittal glance. "Yeah," he said. "My dad's taking some classes. My little brother and sister are here, too," he added grudgingly, looking down at his paper.

"I beg your pardon?" Camilla asked.

"My twin brother and sister," the boy repeated. "They're seven years old. They're in some kind of special class for egghead kids."

"That's our accelerated study group. In fact, I think I'll probably be meeting your brother and sister later this afternoon."

The boy nodded without interest as she moved away.

A couple of tiers higher, Camilla noticed a dark-haired girl laboring over her paper. Tears glittered in the young woman's eyes. Camilla mounted the stairs unobtrusively to stand next to her.

"Is something the matter?" she whispered.

The girl looked up at her in anguish. "I can't do this!"

"It doesn't have to be a masterpiece," Camilla said. "Just a few words about yourself and your goals."

The student shook her head. "I mean this whole college thing. I've been out of school for four years, working and saving to come here. Now I'm in a panic. It's all so hard, and there's a ton of reading to do, and I—" Her voice broke.

Camilla knelt beside the girl's desk and put an arm around her shoulders. "I know it feels pretty overwhelming at this stage," she murmured, "but it'll all fall into place within a week or two. Trust me, you're going to feel a whole lot better after a few more classes. In the meantime," she added, "drop by my office anytime and I'll do what I can to help out."

The girl looked up, her face clearing a little. "Really, Dr. Pritchard?"

Camilla got to her feet, one hand still resting on the student's shoulder. "I was a freshman once, too," she said. "And I was even more terrified than you are. I'll be glad to help."

The girl managed a trembling smile. Camilla smiled back, then moved up the steps to watch as the others toiled away at their essays.

They're my children, Camilla thought. *All these young people are the children I've never had.*

Involuntarily, she glanced at Steven Campbell's bent head and felt a deep wave of sadness.

CONSIDERING ALL the bizarre things that were happening to her this term, it took a lot of courage for Camilla to head over to Gwen's classroom after lunch and keep her appointment with the study group.

She went down the hall and knocked on the door of a comfortable suite of rooms where the gifted children learned everything from chemistry to judo.

"Come in," Gwen called, and Camilla entered to find a lively session in progress.

The students, about a dozen of them ranging from six to ten years old, were constructing a solar system out of papier-mâché, hanging their planets in proper scale from a sunlamp in the center of the room.

"Children, this is Dr. Pritchard," Gwen told the students. "She's going to be dropping in to play games with us and ask some of you a whole lot of questions. Say hello, class."

"Hello," Camilla said, smiling at them.

"Hello, Dr. Pritchard," the children chorused, then went back to their project.

Gwen drew Camilla aside. "Look, I don't know how you were planning to begin your study, but could you possibly take the twins for a few hours?" she whispered. "I need to work out a special program for them, but I haven't had time yet."

She indicated a corner of the room where two curly-haired children lay on their stomachs near the aquarium, sharing a book.

"What are they reading?" Camilla whispered back.

"A. A. Milne. They like to memorize stories."

Camilla chuckled. "Definitely children after my own heart. Why aren't they making planets like the others?"

"They've already done this same project at home with their father, working out the orbits and distances all by themselves. They're bored with the whole idea by now. The thing is, I still haven't had time to work out something that's going to challenge them properly. So if you could…"

"Would I be able to include both of them in my study, do you think?" Camilla asked.

"Kiddo, if you can take those kids off my hands for a few hours a week, I'll be eternally grateful," Gwen murmured.

"Would it be okay if I took them down to my office? I need some time to get to know them properly before I start testing."

"Sure. But you'll find they're pretty tense little

kids," Gwen warned. "It's hard to get them to relax and open up, unless... Jason," she called to the group, "I think we need to move Neptune a little farther out. You'd better check the book, okay?"

She turned back to Camilla who was frowning thoughtfully.

"How about my apartment? They might be more comfortable if they could sit around in a homey setting and play with my cats."

"That's a good idea," the teacher said. "Just tell me before you take them out of the building, okay? I need to know where they are."

"Of course." Camilla moved closer to the two children, accompanied by their teacher.

"Ari and Amy, listen to me." Gwen stood above their prone figures. "This is Dr. Pritchard. She's a very, very nice lady who's going to be working with us quite a bit over the next few months."

Two pairs of wide eyes looked up at them, green and gray, quietly watchful. Camilla was relieved to find that these children, at least, looked nothing at all like Jon Campbell.

She knelt beside the twins, then sat next to them on the carpeted floor while Gwen returned to the rest of the group.

"What are you reading?" she asked.

"Stories about Pooh and Piglet," Ari said. "We like to memorize them."

"Why?" Camilla asked.

"So we can say them to each other when we don't have the book." He pointed at one of the pictures.

"See? Pooh's got his head stuck in the honey pot and he can't get out."

"Piglet's coming to help," Amy chimed in. "But Pooh keeps getting lost."

"Eeyore is my favorite," Camilla said. "I like his cheerful outlook on life."

Ari and Amy exchanged a glance. Camilla could see the silent message passing between them and sensed to her relief that for some reason they'd decided to trust her. Ari giggled, then moved closer to lean against her. "I like Baby Roo. It's neat the way his mother takes such good care of him."

Camilla touched the little boy's rounded cheek, "I like that, too."

Amy smiled and edged toward them, pressing against Camilla's other side. Together they finished reading the story, speaking quietly to avoid disturbing the others, and laughed over the whimsical illustrations.

At last she got up, drawing the twins along with her. "Let's go somewhere to talk, okay?" she said. "I want you kids to help me with something I'm working on."

Ari began to look anxious again. "We're not supposed to go anywhere with strangers. Daddy says…"

"It's all right, dear." Gwen came back across the room. "Dr. Pritchard is a teacher, too, and you can go anywhere she wants to take you."

"Does Daddy know we're going?" Amy asked.

"I told your daddy that Dr. Pritchard will be working with you and he knows we're all taking very good care of you," Gwen replied. "Now, Dr. Pritchard wants to take you to her office and play some games with you, that's all."

"What kind of games?" Ari asked.

"The kind of games that are your very favorite, dear. Flash cards and films, memory games, things like that."

Ari brightened and turned to Camilla with a questioning glance.

"That's right," she told him. "Lots of games."

"Better have them back here by four, okay?" Gwen called. "That's when their housekeeper comes to pick them up."

"We'll be back," Camilla promised.

She walked down the hallway, enjoying the feeling of a little warm hand in each of hers. "What's your housekeeper's name?" she asked.

"Sixty-four," Ari muttered, apparently counting the tiles under his feet. "Amy, what's the square root? Quick!"

"Eight," the little girl said absently. "Margaret," she added with a smile for Camilla.

"The housekeeper's name is Margaret?" she asked.

Ari nodded. "Eighty-one."

"Nine," Amy said.

"Margaret has a boyfriend," Ari said. "His name's Eddie. He works way up north on the oil rigs. And Tom has a girlfriend, but Margaret says they'll never get married."

"Who's Tom?" Camilla asked.

"He's the foreman at the ranch."

"Your father's ranch?"

Amy giggled. "Once, Ari put Tom's brand-new cowboy boots into the rain barrel."

"They were made out of alligator skin," Ari said. "I wanted to see if they'd float."

Camilla laughed. "And did they float?"

Ari shook his head, looking glum. "Tom was real mad at us. He wouldn't let me ride my pony for a whole week. But after that, he said it didn't matter because those boots needed to shrink a bit anyhow."

Something in the child's voice made Camilla stop and kneel beside him again.

"Do you miss the ranch, dear?"

Ari looked away from her while Amy waited silently nearby.

After a moment, Camilla got to her feet again. "I'll tell you what," she said with sudden decision. "Let's forget about those tests for now, okay? Let's go down to the cafeteria and get some ice-cream cones."

They spent a long time in the cafeteria choosing the flavors of their cones. Finally Ari selected pistachio and Amy took raspberry.

"What kind should I get?" Camilla asked.

The twins exchanged a glance. "Butterscotch ripple," Amy said firmly.

"Why?" Camilla said, intrigued.

"Because you're all white and gold," Ari said.

"I see," she sad, smiling.

"How long has Margaret been your housekeeper?"

Camilla asked idly while they were sitting on a rock ledge outside the cafeteria.

"A long time. Since we were babies. Look," Amy said, pointing to a black bird worrying a scrap of bread on the grass. "That's a raven."

"Nevermore," Ari croaked, then laughed. "It's not a raven, it's a crow. Ravens are bigger. Did you know that our daddy goes to this college?" he asked Camilla with one of the lightning changes of subject she was becoming accustomed to.

"I certainly do. He's in one of my classes, and so is your brother, Steven."

The twins considered this. Camilla took advantage of their brief silence to return to the topic of Jon Campbell's household.

"Does Margaret help your mother with the cooking and everything?"

"Our mother lives in Switzerland," Amy said, "where all the mountains are."

"There's mountains here, too," Ari said. "Look, you can see them from here." He waved his hand toward the western horizon.

Camilla felt guilty about pumping small children for personal information, but the temptation was too great. "When did your mother go to Switzerland?"

"When we were born." Ari pulled off some bits of the cone and tossed them toward the crow.

"You mean she took you away to Switzerland?"

"No, she left us here and went by herself because she didn't love Daddy anymore. She says he's a selfish pig who only cares about himself, so she went away.''

The child's tone was flat and unemotional as he stared at the big bird.

Camilla thought about Ari's words. The accusation against Jon Campbell seemed extreme, especially coming from a woman who'd apparently abandoned her own children. But perhaps Jon Campbell wasn't the man she'd always thought. Maybe he was actually the kind of person who'd use his wealth and power to separate a woman from her newborn babies.

"When are we going to play games?" Ari was asking, tugging at her arm.

"Right away." Camilla got to her feet and brushed at her skirt. "Let's go to my office and see how much fun we can have."

They went inside the building again. In the crowded hallway, the twins moved to each side of her and reached for her hands. The three of them walked along the corridor, swinging their arms, and in spite of her nagging fears, Camilla felt a wholly unexpected surge of happiness.

CHAPTER FOUR

"A VITALLY IMPORTANT part of creative writing," Camilla told her senior class, "is the ability to give your reader a sense of place. This is accomplished by means of descriptive passages, but they have to be used sparingly or they'll overpower the narrative."

"Like garlic salt," one of the students suggested, and Camilla smiled.

"Like garlic salt," she agreed. "A little bit is delicious, but too much will spoil the dish. As you work your way through the reading list, I think you'll find that all of the great writers are masters at description. Now, for your next assignment, I want you to take some time this weekend and do a couple of pages describing the most beautiful place you've ever seen."

Hands shot up all over the room. "Can it be an imaginary place? What if it's something that's only beautiful to me, but nobody else? How many words should the essay be?"

She moved around the room to answer their questions, conscious of Jon Campbell watching her steadily from his seat at the back.

This was the fifth session of this class, and she was

becoming accustomed to having him nearby. But it was still disturbing to see him lounge in his desk as he watched her with that thoughtful blue gaze.

By now, though, Camilla was convinced that the man really didn't remember. Maybe the incident had meant so little to him that he'd forgotten it as soon as it happened.

Or maybe, like her, he'd repressed the past, buried all of those memories in some deep place where they were never disturbed.

She still had hopes that he might be intimidated enough by the major assignment he'd been given to drop the course altogether. But even this faint hope was beginning to fade. Jon Campbell didn't appear to be a man who was easily intimidated, and his written work showed a surprising degree of skill.

The main problem for Camilla was that her own dark vault of memory seemed to be opening, slowly but relentlessly.

For instance, the nightmares were creeping back, although it had been years since they'd last haunted her. She found herself waking abruptly at three in the morning, drenched with perspiration, shaking in terror.

And there were other disturbing flashes of memory that leaped at her from unexpected places, things so much at odds with the carefully controlled life she'd made for herself that she could hardly bear the pain....

"That's all for today," she told the class with a glance at her watch. "I'll be in my office this afternoon if any of you want help related to your major research papers. Thank you, and have a nice weekend.''

She went to the desk and began to gather her papers, conscious of Jon Campbell's approach. Her senses seemed to be so finely attuned to this man that her body had some mysterious way of knowing when he was nearby. The fine hairs on her forearms actually lifted, and her pulse quickened.

''I've seen a lot of beautiful things in my life,'' he said quietly. ''It's hard to choose just one.''

What did he mean by that?

She forced herself to look up him, but his eyes were mild and steady, not at all threatening.

Camilla hefted an armload of books and started for the door. ''Why don't you describe something at your home?''

''My home is a ranch on the dry prairie.'' Jon fell into step beside her. ''A lot of people wouldn't think there was anything beautiful about it.''

His sleeve brushed against her arm, and she could smell the pleasant masculine scent of clean skin and shaving lotion. She closed her eyes briefly, struggling to maintain her composure. ''Beauty is in the eye of the beholder, Mr. Campbell.''

''It sure is.'' She could feel him looking down at her, but she was afraid to meet his eyes again. ''I understand you've met my kids,'' he added.

''Yes, I have. All three of them.'' She paused by the door. ''The twins are helping me with some research I'm doing into the development of reading ability. And Steven is in my freshman English class.''

"Actually, I have four kids," he said with a smile. "The only one you haven't met is Vanessa. She's sixteen, in twelfth grade."

"Is she as bright as Steven and the twins?"

"I think so." His smile faded. "I wasn't aware Steve was in your English class. He doesn't seem to tell me things anymore."

Camilla was urgently tempted to ask the man some questions. She wanted to know a lot more about that handsome, unhappy boy who looked so much like his father. And the shy, brilliant twins, and their mysteriously absent mother...

Enrique Valeros passed them with a timid nod, stumbling a little as he went into the hallway. He carried a huge pile of library books, and his face was pale with fatigue. Camilla and Jon watched in silence as the dark-haired boy moved down the corridor with an unsteady gait.

"That poor kid always looks like he's dead on his feet," Jon observed. "His hands were shaking again today. I wonder if he's sick, or taking drugs or something."

Camilla frowned. "No, I don't think it's drugs," she said at last. "His written work is beautiful, very concise and disciplined. It's particularly impressive for somebody for whom English is a second language. The students who abuse drugs tend to be rambling and disconnected, although," she added dryly, "they always believe that their work is wonderfully eloquent."

"Then why do you think Enrique's so tired all the time?"

"I don't know."

She felt a treacherous urge to move closer to Jon Campbell, to nestle against the man and feel his arms around her. It was surprisingly pleasant to stand here with him like this, talking and hearing his voice in reply.

Abruptly the years fell away and she was seventeen again, overcome with a stormy passion she'd never expected to feel....

"Goodbye, Mr. Campbell," she said hastily, starting down the hallway toward the administrative wing. "Have a pleasant weekend."

"HI, GRETCHEN." Camilla stopped at the bursar's office and dropped her books onto the counter with a sigh. "I wonder if you can tell me something about one of my students."

"As long as it's not classified." Gretchen's tanned face was bright with humor. "What do need, Dr. Pritchard?"

"Whatever you can tell me about a boy named Enrique Valeros. Where he lives, whether he's on scholarship, that kind of thing."

Gretchen got up and took a file from the bank of metal cabinets, then sat down at her desk to leaf through it. "No scholarships," she reported after a moment. "And it looks as if he's in the country on some kind of conditional visa."

"Conditional?"

"Apparently he has to stay in college and continue to get good grades or he'll be deported, even though he told the Immigration Service he'd be killed if he went home."

"Where's home?"

"Nicaragua."

"Hmm." Camilla tapped her fingers on the counter. "And he's got no sponsors? A church group that's helping him, anything like that?"

Gretchen looked at the file. "Not that I can see. No sponsors, no relatives. Enrique seems to be all on his own."

"Can you give me his address and phone number?"

"No phone number, but I can tell you where he lives." Gretchen read the address aloud.

"Not exactly a terrific neighborhood," Camilla murmured, writing it down.

"You can say that again," Gretchen said dryly. "But I doubt if the poor kid can afford anything better, when he's carrying a full load of classes. Unless he's got a money tree in his apartment, or some kind of fairy godmother."

Camilla looked at the other woman in concern. "I wonder how he's managing to look after himself," she said thoughtfully.

ON FRIDAY NIGHT, Enrique closed the convenience store at midnight. He washed the floors, cleaned the windows and countertops, totaled the cash in the till and took it next door to the night-deposit box, then came back and prepared all the coffeemakers for the next morning.

Finally, numb with fatigue, he gathered his pile of books and left the building, locked the door carefully behind him and walked a few blocks down the street to the service station where he worked five nights a week from one o'clock until seven in the morning.

With any luck, his shift would be quiet and he'd have time to tackle some of his growing mountain of homework, maybe even snatch a few minutes of sleep between customers. Enrique nodded timidly at the attendant who was going off shift, then settled himself in the little booth and opened his books on the table, getting ready to work on his creative-writing assignment.

The most beautiful place he'd ever seen...

Enrique dropped his face into his hands and let himself drift for a moment on a warm tide of memory. He thought of the swimming hole outside the village where he'd grown up, the richness of the green canopy overhead, sunlight that glimmered on the water and the distant echoes of birdsong in the forest.

A big new car pulled up to the pumps and Enrique rushed outside to wash the windshield. The driver held a can of beer, belching loudly as he searched through his wallet for a credit card.

Enrique carried the gold card back to his cubicle, marveling at the awesome power this bit of plastic represented. He wondered what it would be like to possess such a card, to hand it over with easy carelessness and know that it would pay any expense you wanted.

Like a key to a magic kingdom, Enrique thought wistfully.

He rubbed his aching back and watched as the car pulled away and swerved across a couple of lanes, speeding down the street into the darkness.

Life wasn't so bad, he told himself firmly.

This was Friday night, which meant he had no classes tomorrow and no early bus to catch. After his shift, he could go home, lie down on his cot and grab a few precious hours of sleep, then work on his assignments until it was time to head over to the convenience store for his five o'clock shift.

Enrique lived in the basement of an old apartment building where he had a single room behind the furnace and did some basic maintenance work in exchange for a reduced rent. Even with these primitive living arrangements, as well as two jobs that were virtually full-time, he barely managed to pay his tuition and buy the books he needed for his classes. Food was a luxury, and entertainment was unheard of.

He sighed and trudged back into the cubicle, trying to concentrate on the most beautiful place he'd ever seen. But the lines of the notebook blurred in front of his eyes, and his hands were shaking so badly that it was difficult to hold the pen.

ON SATURDAY MORNING, the Campbell family enjoyed a rare opportunity to eat breakfast together around the big oak table in the kitchen.

Margaret put a platter of pancakes in the middle of the table and brought a jug of warm syrup from the microwave, then paused to pour orange juice into the glasses at the twins' plates.

"Drink your juice," she said.

"It's got stuff in it," Ari told her. "I hate the squidgy stuff."

"That's pulp, you silly," Vanessa said. "Margaret just squeezed the oranges a few minutes ago."

Ari turned in his chair to glare at his older sister, who returned the look evenly.

The small boy was the first to look away.

"Little monster," Vanessa muttered in triumph, helping herself to a tiny pancake from the edge of the platter.

Jon reached for the syrup jug and addressed his older son. "Did you have a good time last night, Steve?"

With a distracted air, Steven glanced up from a book lying open next to his plate. For a moment he gazed blankly at his father.

"Last night," Jon repeated, his voice hardening a little. "You didn't get in until past two o'clock, so I assume you were having fun. What did you do?"

The other children were suddenly quiet, their squabbles forgotten.

Steven's handsome face darkened briefly. "I went out with some friends," he said. "Okay?"

"I don't know if it's okay. Have I met these

friends?''

''For God's sake, Dad. We just moved here a few weeks ago. Do I have to bring every guy I meet over here for your approval?''

''That would be nice,'' Jon said quietly. ''I asked you what you were doing, Steve.''

''Oh, for... We were driving around. Okay? We went to a movie, then had some burgers and rode around for a while. I would have been home on time but I ran out of gas and had to walk to a service station. Is that what you want to hear?''

''I want to hear the truth, son. That's all.''

Steven got up, wadded his napkin into a ball and threw it on the table, then stalked from the room. In a few minutes they heard the roar of his yellow Mustang and saw the cloud of dust as the car pulled onto the graveled access road, heading for town.

Jon watched the disappearing plume of dust. These challenges between them were getting more frequent all the time, increasingly edgy and tense now that Steven was almost as tall as his father.

''What's that book, Daddy?'' Ari said, clearing his throat nervously. He indicated a volume at Jon's elbow, bristling with notes and markers.

''*Pride and Prejudice*,'' Jon told him. ''By Jane Austen.''

''At *breakfast*?'' Vanessa asked with a grimace of distaste.

''Dr. Pritchard gave all of us our individual research assignments yesterday. I have to compare the work of five modern British novelists with five others from the nineteenth century.''

''Wow,'' Vanessa muttered with a rare show of sympathy. ''That's brutal, Daddy.''

''I know. This English class is going to be a lot more work than the others.''

''Why don't you drop it?'' Vanessa asked. ''I heard lots of people are dropping classes.''

''Well, I'm not one of them, Van. I believe in finishing things once I've started them.''

She shrugged and wrenched the syrup jug away from her little brother.

''I can't wait to go to the ranch,'' Amy murmured, her face shining with happiness. ''I just can't *wait*. When are we leaving, Daddy?''

''In a few minutes, pumpkin. There's lots of work to do out there this weekend. Tom needs help getting the yearlings ready for market, and we have to buy a few loads of feed, too. But I'll sure be burning the midnight oil with all this reading I have to do.''

Jon smiled at the twins, pleased to see how happy they looked. Now it was his older children who worried him the most.

Vanessa seemed more self-absorbed and combative than ever, and he was increasingly worried about Steven...

Jon sighed and returned his attention to his twins. ''So, what are you kids planning to do this weekend at the ranch?''

''Stuff,'' Ari said serenely.

Jon reached out to stroke Amy's hair. ''How about

you, sweetheart? Have you got anything special planned?''

Amy shook her head and gave him a shy smile that tugged powerfully at his emotions. Of all the children, this one was probably the easiest to love. Amy shared her father's attitudes about many things. She was a thoughtful, gentle child with a vivid imagination.

Jon sometimes wished that the twins weren't so wrapped up in each other. He would have liked to spend more time alone with each of them separately.

But Amy and Ari were a package deal. If you had one of them, the other was almost always there, too.

"Well, it's a beautiful fall day." Jon touched Amy's rounded cheek with the backs of his fingers. "You kids should have lots of fun playing outside. Maybe you can saddle your ponies and help Tom move the yearlings up to the corrals."

The twins exchanged a delighted glance but said nothing.

"So, Daddy, what do you think of Dr. Pritchard?" Vanessa picked daintily at her pancake.

"She's a pretty tough professor," Jon said, then put down his fork and looked at his daughter in surprise. "How do *you* know Dr. Pritchard, Van?"

Before Vanessa could answer, Ari spoke. "We know her too. She's the lady who gave us our tests."

"I know, Ari," Jon replied. "Gwen told me you sometimes go to her apartment."

"Well, I think she's wonderful," Vanessa sighed dramatically. "She came to career day at our school yesterday, to talk to us about freelance journalism and to tell us which English courses we need to take next term to get into the right program at college. She's *so* gorgeous.''

"Yes, she's a good-looking woman," Jon agreed. He hesitated, frowning. Then, "You know, I keep wondering if I've seen her somewhere before. There's something familiar about her, but I can't put my finger on it.''

Vanessa looked at her father with sudden interest. "Did you meet her somewhere around here?"

"I don't think so. I have the feeling it was a long time ago, but I can't remember where."

"Well, she certainly didn't grow up on the prairies." Vanessa added a packet of artificial sweetener to her coffee. "She just moved to Calgary a few years ago."

"Where did she come from?" Ari asked.

"I think she got her degree at Montreal and did graduate work at Harvard." Vanessa was clearly pleased to be the center of attention. "She's an American, you know. Her family is one of the wealthiest in the country, but she never talks about them. She grew up in Massachusetts and dated one of the Kennedy boys. And she was also a world-class equestrienne. I think she rode in the Olympics in Seoul."

Jon gave his daughter a skeptical glance. "Who told you all this, Van?"

"Everybody knows. There are tons of stories about Dr. Pritchard." Vanessa sighed again. "She's so classy. I'd just love to meet her. I think she's fabulous."

Jon sipped his coffee thoughtfully. He thought of Camilla Pritchard's elegant, fine-boned face, her aloofness and academic discipline. Had she really dated a Kennedy and ridden in the Olympics, or was that just campus gossip?

If the rumors were true, perhaps they explained why the woman seemed so hard to approach. She probably had no time for a man who dressed in blue jeans and helped the cowhands with chores around his ranch. No doubt she'd find Jon Campbell's life-style far too primitive for her tastes.

"Do you like her?" Ari asked.

Jon looked at his son in surprise.

"Camilla. Do you like her, Daddy?"

"Yes," Jon said after a brief hesitation. "Yes, Ari. I like her."

"Do you think you'd want to marry her?" the little boy asked.

Vanessa hooted with laughter. "Marry Dr. *Pritchard!*" she jeered. "Can you imagine her living with us at the ranch and putting on rubber boots to go and help feed the calves? I'll bet she'd just be really tickled with all that."

Jon quelled the girl with a stern glance and turned to Ari, who was waiting for an answer.

"Why are you asking me about this, son?"

"I just wondered, that's all. She's a really nice, pretty lady and you like her, so wouldn't you want to marry her?"

Jon thought about that slim body, the smooth blond

head and remote look, and the sudden, surprising glow of warmth when she smiled at Enrique Valeros.

"Well, now, I just might consider it," he told the child solemnly. "Matter of fact, if I were planning to get married again, which I'm definitely not, then yes, I think a lady like Dr. Pritchard could probably be a serious candidate."

Ari scrambled up eagerly to kneel on the chair and lean across the table toward his father. "So will you ask her?" he said.

Jon chuckled. "No, son. I won't be asking her anytime soon. Look, I haven't even had a chance to talk with her. I'm hardly ready to propose marriage."

"Why not?"

"Marrying somebody isn't the same as buying her a cup of coffee, Ari. Why?" he asked suddenly. "Do you like her a lot, son?"

Ari squirmed uneasily on the chair and exchanged a glance with Amy, then took a sip of milk. "She's nice," he said, wiping his mouth with the back of his hand. "She has two cats named Elton and Madonna. Elton's really funny."

Amy nodded in agreement. "We like her a lot. She gave us cookies yesterday."

"Camilla was wearing blue jeans," Ari volunteered. "And a Calgary Stampeders football shirt. She really likes to watch football games."

"She wears jeans and likes football," Jon echoed, trying to adjust his mental image of the woman. "What else does she like to do? Did you—"

"Hey, Ari, what's her house like?" Vanessa interrupted, breathless with interest. "I'll bet it's really beautiful. Where does she live?"

But the twins were losing interest in the conversation. Ari slid down from his chair and headed for the door, followed closely by Amy.

"Hurry up, Daddy," he said impatiently.

"I'll be ready in a few minutes." Jon got up and smiled his thanks to Margaret, strolled to the back entry and put on his hat.

"Pay attention to Margaret while I'm gone," he told Vanessa, opening the kitchen door and starting outside. "And remind Steve that he still has a one o'clock curfew on weekends, and there'll be some serious discussions between us if he doesn't keep it."

"I'll tell him," Vanessa promised. "Have a good time, Daddy."

"Say hi to Tom," Margaret called. "Tell him he'd better propose to Caroline before some other cowboy grabs her."

Jon smiled again at their laughter. He left the house, enjoying the mellow autumn sunlight, and strolled across the yard toward the hangar, where the twins were already waiting near the plane.

IT WAS AFTER MIDNIGHT and the autumn air was getting chilly. Camilla pulled an old cardigan tighter around her shoulders and blew on her fingers to keep them warm. She was inside one of the main-floor rooms of a derelict apartment containing little more than a scarred wooden desk, a rickety file cabinet and a few cardboard boxes full of donated coats and blankets, as well as some emergency medical supplies.

The street kids referred to this room as an "office," but Camilla and the other volunteers were constantly frustrated by their lack of work space, to say nothing of the money and supplies necessary to provide any kind of worthwhile help to the city's booming population of homeless youth.

A ragged boy popped his head into the room, grinning widely, showing a couple of missing teeth. He was accompanied by a thin girl with hair cropped short and dyed a shocking shade of red. The girl was very pale, whimpering and hugging herself as she swayed on her feet.

"Hey, Queen," the boy said to Camilla. "How ya' doin'?"

"Queen" was Camilla's street name, given apparently because of her regal bearing. Street kids shunned the use of given names or titles of any kind, preferring to reduce everyone in their world to a single level. They knew little about the everyday lives or backgrounds of the volunteers who helped them, and didn't care. Nothing really mattered to them except the harsh realities of their own lives. They'd tagged Camilla with the name at once, and in the beginning it hadn't been particularly friendly.

But now, after more than five years of volunteering at the hostel almost every weekend, Camilla was a favorite with the kids. She never pried, never acted judgmental or disapproving. Instead, she listened quietly, sympathized and helped whenever she could.

"I'm doing fine," she told the boy. "Who's your friend?"

He put his arm around the girl to support her more firmly. "This is Rosie. She's not feeling too good. Ate something that made her sick. But Queen, there's real bad stuff on the streets tonight. So you'll be seeing some kids sick from bad drugs."

Camilla looked up, suddenly alert. "What kind of stuff? Where's it coming from?"

"Dunno. But people are going down all over. It's a bad scene."

Camilla sighed and looked at the papers on her desk, knowing she'd probably have a busy night.

"Tell the kids I'm here if anybody needs help. Shouldn't Rosie see a doctor?"

"Are you kidding?" he asked in disbelief. "A *doctor*?"

Camilla rummaged in her pocket and handed ten dollars to the boy. "Well, see if you can get her to at least drink something. Or maybe get her some clear soup, okay?"

The boy pocketed the bills gratefully and made his way back onto the sidewalk, supporting his woozy friend. Camilla watched them through the cracked window, then returned with an angry frown to the stack of English papers she was marking.

If she could do anything personally about the people who poured drugs onto these streets, she'd have no compunction about condemning them to life in prison. The volunteers at the hostel saw firsthand the results of the dealers' greed. They saw the damaged young minds and bodies, the wrecked hopes and heartbroken families.

But they couldn't intervene. A private operation without formal mandate, public funding or governmental support, the hostel was simply a final resource for homeless youth. Camilla could only wait here in the shabby, poorly equipped little room until the kids came to her for help.

Camilla pushed her hair back wearily from her forehead and returned to the essays.

Eventually she came to Steven Campbell's impromptu treatise on personal goals, and looked at it with quickened interest.

"My goal is to be a modern-day Robin Hood," the boy wrote. "I want to steal from the rich—people like my parents—and give to the poor who really need help. I see nothing morally wrong with criminal activity as long as it results ultimately in a fairer distribution of wealth."

Nothing morally wrong with criminal activity…

Camilla thought about the boy's handsome face, his moody, withdrawn look and the stubborn set to his mouth, and wondered if perhaps Jon Campbell was having some serious problems with his elder son.

Not that it was any of her business, of course.

But the twins…

Camilla smiled wistfully and nibbled on her marking pen.

The twins were a different matter, baffling, intriguing and funny.

It was a rare experience for Camilla to enter the

world of these small children. In fact, she was beginning to realize, as she spent more time with Ari and Amy, that she'd never really had a childhood herself.

And the twins had never had a mother. Camilla knew their mutual needs and yearnings made the three of them a potentially explosive combination, but she couldn't resist the charm of these brilliant, winsome children.

If only they didn't belong to Jon Campbell, who posed such a terrible threat to her own safety...

"Queen!" A girl clattered down the hall and tumbled through the door, breathless and pale. "Thank God you're here."

"Hi, Marty. What's up?"

The girl wore denim coveralls with one strap hanging, a filthy plaid shirt and a pair of men's running shoes, riddled with holes.

"Is it Chase?" Camilla asked.

Marty nodded and rubbed her eyes with blackened fingers. "He's in terrible shape. He...got some really bad stuff."

"I heard there was bad stuff around tonight. How is he, Marty?"

"I think...God, Queen, I think he's dying!"

"Let's go. Hurry!" Camilla got up from the desk, grabbed her cellular phone and box of medical supplies and ran out of the room. She followed the girl through dark alleys piled with garbage, heading for a row of fire-damaged, abandoned warehouses.

CHAPTER FIVE

CAMILLA STOOD ALONE on the windswept street, watching the flashing red lights of the ambulance as it screeched off into the darkness.

The ambulance attendants hadn't wanted to take Marty with them. Only Camilla's passionate insistence had finally convinced them that the girl should be with Chase when he was admitted to the emergency room.

People tended to look on street kids as less than human, somehow lacking in the emotions that other people had. But Marty was a nice girl, and Chase, too, was a decent person, shy and pleasant, with a rare talent for music. He'd been supporting himself and Marty for more than a year now, playing his guitar on downtown-street corners while people dropped coins into a bowl that Marty held as she sat cross-legged on the sidewalk nearby.

Camilla often wondered where the boy had come from, and what he might have become if drugs hadn't claimed him. She'd never know, of course. Street kids kept their pasts to themselves. Every young face was a secret, a closed book.

Probably that was why she felt strangely comfortable in this grim environment. The streets were a place where nobody shared their childhood memories or discussed the past at all.

Never look back, that seemed to be their motto.

And until now, Camilla hadn't looked back, either. She'd kept the door firmly closed on all those dreadful images from the past.

But the sudden reappearance of Jon Campbell in her life was changing all that. Camilla knew he was responsible for the painful flashes of memory, the trauma and the nightmares.

At some level, of course, she understood that she needed to find a way to talk about these things. As long as they were hidden inside her mind, unspoken and darkly powerful, her memories would continue to shadow her life and make it impossible to trust anybody or form any kind of close relationship.

She should probably go into therapy, find a self-help group, develop enough confidence in somebody to confide the truth about herself and her past. But she couldn't. The very thought of talking about those things made her feel ill.

Camilla sat down on the curb and hugged herself, still shaken by the memory of Chase's frantic white face, his enlarged pupils and convulsed body, and Marty's terror.

It was well past midnight, with little traffic moving in the city core. A few people wandered past, ignoring Camilla as she huddled on the curb. The autumn wind tugged at her hair and chilled her shoulders. Scattered drops of rain began to fall, pattering lightly onto the dirty pavement.

Camilla buried her face in her hands, shivering. With the rain, memories came flooding back and she couldn't hold them at bay...

July 1977

I'M ON THE BACK of his motorcycle. The wind whips at my hair and roars in my ears. I'm so weak that it's all I can do to hold on to him. I have no idea where he's taking me or what's going to happen.

I try to remind myself that it doesn't matter what he does to me. But I'm still scared...

He pulls up at a shabby building just off the highway. It looks sad and deserted in the morning light. A couple of pickup trucks are parked outside, and tumbleweeds bounce across the parking lot. He lifts me down and sets me on the curb like a little kid.

"I'll be right back," he says. "Don't go away."

He must be joking, because I can't even stand up. I hug my knees and put my head down so I don't have to look at the glaring sunshine and the litter of garbage in the vacant lot next to the motel. The strong light is making my head ache.

He's back almost right away, holding a key. He unlocks one of the rooms, then picks me up and carries me inside.

I have a confused impression of lurid colors, of old furniture, a dirty brown carpet and a little bathroom behind a half-closed door.

It's not much, but it looks a whole lot better than the place I've been living.

He puts me on the bed and goes into the bathroom. I can hear water running. Now he's back. He strips off his leather jacket, then starts to tug at my clothes. Instinctively I fight him, try to grab his hands. But he's too strong.

Soon I'm completely naked. It's almost a relief to have all those filthy clothes gone from my body. Still, I curl on the bed and try to hide myself from him. I don't even know who he is.

"I'm sorry," he whispers in my ear. "I'm so sorry to do this to you. But I promise it won't take long."

I brace myself for the invasion, the searing pain and horror of it. But instead, he lifts me again and carries me into the bathroom, lowers me carefully into a steaming tub of water.

It feels like heaven. I'm so shocked that I forget to be terrified and stare up at him. He's flushed with embarrassment under his tan.

"I'll just go away now," he mutters, "and let you…" He edges out the door.

The water helps to revive me. For a long time I revel in the steaming bliss, scrubbing my arms and legs, washing my hair with the shampoo he's left on the floor. Finally, reluctantly, I climb out and wrap myself in one of the towels, then try to dry the rest of my body.

But heat and hunger have made me really dizzy. I stumble and bump my elbow against the door. He's there in a second, looking at me in concern. He takes the towel and helps me.

When I'm dry he carries me into the other room,

pulls the covers back and tucks me into bed, then crosses the room to open his knapsack. He takes out a white T-shirt, neatly folded, and pulls it over my head. It smells like him, clean and sunny, faintly masculine.

I lie back against the pillows, my wet hair in tangles all around me. He comes back with a hairbrush and raises me, then begins to brush my hair, taking care not to pull at the snarls. When it's smooth, he braids it and fastens an elastic in place.

This whole situation is so weird. We're complete strangers involved in this homey, intimate act. But I'm too tired to think about it very much. By the time he finishes with my hair, I'm drowning and the world is spinning around me in multicolored flashes of heat. I feel as if I'm going to pass out.

He tucks me down among the pillows and draws the covers up around me. For a moment I luxuriate, warm and safe and marvelously comfortable. Then I tumble down into sleep like a person falling off a cliff.

A CAR SWERVED near the curb. A beer bottle smashed at her feet, spraying bits of broken glass over her shoes. Camilla looked up in confusion, still lost in the depths of her memory. The car drove past, full of young men, all of them laughing raucously.

It was a bright yellow, sporty model. Camilla recognized a couple of the boys inside the vehicle from the years she'd been working with street kids, although these particular youths had long since been banned from any contact with the hostel.

After the vehicle pulled away she got slowly to her feet, picked up her box of supplies and made her way down the street toward the hostel, fighting a dizzying sense of unreality.

Twenty years later, the face in her memory was still vividly clear to her, the handsome boy who'd knelt beside her to lift her out of the mud on a long-ago summer morning.

But just moments ago, in the sudden glow of a cigarette, Camilla had seen that same face behind the wheel of the yellow car.

ON SUNDAY NIGHT, two weeks after the start of classes, Enrique got home from the convenience store at about one o'clock. Because he didn't have to go to his job at the service station on weekends, he'd spent an extra half hour cleaning the floors and tidying the storeroom. He was exhausted, covered with greasy dirt from a pail of water that he'd accidentally spilled on himself.

Late at night was the best time for a shower since he shared the bathroom with four other tenants and there was usually somebody pounding on the door in the daytime. After midnight, there was even a chance for some hot water.

He sighed in anticipation, thinking about those steaming jets of water, and began to unbutton his jacket. But all at once a strange thing happened. The lights flared, then gradually darkened. Enrique found himself lying on the floor, feeling the gritty hardness of the linoleum under his cheek.

This isn't right, he thought in confusion. I shouldn't be lying here with all my clothes on. I need to have a shower and then cook something to eat. I need to get up.

But try as he might, Enrique couldn't heave himself to his feet. It was as if his body was some huge, inert mass, far too heavy to move. Nausea flowed over him in huge, smothering waves.

After a few moments the world began to darken again.

CAMILLA HAD A three-hour break after her first class on Monday. She took advantage of the time to work in her office, grading assignments, planning lectures and putting the finishing touches on an article she was writing for an American scholastic journal.

Toward noon the secretary knocked, then popped her head in the door. "Dr. Pritchard, one of your students is here. Do you have a minute?"

Camilla glanced at her watch and ran a distracted hand through her hair. "All right, Joyce."

The secretary vanished and Jon Campbell appeared in her place. He closed the door behind him, approaching Camilla's desk while she watched in startled, wary silence.

Camilla's mind began to race, assessing her situation.

The two of them were alone in a room behind a closed door. Perhaps he'd remembered everything.

Now he was about to make his move, tell her what he planned to do with all that damning information he possessed.

But he said nothing, merely folded his long body into one of the leather armchairs and gave her a courteous smile.

"Hello, Mr. Campbell." She looked down at the papers on her desk. "How may I help you?"

"I'm having some trouble with this assignment on modern and nineteenth-century British novelists."

Camilla felt a brief surge of hope. "Well," she said carefully, "if you're finding the course too difficult…"

"It's not too difficult," he said. "In fact, it's really interesting. I'm just having a hard time getting hold of some of the books, that's all. I wondered if you had any idea where I could pick up a few of the modern novels."

"Could you show me your list, please?"

He handed the sheet across the table, and Camilla checked the books he was missing. For a moment, her sense of academic fairness warred with the urgent need for self-preservation. Ultimately, professionalism triumphed.

"I can loan you those books," she said without looking at him. "But please be careful with them. I'd hate to lose them."

"That's very generous of you, Dr. Pritchard."

Camilla got up and moved to the wall of books at the far side of her office. As she searched the shelves, she was conscious of his gaze resting on her back.

Don't look at me, she wanted to shout. *Don't sit there thinking about my hair and posture, the shape of my body, your memories...*

"Here they are." She handed the books to him and retreated behind her desk.

"Thank you." He opened one of them to read the name inscribed on the title page. "Camilla Pritchard," he said. "That's a pretty name."

She continued to look down at the papers, wishing he would go away.

Callie, he'd whispered long ago. *That's a pretty name... You're so sweet. Give me a kiss, Callie... Let me touch you...*

The silence lengthened.

"Are you...progressing with the assignment?" she said at last.

"I'm reading a lot and making some notes. At the ranch last weekend, I stayed up working until about three o'clock every night."

"Where is the ranch?" she asked without looking up.

"In Saskatchewan, just across the border. We run about fifteen hundred cows and calves over near the Great Sandhills."

She knew that, of course. He'd told her about the sprawling family ranch more than twenty years before. Besides, the twins talked about it all the time. They loved the ranch.

Camilla felt a pang of guilt. "You must miss it."

"I do. But luckily I fly my own plane," he said casually. "It just takes an hour to get there. And the place I've bought on the western outskirts of town is not exactly a ranch, but there's enough room for my family to spread out a bit.''

"The twins..." She paused, then, "They seem to miss the ranch a lot."

"I gather they talk to you quite a lot. In fact, you seem to have made a big hit with them. They're usually kind of shy with strangers."

"They're very unusual children. I don't know if I've ever encountered such advanced intellects in seven-year-olds. And yet..."

"Yes?" he prompted.

"Despite their intelligence, they seem quite natural in their reactions. Not at all spoiled or self-consciously precocious like some of the children in our program."

He glanced at her with interest. "So what does all that mean?"

Camilla smiled. "I suppose it means you're doing a good job."

He smiled back, his face creasing with humor. The smile was so warm and pleasant that she felt herself being drawn to him again, and had to fight her reaction.

"I keep trying," he said. "But it's not easy."

"Their mother..."

"She's not in the picture very much. They don't see her more than a couple of times a year. I know it's hard on them."

Camilla couldn't help herself. "It's a little hard to

understand,'' she murmured. ''I honestly don't know how anybody could stay away from them.''

''That's because you haven't met my ex-wife.''

Then why did you marry her? Camilla asked silently.

As if reading her mind, Jon said, ''I'll bet you're wondering what possessed me to marry a woman like that in the first place. Aren't you?''

She felt her cheeks warm and turned away hastily, then got up and pretended to search for a book.

''It's certainly none of my business.'' Camilla selected a volume at random and returned to the desk. ''I prefer not to involve myself in the personal affairs of my students, Mr. Campbell.''

''Do you think you could bring yourself to call me Jon? After all, you're getting to be best friends with my kids, so you and I might as well be a little less formal.''

''I really think it's best if we keep our relationship formal.''

''Do you?''

She felt herself growing increasingly nervous under his steady gaze.

''Steven is also a very gifted student,'' she said at last.

''I know. When he was younger, he always had good grades. He used to be such a wholesome, happy kid, too. But during the past few years, he's seemed to change completely.''

''Do you think... Could it have something to do

with the family relationship?'' she asked. ''In a couple of his essays, I've sensed quite a lot of hostility.''

Jon's face hardened with concern. ''I suppose it could.'' He was silent a moment, shaking his head. ''A man pays all his life for the mistakes he makes when he's young. If it was just me who suffered, I wouldn't mind so much. But I hate to realize that my kids have to keep paying for my blunders, too.''

She leafed through the book, wondering what to say.

''Have you ever been married, Dr. Pritchard?''

Camilla shook her head.

''Ever been in love?'' he asked with a brief teasing light in his eyes.

Only with you, she thought.

''How much do you know about Steven's friends?'' she asked abruptly.

''His friends? I haven't met any of them. At least, not since we moved to the city. Steve's past the age when he brings kids home for me to examine. He goes out, and I have no idea where.'' Jon leaned forward. ''Why? Is there something I should know?''

Camilla shrugged, reluctant to involve herself any further. ''I just wondered. It seems to me perhaps I've seen him lately in the company of some boys who were…''

''What?'' Jon urged.

''Maybe not the best company for him,'' Camilla said. ''It's really none of my business, so please don't tell him that I said anything to you.''

"I won't, but I'll certainly talk to him. Were these boys college students?"

"I hardly think so," Camilla said dryly. She was conscious of him watching her curiously.

They were silent for a moment. A flood of warm autumn sunlight poured in the window, shimmering on a lush fern near her desk and gilding the rows of books on the shelves.

Jon leaned back in his chair, apparently reluctant to leave. "Enrique Valeros wasn't in class this morning," he said finally.

Camilla felt a brief tug of worry. "I know. It's the first time he's missed. And he's been looking even more exhausted lately."

"Does that concern you, Dr. Pritchard?"

"Of course it does."

He smiled. "You're not nearly as tough and heartless as you like to pretend. Are you?"

She felt a rising alarm and closed the book with a dismissive gesture. "If you'll excuse me, Mr. Campbell, I have to…"

"Do you happen to have his address?" Jon said, clearly ignoring her attempt at brusqueness. "In fact, that's one of the reasons I came to see you this morning. I'd like to stop in and check on him."

Camilla opened a ledger. "It's right here." She read the address aloud, watching as he copied it down. "I've dropped in a couple of times but he's never home. I assume he must work somewhere after class."

Jon's eyebrows shot up.

"I was just passing by," she said casually, before he could ask any questions. "It's really quite an awful place," she added after a moment.

"Well, I'll see if I can find out what he does after class." Jon got to his feet, and Camilla smiled up at him.

"Thank you," she said. "I'd appreciate that very much."

"Dr. Pritchard." He paused by the door.

"Yes?"

"Would you like to go out for coffee? I'd really enjoy talking with you about something other than school and kids."

When Camilla made no response, he pressed his advantage.

"Maybe I could stop by in another hour or so and take you to lunch."

She looked up, then away, finding it hard to meet his eyes. For a brief, treacherous moment she remembered the sweetness of his mouth, the hard young body and thrusting sexual hunger...

Just then, Gwen Klassen appeared in the doorway and gave Jon a cheerful smile, then looked at Camilla. "May I?" she asked.

"Come in, Gwen," Camilla said with relief. "Mr. Campbell was just leaving."

Jon made no move to go. He looked large next to the petite gray-haired professor.

He was like a big, prowling lion, Camilla thought with growing alarm. Definitely a threat to her safety, unless she could...

"Hi, Jon," Gwen said. "How are you?"

"Fine. How are my kids doing today?"

Gwen smiled again. "They're having lunch with a couple of graduate students and playing on the computer. You should drop by."

"I'm trying to take Dr. Pritchard to lunch. Maybe she'll come with me to see the kids."

"What a good idea. Camilla, why don't you go?" Gwen gave her colleague a teasing wink. "You can watch the twins surfing the Internet. It's really a sight to behold."

Camilla cast the other woman a look of urgent appeal as she shook her head.

Jon turned to Camilla again. "So, how about it, Dr. Pritchard? Are you going to have lunch with me?"

"No," she said calmly, though her heart was pounding. "I'm afraid not. I'll see you in class, Mr. Campbell."

He inclined his head politely, closed the door and left them alone.

When he was gone, Gwen sat in her customary perch on the edge of the desk, watching Camilla with a bright, inquisitive glance.

"What?" Camilla said at last.

"Why won't you go to lunch with him?"

"Because I don't want to." Camilla got out her pile of essays and began marking furiously. "Go away."

"Now, let me think about this." Gwen leaned back, swinging her feet, clearly not at all intimidated. "Why wouldn't a woman want to go out with a man

like that? Could it be his looks?" she mused aloud.
"After all, the man's absolutely gorgeous. And he
seems very nice, and I understand he's rich and single, to say nothing of his adorable little kids. You're
right, definitely not a good prospect at all. Best to
avoid him."

"Your sarcasm is unbecoming." Camilla smiled in
spite of herself. "Really," she pleaded, "I don't want
to talk about this anymore."

"But I'm not finished yet."

Camilla sighed. "Gwen, he's a student."

"Oh, come on. You're both grown-ups, aren't you?
Why should it make the slightest difference?"

"It's just not a good policy, that's all."

"Well, it certainly won't be the first time a prof
has dated a student around here," Gwen said.

"We're not dating!"

"Just tell me why you don't want anything to do
with this man. Give me one good reason and I'll leave
you alone. I promise."

Camilla hesitated, toying with her pen. "Did you
know that the twins' mother hardly ever visits them?
She's got four kids and she doesn't even seem to care
about them. Apparently, she's living in Switzerland,
hanging out with a ski instructor."

"So?" Gwen asked. "Why does that keep you
from going to lunch?"

"What kind of man…" Camilla paused, feeling
her face redden with embarrassment.

Gwen gave her a shrewd glance. "You're assuming
he's a shallow person or he wouldn't have been at-

tracted to this woman. Is that what you're trying to say?''

''Something like that, I suppose. Gwen, can't we just—''

''You don't think people can make mistakes, especially when they're young?''

''I don't know.''

''How old is Steven?'' Gwen asked.

''About eighteen, I guess. Why do you ask?''

''Because that means Jon Campbell was in his early twenties when the kid was born. Not exactly old enough to make all the right decisions. Maybe he'd fallen in love with somebody else who'd left him. So he married this woman on the rebound because his heart was broken.''

Camilla felt the color drain from her face. She looked down in confusion, gripping the pen until her fingers ached.

''Anyhow,'' Gwen said, slipping off the desk, ''all kidding aside, you really have to build some kind of comfortable relationship with this guy if you're going to be working with his kids for the rest of the year.''

''That's a big part of the problem,'' Camilla said. ''I've never gotten so wrapped up in any kids I've worked with. The twins are irresistible.''

''I hear you took them to the zoo on Friday afternoon.''

''The zoo's an ideal place for symbol recognition,'' Camilla said with dignity, though she couldn't hide her smile. ''It's full of symbols.''

''And hot dogs and cotton candy,'' Gwen said with

a cheerful wink. "Don't worry, I know what's been going on. They're getting to love you as much as you love them, and they're not easy kids to get close to. I'm really jealous of your relationship with them."

Camilla's smile faded. "I'm afraid it makes me… vulnerable."

"It's not so bad to be vulnerable, sweetie," Gwen said gently. "You have to take risks if you're ever going to care about people."

Camilla shook her head, not trusting herself to speak.

"You can't stay forever in that ivory tower of yours," Gwen said. "It may be safe up there, but it's awfully lonely, isn't it?"

"I'm used to loneliness."

Gwen stood in the doorway, looking at her with compassion. "Why not take a chance, dear? Safety isn't everything, you know."

Then she was gone. Camilla stared at the closed door. The sun was warm on her face, and her eyes burned with unshed tears.

CHAPTER SIX

JON LEFT Dr. Pritchard's office and strode off through the halls of the arts building, deep in thought. He couldn't recall the last time anyone had interested him so profoundly, but left him feeling so hollow and frustrated.

The woman was like a rainbow, lovely and tantalizing but impossible to reach.

Maybe it really *was* impossible, Jon told himself moodily.

Perhaps no man could ever get close enough to Camilla Pritchard to explore the depths of her mind and learn the secrets behind those remarkable eyes.

Of course there were other things about her that would be delightful to explore, as well, but Jon no longer allowed himself to pursue those thoughts. Fantasizing about her body was too unsettling, and tended to interfere badly with both his sleep and peace of mind.

He wandered into Gwen's bright classroom. It was empty except for the twins and a young man with thick glasses and a ponytail. This was Gordon Ames, one of Gwen's assistants, who was doing his master's thesis on creativity levels in exceptional children.

"Hi, guys," Jon said, pausing behind Amy's chair. "What's up?"

The children were seated at computers, while the graduate student hovered nearby and watched as their small hands flew over the keyboards. He nodded at Jon and gave him a shy smile, then turned back to the two computer monitors.

"Hi, Daddy," Amy said absently, offering her cheek for a kiss without turning around. "We're looking at beetles."

Jon patted her head fondly. The twins had been deeply interested in beetles for the past few weeks, and now had a small collection of them lumbering around a plant-filled terrarium in the kitchen at home.

"This is awesome," Ari said. "Look, Daddy."

He waved his hand at a cut-out diagram of an army tank on the screen, showing the inside of the turret and the undercarriage.

Jon leaned forward to study the diagram. "What's that got to do with beetles?"

"They noticed a similarity." The young student shook his ponytail, looking dazed. "Now they've started pulling stuff off the Internet, checking design components of military tanks and comparing them to the natural structure of beetles."

"See, Daddy?" Amy showed him a beetle on her screen, then enlarged the image so it was proportionate to Ari's tank. "They're just the same."

"Next we're comparing dragonflies and helicopters," Ari said happily.

"In a couple more years they'll probably be able

to design a jumbo jet, Mr. Campbell.'' Gordon took Jon's elbow and drew him away from the computers. "I've never seen anything like this," he muttered in awe.

Jon glanced over at the curly dark heads of his children. "They're just little kids," he told the young man in a low voice. "Don't treat them like they're different, okay? I want their lives to be as normal as possible."

"That's what Dr. Klassen and Dr. Pritchard keep telling us. But it's really hard not to get excited about what they can do."

Amy looked over her shoulder. "Are you going home now, Daddy?"

"In a few minutes. I don't have any classes this afternoon. Why?"

"Tell Margaret we want meat loaf for supper. She promised yesterday, but sometimes she forgets."

"And no cheese melted on top of it," Ari warned. "That's *so* yucky."

Jon and Gordon exchanged an amused glance and went back to watch the computers for a few more minutes, chatting with the two children and enjoying their animated discussion.

He had been right to bring them here, Jon thought. Despite their homesickness, as well as the general upheaval in his family life, all of his children needed this kind of challenge and mental stimulation.

He glanced at the door wistfully, hoping Camilla might change her mind and decide to come down and visit. But it clearly wasn't going to happen today.

Finally he got up, kissed both children and left the room, heading out to the parking lot.

Jon settled behind the wheel and took out the sheet of paper with Enrique Valeros's address. He stared at it, debating.

Maybe it was none of his business. After all, the kid was living on his own, older than Steven, taking a full load of classes. Maybe he wouldn't appreciate a classmate coming around and poking into his personal affairs.

But Camilla had mentioned being concerned enough to stop at the boy's apartment. The thought of his elegant professor actually entering such a squalid neighborhood was the deciding factor for Jon. He shifted his car into gear, drove south on Crowchild Trail and crossed the river, then turned and headed for the downtown core.

The building where Enrique lived was so dilapidated and filthy that Jon hesitated in the foyer for a few minutes, looking around at the smeared walls and broken floor, the shards of glass and discarded hypodermic needles behind the radiator.

Jon made his way downstairs into the basement, where the squalor was even worse. He paused outside Enrique's apartment and knocked but there was no answer. Jon waited, shifting restlessly on his feet. He knocked again, then tried the doorknob. The door was unlocked and swung open loosely, sagging on a broken upper hinge.

He stepped inside to wrestle the door back into place, then looked around, feeling guilty at this invasion of privacy. But Enrique clearly didn't have much of a private life. There was nothing at all in the room but a cot fitted with a coarse gray blanket, a folding table and metal chair, two cardboard boxes and a pile of books.

Despite the barrenness of the place and an unpleasant smell that was now almost overpowering, Jon could see that an attempt had been made to keep things clean.

Suddenly he tensed and caught his breath. Behind a ragged curtain in an alcove, he could detect a bulky shape on the floor, and the sole of a running shoe. He hurried across the room, pulled the curtain aside and knelt over Enrique's body.

The boy was curled in a fetal position, his face deathly pale. He wore filthy, grease-smeared clothes and had vomited on the floor nearby, obviously the source of the offensive smell. At such close quarters, it almost made Jon's stomach heave, as well.

He felt for a pulse, and discovered that the boy's heartbeat was faint but regular. Hastily he got to his feet, found a cloth in the sink and soaked it in cold water, then knelt to wipe Enrique's face and neck. After a few moments, the boy's eyes fluttered open and focused blankly on Jon's face.

"Hey, guy," Jon said, trying to smile. "What's going on? This is a pretty weird place to fall asleep, you know."

Enrique blinked in confusion and turned his head away. Suddenly his face turned crimson with embarrassment.

"I was sick," he whispered, struggling to sit up. "I am...so sorry. Please don't bother about me. I will be fine."

"Do you think you can sit up?" Jon reached to put an arm under the boy's thin shoulders and help him to a sitting position.

"I must clean my floor. Please, Mr. Campbell, I don't want you to..."

"I'm used to messes, son," Jon told him comfortably. "I've raised four kids and cleaned up more messes than you could imagine. Quit fretting and tell me what's going on here. Are you just hungry, or what?"

"I'm fine," Enrique said with a touch of stubborn pride. "I can look after myself now."

"Sure you can." Jon helped the boy stand. "Do you feel dizzy?"

But Enrique couldn't reply. He turned white again and sagged in Jon's arms, clearly unable to support his own weight.

Without further hesitation, Jon swept him into his arms and carried him outside, pausing to pull the door shut behind him. He settled Enrique in the back seat of the car, over the boy's feeble protests. Finally he turned the car around and started toward the hospital.

ENRIQUE FELL ASLEEP again while they were driving home and hardly roused as Jon parked and lifted him from the car. Margaret was in the kitchen when he carried the boy into the house. She rushed across the room, wringing her hands in her apron.

"He's one of the kids I go to school with," Jon told her as he strode down the hallway toward a guest room, with his housekeeper close behind.

"What's wrong with him? Shouldn't he be in the hospital?" she asked.

"I took him to the emergency room. The doctor said he's just worn-out, dehydrated and hungry. He needs a good rest and a lot of warm fluids." Jon entered one of the rooms and placed Enrique on a quilted bedspread.

Margaret stood by the foot of the bed and looked down at the thin white face, the dark eyelashes and ragged hair. "Poor thing," she whispered.

Jon unbuttoned the boy's shirt. "I'll undress him and wash him," he said over his shoulder. "Margaret, could you please find me one of Steve's shirts and a pair of shorts? And then maybe we'll see if we can get him to eat something."

"I have a big pot of soup on the stove. That'll be perfect for him." Margaret started briskly toward the hall. "Hello, dear," she said, greeting Vanessa, who paused in the doorway and peered at her father.

Jon was removing Enrique's shoes while the boy lay limp and unmoving.

"Who's that, Daddy?" Vanessa asked.

"It's a kid from one of my classes at the college." Jon pulled off one of Enrique's socks and dropped it on the floor, then tugged at the other one.

Vanessa edged closer to the bed, wrinkling her nose in distaste. "Why is he here?"

"Because he's sick and he needs our help for a while."

Vanessa looked shocked. "You mean he's going to *live* here?"

"I don't know." Jon pulled off the other sock and unfastened the boy's ragged belt. "He's probably going to stay until he's feeling a little stronger, at least. You should have seen where this poor kid was living, Van. You couldn't even imagine a place like that."

"But he's..." She looked in alarm at the limp form on the bed. "He's so *dirty*."

Jon turned and stared at his daughter in disbelief. "For God's sake, Van, look at him! Don't you have any feelings at all?"

She met his gaze in silence, her pretty face flushed and rebellious. At last she turned abruptly and ran from the room before her father could say anything else.

THE NEXT DAY Camilla went down the hall at two o'clock to collect the twins for their regular appointment. She took them back to her office, listening with pleasure while they trotted along beside her and chattered about beetles.

"There's more than a quarter of a million different species. They're one of the oldest things in the whole world," Amy said. "Did you know that, Camilla? Beetles were here before dinosaurs, even."

"That's because they're such a good design." Ari stopped at the water fountain and waited for Camilla to lift him so he could drink. "Like army tanks."

"What's so special about the design of beetles?" Camilla asked as she lowered him carefully to the floor again.

"They have wings and armor," Ari said. "Nothing else does."

"Army tanks don't have wings," Camilla said. "Maybe it would be a good idea if they did. What do you think?"

The twins looked startled, then interested. "Hey, we could design a tank with wings," Ari told his sister. "Let's do it on the computer at home and show it to Gordon tomorrow."

"Can we work on your computer today, Camilla?" Amy asked.

"Not today, dear. We're doing symbols again this afternoon."

"Concrete or abstract?" Ari said.

He took a deep interest in all the tests that Camilla administered, and liked to know the proper names for them.

"Concrete. Words and pictures that have to be matched."

Camilla unlocked her office door and watched while the twins settled themselves at the miniature table near the window, looking up at her in anticipation.

She sat in an armchair nearby and took out a set of big printed cards.

"Did Daddy have an English class this morning?" Amy asked.

"Not today. His class is tomorrow morning."

"He stayed home to help Margaret look after Enrique," Ari told his sister. "Remember?"

Camilla looked up, startled. "Enrique?"

"That's a boy who goes to school with Daddy. He's really nice."

"I know. But I wasn't aware... Is Enrique at your house?"

"Daddy brought him home." Amy riffled through a pile of books on the table, looking happily at the pictures. "He was real sick at first. But Daddy thinks he's better now because Margaret made bean soup and he ate almost all of it."

"And some meat loaf," Ari volunteered. "But not very much. Daddy says that Enrique's too weak to eat meat loaf yet."

"My goodness. I had no idea all this was happening." Camilla gripped the pile of cards in her lap. "Is Enrique going to stay at your house?"

Ari shrugged. "I guess so. Daddy says Enrique doesn't have a very nice place to live, and he needs somebody to look after him."

"Your father seems to—" Camilla bit her lip abruptly.

She'd been on the verge of saying that their father seemed to make a habit of picking up strays, feeding and caring for them. But she stopped herself just in time.

"Look, Ari." Amy held out one of the books. "It shows all different kinds of seeds. These are like little propellers."

Ari climbed up, kneeling on the chair, and leaned

across the table in excitement as he examined the picture book.

"We could use those wings for our tank. And then they'd fold inside the roof when it wasn't flying." He began to scrabble through the pencils and paper on the table.

"Not now," Camilla told him gently. "Let's do half an hour of cards first. Then you can work on your tank for half an hour, okay?"

"Okay," the twins chorused obediently.

Camilla began to display the cards and mark the children's response time as they named the objects and matched them to printed words.

After their session was completed and the twins were working contentedly at the table on their own project, Camilla settled behind her desk to transcribe the results of the test.

Their intelligence was phenomenal, and yet in so many ways these children were normal seven-year-olds. In fact, their emotional development and grasp of adult relationships and concepts was no different from any other child's.

As her research progressed, Camilla was growing more convinced that their brilliance was related to something inside their brains, a rare ability to grasp and process symbols with lightning speed. The study excited her, and promised to become the most important piece of research she'd ever done.

But with increasing frequency, she found herself wanting to put all the cards and tests aside, gather the twins into her lap and cuddle them.

She smiled at their curly dark heads glinting in the sunlight as they worked close together at the little table.

Her phone rang and she picked it up, still watching the children. "Dr. Pritchard speaking."

"Camilla? It's Simon."

"Hello, Simon," she said, a little surprised that he was calling her at work. Simon Constable was the senior administrator at the youth hostel.

"I know you don't like to come down here on weeknights, but we're really short-staffed. Could you possibly do the eight o'clock shift tonight?"

"All right. Eight o'clock, you said?"

"That's right. I think you'll probably only have to stay until midnight, unless there's some kind of new crisis."

"I'll be there."

"Thanks, Camilla. I don't know what we'd do without you."

"Wait, Simon. Have you heard how Chase...."

But he was already gone. She hung up and turned to find both twins watching her with wide, thoughtful eyes.

"Do you have a date?" Amy asked.

Camilla hesitated. "Sort of."

"Is it somebody you really like?"

"It's not that kind of date, dear. More like a job I have to do."

Ari selected a crayon. "Daddy had a date once," he volunteered.

"Who with?" she asked.

"It was a lady who was visiting at another ranch. She had red hair."

"Did you like her?" Camilla asked, feeling treacherous.

"She was awful," Amy muttered. "She laughed at us."

"She *laughed* at you? Why on earth would she do that?"

Ari's round face turned pink with distress. "Vanessa made us sing a song for the lady, and she laughed. She said we sounded like chipmunks."

"Well, that was silly of her," Camilla said indignantly. "I'll bet your song was really good."

"Daddy didn't like it when she laughed at us." Amy brightened a little. "He never had any more dates with her."

"I wish *you'd* have a date with Daddy," Ari said. "Why don't you, Camilla?"

Camilla was conscious of both children watching her intently. An uncomfortable flush warmed her cheeks, and she looked down at the record book on her desk. "Your father's one of my students, Ari."

"But does that mean you can't ever go out on a date with him? Could he be your boyfriend if you wanted him to?"

"I don't think so. Teachers shouldn't really go out on dates with their students. Tell me, how's that army tank of yours coming along?"

She got up and crossed the room to look at their drawing. Soon, to Camilla's relief, the children were absorbed in showing her the intricacies of their new design, and there was no more dangerous talk about boyfriends and dates.

HOURS LATER Camilla settled behind the old desk at the hostel, took out her ever-present stack of papers and began marking. This was the essay from her senior English class, describing the most beautiful place they'd ever seen.

She worked carefully, making notes and comments, circling the errors. Her students had chosen to describe the usual places…cathedrals, waterfalls, mountain scenery.

Idly, she wondered what the response would be if she asked Ari and Amy to describe the most beautiful place they'd ever seen. There was absolutely no way to predict their answer, which was part of the fun of being with them.

She wound a strand of hair around her finger, thinking about Jon Campbell.

He, too, had a brilliantly original mind, something she was becoming increasingly conscious of as she marked his essays and graded his tests.

Was it feasible that a man like him would really have forgotten their encounter? He'd been so kind to Enrique and so sincere that she no longer thought him capable of outright deception, yet he showed no recollection of her.

Camilla couldn't believe that she'd changed so much in twenty years. Inside she often felt like the same lost, terrified child she'd been when Jon Campbell first met her.

She was strongly tempted to rummage through the pile of essays and find the one he'd written. The man's opinions and observations were becoming more fascinating all the time. But she forced herself to keep on marking, to wait until his essay appeared.

As she worked, she was interrupted regularly by street kids coming into the hostel and settling down for the night. About a dozen were in residence tonight, sleeping in the big adjoining room on old blankets and makeshift cots. They weren't allowed to leave once they'd checked in, so after greeting Camilla they passed the evening playing cards and talking among themselves.

She got up every half hour and went to check on them, enduring their teasing sallies with calm good humor. The building was old and decrepit, but the tumbled blankets and noisy group of young people made it seem cozy, almost cheerful.

It was a bit like a slumber party, Camilla thought. Not that she'd ever been invited to slumber parties when she was a girl, but she'd often fantasized about them in those days, wondering how it would feel to spend the whole night with a laughing bunch of friends.

Still, there was a grim edge to this scene, too. She didn't like to think where these kids would be tonight if the hostel weren't in operation.

"Hey, Queen," a voice said behind her. "How ya doin'?"

It was Marty, carrying Chase's guitar and an old yellow pillowcase that bulged with clothes.

Camilla hugged the girl, delighted to see her. "I've been wondering about you," she said.

Marty shifted on her feet, clearly touched by the embrace. "I thought maybe I'd crash here tonight if you've still got room. It's scary over at that place when Chase isn't there."

"Of course I've got room. How is he, Marty?"

Camilla led the way into the office and gestured for the girl to sit opposite her. Marty put down the guitar and settled wearily on the chair, stashing her bundle of clothes out of sight behind her old running shoes.

"He's getting better." She glanced shyly at Camilla. "He's going into drug rehab at the hospital. He'll be there a few more weeks, I guess."

Camilla smiled at the girl. "Really?"

"We talked for a long time after he woke up the other day. He's ready to give it a try. That whole scene really scared him." Marty lowered her head to look at the floor. "It scared both of us."

"Sweetie, that's such wonderful news!" Camilla got up and hugged Marty again. "I've been praying for this to happen."

"Me, too. And he's ready. I know Chase. He can do anything if he sets his mind to it." Marty smiled shyly through her tangle of hair. "We've got all kinds of plans. I just got a job as dishwasher at a pizza restaurant over on Sixth Avenue. They said Chase can come and work there, too, as soon as he's out of the hospital. We figure if we save everything we make and he's not buying drugs anymore, we can maybe get a place of our own in a few months."

"That's great, Marty. Really wonderful. I'm so glad to hear it."

Marty smiled again. "You know what I did yesterday, Queen? I opened a bank account and put in some of the money Chase made while he was playing. We were keeping it in a sock under the floorboards. Just imagine," the girl said in wonder. "Me, with a bank account."

On impulse Camilla reached for her handbag, took out a leather folder and wrote a check. "Add that to your bank account, honey."

Marty took the check and looked at it. Her eyes widened.

"But this...it's too much. You can't give me all this."

Camilla smiled. "Of course I can. I love to hear about a girl who's trying to make her life better."

"Queen, I..." Marty hesitated and glanced down at the check. "Camilla Pritchard," she said awkwardly. "I've known you for years, but I never even heard your name before."

"Well, now you know it. I teach English at the university."

"Wow," Marty said. "And you spend every weekend in a dump like this. Why?"

Because I've been there and I know what it's like. Because somebody helped me once and turned my life around with kindness, and I've never forgotten it.

She longed to tell somebody the truth. But she simply couldn't do it. Not even with Marty, who'd lived the same nightmare.

I can't escape from my past, Camilla thought in despair. *It's going to haunt me forever because it's too awful to talk about.*

The girl was watching her in concern. Camilla gathered herself together and smiled. "I guess I'm just fond of kids," she said. "Now, you'd better go and find a space for yourself before anybody else gets here."

"Can I leave Chase's guitar in here? I don't want those guys to touch it."

"Of course you can. Marty…"

"Yeah?"

"Do you know anything about Zeke and Speedball?" Camilla asked. "What are they doing these days?"

Marty grimaced in distaste. "Nothing good, that's for sure. I heard Zeke was in detention for a while, used a knife to rob some little old lady's grocery store. The guy's a total jerk."

"Do you see him around much?"

"Not anymore. But I heard Speedball's been bragging that they've got a good deal going."

Camilla's heart sank. "What kind of deal?" she asked, though she was fairly sure what the answer would be.

"They've got some rich kid hanging out with them, a guy with a car and lots of money. I don't know what they're planning to do with him, but I wouldn't want to be in his shoes."

Camilla looked down at the papers on her desk. "Thanks, Marty."

I see nothing inherently wrong with criminal activities, Steven Campbell had written.

Camilla watched as Marty trudged out of the office, her torn soles flapping against the splintery planks. Still troubled, she went back to her work, riffling through the pile of essays to find Jon's.

The most beautiful place I ever saw was a room in an old motel in Saskatchewan. The carpet was dirty brown, the furniture was faded orange plaid and the curtains had big blue flowers all over them. The toilet was cracked and the dresser was made of wood-grain plastic. The place reeked of cigarette smoke and had a colony of ants living under the heating unit.

But it was beautiful. I'll never forget that room. What made it so beautiful was the girl who stayed there with me. Her name was Callie, and I've thought about her a thousand times in the years that have passed since then, even though I only saw her for a few days. Afterward I was...

Camilla's eyes blurred as she stared at the paper, frozen with shock. Her face drained of color and her heart pounded.

She read the rest of his essay slowly, holding her breath. When she was finished, she put her head on her folded arms, dropped the marking pencil and began to sob.

CHAPTER SEVEN

July 1977

WHEN I WAKE UP he's sitting across the room, watching television with the sound turned low. He leans back in the old vinyl armchair holding a can of juice. He's wearing a T-shirt like mine, a pair of faded jeans and clean white socks. His feet are propped up on the edge of the bed.

Everything about this guy is so clean. I pretend to be asleep while I'm watching him through half-closed eyes.

He's handsome in a wholesome, clean-cut way, like somebody's older brother. He doesn't look particularly scary, but I know you can't judge by looks.

He's gone to a lot of trouble to get me into this room. We're alone together and I'm naked except for his cotton T-shirt. God knows what's going to happen to me next.

Now that I've had some sleep and I'm not feeling so weak, I have enough energy to be worried about my safety. I wish I could pass out again and wake up by myself, but it's a pretty faint hope.

This guy doesn't look as if he's going anywhere.

He's just sitting there, waiting for me to open my eyes.

Suddenly he notices that I'm awake. When he smiles, his whole face lights up. I try to feign sleep again but it's no use. He pads across the room and sits next to me on the bed.

"Hi, kiddo" he says, his voice husky. "I'll bet you feel a lot better now. I thought you were never going to wake up."

I look up at him, but I still can't talk. I'm actually getting a little worried about my voice. Maybe I won't ever be able to talk again. What if I have to go through the rest of my life writing notes to people because I can't say anything?

But then I remember that the rest of my life doesn't amount to much anyway, so it doesn't matter.

"What happened to your nose?" he asks.

I watch him in wary silence, still trying to figure out what he plans to do with me.

"It looks like maybe it was broken," he says, bending closer with a worried frown. "And I think you've had a couple of black eyes, too, but they're mostly healed now. Can you tell me who hurt you?"

He touches the bridge of my nose with his fingers. I wince automatically but his hands are gentle and they don't hurt.

"I've got some sandwiches here." He gets up and crosses the room again to take a paper sack from the dresser. "And cookies and a few bottles of fruit juice. I didn't know what you'd like."

He unwraps the sandwich. I can see thick slices of

roast beef, lettuce, mayonnaise. My stomach rumbles. All at once I'm so hungry I can hardly keep from grabbing the bread and stuffing it into my mouth like a starving animal.

He hands me the sandwich and watches while I eat. "Orange juice?" he says casually, as if we've spent our whole lives eating together.

I nod and he pops the can, holding it out to me. I've never tasted anything as delicious as this sandwich and juice.

It's like ambrosia. That's something we learned about in history class. It was the food and nectar of the gods.

I'd like to tell him all about the ambrosia. There's something in his face that makes me think he'd understand. But I'm nervous and the words still won't come.

"Guess what time it is?" he says.

He gets up and opens the drapes. There's a strange pearly light shimmering against the dirty windows. I can't tell where it's coming from.

When I don't speak, he answers his own question. "It's just a bit after dawn."

He comes back to unwrap another sandwich for me while I watch him in confusion.

How can it be dawn? It was early morning when I went to sleep.

"You've slept for almost twenty-four hours," he says as if I'd spoken aloud. "I've had a chance to explore every inch of this crummy little place. There's an old dog with a litter of puppies in a cardboard box behind the office. And the manager used to be a rodeo champion. He's got all his trophies on a big shelf next to the check-in. He's a really neat guy.''

I begin to eat the other sandwich. There's such a big hole in the center of me, it feels as though I'll never be full again. He opens a second can, apple juice this time, and hands it to me. I realize that I need to go to the bathroom, but I'm too shy to do anything about it while he's sitting there.

''How old are you?'' he asks.

''Seventeen.''

We're both astonished that I've actually spoken. My voice is practically a croak but at least it's audible. We smile at each other and I have to turn away quickly. His smile makes me feel strange, warm and melting inside. It's a weird sensation but not unpleasant, just a little scary.

''Did you run away?''

I nod and gulp the juice.

''Why?''

I shake my head. He's so nice, so boyish and gentle and kind. How can I tell him about the squalor of my life, and the things that have happened to me?

When I remember, I feel ashamed and dirty again, tense with misery. Tears fill my eyes and begin to roll down my cheeks.

His face twists in sympathy. ''Hey,'' he whispers, touching my shoulder. ''Come on, don't do that. Please don't cry. What's your name? Mine's Jon.''

''Callie,'' I whisper.

They've always called me that. Actually, my real

name is Camilla, but nobody uses it. I've always secretly wished people would, because it sounds like such a quiet, elegant kind of name.

But I'm just poor Callie Pritchard from the trailer park, the girl whose mother drinks and brings men home all the time. I'm trash. No wonder they don't call me Camilla.

"That's a pretty name," he says. "Callie." He repeats it softly, making it sound a whole lot nicer than it is.

Everything about him is nice. He's strong and brown, and his teeth are so white when he smiles.

"I went downtown on my bike yesterday afternoon while you were sleeping," he says. "I bought some stuff for you."

Again I'm confused, trying to grasp how long I've been lying in this bed. And I really need to go to the bathroom.

Before I can move, he's on his feet again, dumping a mound of packages onto the covers, opening them to display their contents. There's a new pair of jeans, a couple of T-shirts, a warm jacket, socks and running shoes, even a pack of cotton panties.

"I don't know much about girl's clothes," he says, looking shy and embarrassed. "I hope this stuff is the right size."

I can't think of anything to say. I stare at the clothes, then back at him. Nobody's ever done anything like this for me.

Finally I scramble off the bed, gather up the packages and take them into the bathroom. I get dressed slowly, savoring the feeling of new denim and cotton.

I must not be as close to death as I'd thought, if new clothes can still make me feel this good.

When I'm dressed I stand and look at myself in the mirror, reluctant to go back into that other room where he's waiting. My nose is still swollen across the bridge, though the rainbow of bruising has begun to fade from around my eyes.

How can he look at me with such warmth and admiration? I'm ugly. My face still carries the mark of that man's hand. And my body...

I shudder and turn away from the mirror. When it can't be delayed any longer, I open the door timidly and venture out into the other room.

He's waiting, and he examines me with obvious delight. "Hey, those jeans are a perfect fit," he says. "Aren't they?"

I nod and search for my voice. "I can't...I can't pay you for all this stuff. I don't have any—"

He waves his hand, looking awkward. "Forget it, okay? I've got lots of money left over from the trip. Besides, it was kind of fun, buying all that stuff. Like dressing a doll."

I hate the thought of being somebody's doll, but I know he means well so I don't say anything.

"Are you feeling okay now?" he asks. "Not so weak anymore?"

"I'm a lot better. Thank you," I add a little stiffly, because I owe him so much that I can't begin to express it.

His face lights up again with that luminous smile, making my heart beat faster. He lifts his rangy body out of the chair and reaches for my hand.

"Come on, Callie," he says. "Let's go look at the puppies."

We spend the rest of the morning wandering around in the sunshine, playing with the litter of fat puppies behind the motel, talking with the old cowboy who runs the place.

After lunch we go for a long walk on the prairie and he tells me about the ranch where he lives, about his family, their horses and pets.

He's an only child and both his parents are already in their sixties. It sounds as if he's always been the center of their existence. No wonder he walks with such easy confidence, as if the whole world was made for him and nothing's ever going to be denied him.

Early in the evening we climb onto the motorcycle and go downtown for a pizza. The restaurant is full of young people like us, laughing and fooling around.

It's the first time I've ever done anything like this. I feel like a normal teenage girl, out on a date with her boyfriend. Actually, it's just what I've always dreamed of, a night like this.

But it's too late for the experience to bring me any real pleasure, because I know that if I told him the truth about myself, he'd turn away in disgust. Even if he were polite enough to hide his reaction, I'd be able to see it in his eyes.

We go to a movie, the only one playing in this little town. The film is violent and juvenile, and we both hate it. Later, walking back to the pizza parlor for a snack, we talk about our tastes and find that we've read a lot of the same books.

He's in his second year of college. I tell him how much I've always wanted to attend college, how I've dreamed of getting an education but it's never going to happen. He takes my hand and leans toward me earnestly, telling me nothing's impossible if we want it badly enough.

I have to look away so he can't see my sudden flare of contempt.

What does he know about it? Nothing's ever going to be difficult for him, let alone impossible. The world's been handed to him on silver platter, all he has to do is reach out and take it.

But he's so sincere, so genuinely nice that I can't stay angry with him. I just nod and keep looking down at the sidewalk.

Sounding a little shy, he begins to tell me some of his own dreams. He wants to finish college, then travel around and see the world for a few years before he settles down.

"Will you go back to the ranch?" I ask him.

"Of course," he says, looking surprised. "It's the most beautiful place in the world. I want to get married and a raise a bunch of kids there. But first I'll have to find the right girl."

I can feel him smiling down at me. My stomach tightens and a little chill of excitement whispers through me, making me feel warm and trembly.

Maybe this is how it feels to be in love.

But I can't fall in love with this boy! He's a prince, an aristocrat...

And I'm Callie Pritchard.

When he finds out, he won't even want to talk to me anymore.

We go for a ride on the motorcycle before we head back to the motel. It's dark out on the prairie highway, and the sky hangs above us like a canopy of black silk dusted with silver. There's a damp fragrance of grass and sage. The air is warm and cool in patches, and I cling to him and lift my face to the wind.

I can see his broad back, his shoulders and the tanned curve of his cheek as he turns to shout something over the roar of the bike. I have a sudden urge to cuddle against him and press my face into his jacket. Instead, I take my arms from around his waist and cling to the luggage rack so I won't have to touch him.

"Are you okay?" he calls.

"I'm fine."

But he seems concerned. Finally he pulls the bike around and heads back to the motel.

There's a moment of awkwardness when we enter and turn on the lights. It feels different now that I'm healthy and strong again, not some helpless little starved kitten that he's carrying around. We don't quite know how to behave with each other.

A last I get his white T-shirt from under my pillow and head for the bathroom. "I'll go first," I tell him, and he nods.

I undress quickly and wash my face. He's even bought me a toothbrush and some other stuff, soap and perfumed hand lotion, toothpaste and a plastic hairbrush. It's all in a new red duffel bag on the floor. I can't believe anybody would be so generous.

When I'm ready, I come nervously back into the room and duck under the covers, staying close to my edge of the bed.

"I'll spend another night in the armchair," he tells me, looking away so I can't see his face. "It's pretty comfortable, actually."

I'm consumed with guilt. He's done so much for me already. Last night he sat in that little chair for hours while I slept like a log.

"Look, it's a big bed," I tell him reluctantly. "I guess we can share if you like. You need to get some sleep, too."

His face creases briefly into a smile. "Thanks for the thought, but I'm not sure I could stand it."

I understand what he means and my cheeks flame with embarrassment.

"I've got an idea," he says.

He fetches his knapsack and my new duffel bag and puts them beside me under the covers, forming a long barrier down the middle of the bed.

I lie on my side of the nylon hedge, watching him.

"How's that?" he asks.

"It's...I guess it's okay."

"Good."

He vanishes into the bathroom and I hear water running. He's having a shower. I try not to picture him naked under the streaming jets of water. When he comes out, his hair is damp, showing the neat tracks of a comb. He's wearing a T-shirt and undershorts, and his legs are hairy and muscular, making him look like a man instead of a boy.

His body gives me a brief shiver of terror and I turn away quickly. But when he climbs into bed and switches off the light, I find that I like having him over there beyond the knapsacks. It's a safe, cozy feeling, knowing I could touch him if I wanted. And nobody would ever dare hurt me while he's so close to me.

We lie in the dark, talking quietly. I don't know how it happens, but I find that I'm telling him all about myself.

This is something I never do. I don't talk about my own life, not even with the counselor at school who tries hard to be helpful and understanding. But he's listening so intently that I can sense his concern wrapping all around me, and I feel safe.

I tell him about our awful poverty and my mother's erratic behavior, and how terrifying it used to be when I was a little girl, never knowing what shape she'd be in when I woke up. I tell him all of it, the squalor and the hunger, the pain of being mocked by other kids because of the way we lived. I let him know everything except my full name and the town my mother lives in.

When I get to the part about the boyfriends and how scary they've been lately, he reaches over and takes my hand, holding it gently.

I falter a little but keep on talking. I tell him about the newest boyfriend, about the increasing drunkenness and the threatening looks, about the knife under my pillow. His hand tightens on mine but he makes no other response.

Finally I get to that last terrible night. My voice catches in my throat and I can't go on.

"Tell me, Callie." He leans up on his elbow and looks at me earnestly across the knapsack and duffel bag, his face silvered by the moonlight. "You need to talk about it. Tell me what happened."

So I do. I tell him about the man coming into my room, about how easily he got the knife away from me and what happened next. By the time it's finished, I'm sobbing and the sacks are gone from between us. He's holding me tenderly, brushing at my hair, soothing me like a little child.

With infinite gentleness he kisses the damaged bridge of my nose, then cuddles me in his arms.

"It's okay," he whispers. "It's okay, honey. Everything's going to be all right."

I know nothing's going to be all right, ever again. Still, it feels good to hear him say it.

After a long time I fall asleep. He's still holding me and the closeness of his body isn't terrifying anymore, just tender and strong and comforting, like the father I've never had.

NEXT MORNING I wake in the pale light of dawn to find him sound asleep beside me. I rub my eyes, then roll my head on the pillow to study his face. He seems so young when he's sleeping like this. Despite his broad shoulders and the sinewy, muscular look of his arms, he's like a boy. His breathing is deep and even, and his brown hair stands up in an unruly cowlick that makes me smile.

I reach out to touch his head, trying to smooth the cowlick. He opens his eyes and watches me.

"It's standing right on end," I tell him, stroking the back of his head. "You look like a little kid."

He grins lazily and stretches. "I'm not a little kid."

I know what he means, and realize it's dangerous to keep touching his hair. He's watching me now with a warm, intent look that scares me a bit, but I'm gripped by a kind of recklessness. I run my hand down the tanned curve of his cheek, marveling at how soft his skin feels.

He grasps my hand and brings it to his mouth, kissing my fingers, then my palm. I shiver at the feeling of his lips on my hand. Everything about him is sweet and exciting, like heady wine. I don't even know what I'm doing.

He reaches out and gathers me close to him. Our legs are bare, and his skin is warm on mine. He tickles my ankles with his feet and laughs softly.

"You're so sweet," he murmurs. "Give me a kiss, Callie."

I lift my head and feel his mouth on mine. It's a dizzying sensation, like drowning in sunshine. He begins to stroke my body with a long, slow movement of his hands, as if he's a sculptor shaping something beautiful. I press myself against him. Suddenly I can't get close enough. Something in the back of my mind tells me this is crazy, that he's going to hurt me and I should get up and run. But I'm intoxicated by him.

"I won't hurt you," he whispers. "I'd never hurt you."

He kisses me again, gently, tenderly. He strokes my hip, nestles against me. "We don't have to do anything. I'll just hold you if that's what you want."

I don't know what I want. I need to be close to him, that's all. I press myself against him and kiss his neck.

He holds me and strokes my back. He kisses my eyelids while I drift off to sleep.

When I wake up, there's a wash of bright daylight from the windows. He's standing above me, fully dressed, holding something in his hands.

I try to shade my eyes from the light. "What time is it?"

"Almost noon. Get up, lazybones. I'm starving."

"What's that?" I ask, looking at the cone of paper in his hands.

He unrolls the newspaper to show me a bunch of yellow flowers, wild daisies from the ditch along the highway.

"They're for you," he tells me shyly. "I really wanted to get you a dozen yellow roses because you're a golden princess. But this was the best I could do on short notice."

I pull on a shirt, take the flowers and put them in one of the chipped water glasses. "They're nicer than yellow roses," I tell him.

"Why? They're just wildflowers from the ditch."

"But you picked them yourself. That's what makes them so beautiful."

He smiles happily and my heart aches with love and sadness.

We go about our day, playing with the puppies again, riding downtown on the bike. Later we come back to the motel, carrying our pizza in a box this time, and go to bed. While we eat, we snuggle companionably beneath the covers and talk about everything under the sun. He's full of plans.

"First we need to buy you some more clothes," he says.

"No way. You've already spent too much on me."

He brandishes a wedge of pizza at me, frowning with mock sternness. "Quit arguing with me, woman. I've still got hundreds of dollars in my wallet. We're going to buy you some more clothes, and then I'm taking you home with me."

"Home?" I ask in alarm.

"You've got to meet my parents," he says placidly, so busy with his plans that he's not even aware of my frightened reaction. "And then we'll need to find a place to live in Saskatoon before the fall term starts."

I look at him blankly.

"I have to go back to college," he tells me, bending to kiss my neck. "You can finish high school there and enroll in some freshman classes next term. You're so smart, you'll probably catch up to me in no time."

It all sounds so simple when he says it like that, as if it were really possible for me to meet his parents, share an apartment with him in the city and go to college like a normal girl.

We eat the last of the pizza while I talk and laugh with him to hide my breaking heart. Afterward, we watch television for a while, and fall asleep in each other's arms.

I wake after a few hours. The world is plunged into darkness and the only sound is a chorus of coyotes as they hunt somewhere on the prairie. While he's sleeping close to me, I lie awake and brood about what I'm going to do.

Because of him, something odd has been happening to me. I don't want to die anymore, or embark on some kind of crazy, self-destructive life. I'm determined to survive and make something of myself.

But to do that, I'll need to leave him behind. He knows all about my past. If I'm going to have a future, that other life has got to be erased completely, wiped out as if it never existed. I can't be with anybody who knows who I am or what I used to be.

The old Callie Pritchard needs to die if the new one is going to survive.

Besides it wouldn't be fair to let him believe we could have a future together. He's so good and so kind he deserves someone better than me. His parents and his friends would hate me. The thought of leaving him floods me with agony. I feel tears stinging behind my eyelids, and have to bite my lip to keep from sobbing out loud. My mind darts around, trying to think of some other way. But there's simply no choice, and I know it.

At last I slip out of bed, moving with infinite care so I won't wake him. I gather my new clothes and dress in the bathroom, then grab the rest of the things he bought and stuff them into the red duffel bag.

I creep around the room in the moonlight, looking nervously at his still form in the bed. He mutters something and turns over, begins to breathe deeply again.

His wallet is lying on the dresser. I open it and take out all the bills, then hesitate. He'll need enough money to get home. I think he has a credit card, but I still can't bear to leave him with nothing.

Actually, it would probably be better to take all the money. He'd really hate me then, and be less likely to come looking for me. I waver, trying not to cry. At last I stuff a couple of bills back into his wallet and pocket the rest.

Finally, I shoulder the duffel bag and slip out the door. The night is cold and still, with a pale shimmer of light along the distant horizon where the sun will be rising in an hour or so. I lower the bag to the ground, fighting with myself.

I know it's crazy, but I can't keep myself from creeping back into the room and bending over him. I don't want to risk waking him, so I drop a kiss on the pillow beside his cheek.

"Thank you," I whisper to his dear, sleeping face. "Thank you for everything. I'm so sorry. I'll never stop loving you as long as I live."

Then I leave, closing the door soundlessly behind

me. I head out onto the highway and start to jog, turning around with my thumb extended whenever headlights pierce the darkness.

A woman picks me up. She's middle-aged, sour and tired, heading off to a Bible class she teaches in one of the rural school districts. She preaches at me for a hundred miles while I rest my head against the back of the seat and try to look as if I'm paying attention.

Finally she lets me off and a trucker picks me up almost immediately, taking me all the way to Regina. He's kind and quiet, and tells me a lot about his three daughters. When I promise him I'll go back to school and not hitch rides anymore, he drops me at a youth hostel in the downtown core, near the warehouse where he's going.

My heart is frozen, hard as stone. I know what I'm going to do and where I have to begin. But I know, as well, that I'll never really be happy. And I'll never love anybody again.

I always thought cruelty and neglect were the most painful, but I was wrong.

Love is the real agony. Love hurts more than anything....

"QUEEN! What's the matter? Hey, guys, come and look at the Queen. Oh man, is she *crying?*"

Camilla came back to reality with a start. Three ragged teenage boys stood watching her, their faces puzzled and worried.

She shook her head, rubbing hastily at her eyes. "I

was…I guess I must have been daydreaming. What's happening?''

"A couple of kids want to get in. Have we got enough room?"

"I…I think so. Do we know them?"

"Zippy does. He says they're buddies of his, and one of them's sick."

"Okay. I'll let them in."

Still dazed, Camilla got up to unlock the door, dealing mechanically with the new arrivals. When they were settled in the other room and the street door was safely locked again, she came back to the office and sat down at her desk, staring at the final words of Jon Campbell's essay.

After she disappeared, I went tearing around the country on my bike for a few days, trying to find her. At last I headed for home, got my truck and started to search the whole province, then all of western Canada. I quit college and spent a year looking for her, following up every lead I could think of, going into every little town I passed and asking if a blond girl named Callie had ever lived there. But I couldn't find any trace of her. She'd dropped off the face of the earth.

After a few years the memories began to fade. Now I can't even recall exactly what her face was like. But I'll never forget those two days I spent with her in an old motel room that was the most beautiful place I've ever seen.

CHAPTER EIGHT

JON STOOD in his bathroom, examining his face absently in the mirror as he shaved. He was thinking about the essay he'd written, wondering if the professor had read it yet.

He frowned and lifted his head to shave his jawline.

What had possessed him to tell that story, anyway? Especially to a woman whose opinion was growing more important to him with every passing day...

She'd probably think it was ridiculous, a boyish, overly sentimental reminiscence about his long-ago encounter with a girl.

After so many years of keeping the story to himself, he should never have broken his silence. But lately, for some reason, he'd found himself thinking about Callie again.

Sweet little Callie. He smiled and moved his head to shave the other side.

Even after all this time, he couldn't think of her without a powerful surge of emotion. For years, he hadn't been able to summon up an accurate memory of her face. But he could still see brief flashes of the girl...her sober gray eyes and that glorious mane of silvery-blond hair, her gentle hands, the small shapely body.

Still, it wasn't just her body that he remembered with such wistful fondness. It was her mind and spirit, the very essence of her. They'd only spent a couple of days together, he and Callie. But in all his life, Jon had never felt such a sense of total connectedness to any other person.

Callie had understood and trusted him, and she'd allowed him to see the depths of her mind, her remarkable intelligence and shy, playful imagination.

He thought about the awful story she'd told him that night, the way she'd been neglected and abused, how she was certain she'd committed a murder.

His jaw tightened with pain.

Ever since that encounter, Jon had found himself unable to bear the thought of children and adolescents suffering any kind of abuse. Nowadays, he was a silent benefactor to a number of charities that assisted runaways and teenagers at risk. He understood a lot more, too, about the devastating effects of neglect and cruelty on young people.

Maybe if he'd known more back in those days, he could have helped Callie and kept her close to him while they tried to work out her problems. But he'd been too young to understand, and had handled the whole situation so clumsily.

As a result, Callie vanished from his life and he'd never been able to find her. The pain had been so devastating that it almost killed him.

Even now, he was stunned by remembered grief.

For the thousandth time, Jon found himself wondering what might have happened to her during these twenty years. He simply couldn't picture her as a mature adult woman. In his mind she'd be forever seventeen, a shy, sweet waif with her bruised face and wondrous smile. But Callie had been only a few years younger than Jon, so she must be in her late thirties by now.

That is, if she'd managed to survive whatever happened to her after she ran away from him....

He finished shaving, put away his razor and went down the hall, pausing at Steven's closed door. After a brief hesitation he rapped sharply, then opened the door and glanced inside.

His son lay in bed, looking bleary and annoyed.

"Time to get up," Jon said. "You've got a class at nine."

"I'm not going today. I've got a headache."

"Why?" Jon came into the room and stood at the foot of Steven's bed, eyeing the boy steadily.

"How should I know? My head hurts, okay? I'm going back to sleep."

"No, you're not," Jon said. "You're getting up and going to class. Take a couple of aspirin if your head aches."

The boy watched him stubbornly from the pillow. For a long moment their eyes locked in silent challenge. At last Steven cursed under his breath, rolled out of bed and trudged toward his bathroom.

Jon followed him to the door.

"Look," Steven said with heavy sarcasm, "do you think I could have a little privacy? Or is that too much to ask?"

"Where were you last night, Steve?"

"I was out with my friends."

"Who are these friends? I've told you before that it's about time I met them."

"Well, maybe they're not so anxious to meet you."

Steven ran water into the sink and splashed it angrily on his face. He looked pale, and there were dark circles around his eyes. A soft golden stubble dusted his cheeks.

Jon watched in silence, thinking how passionately he'd loved this son of his when Steven was a baby, a pudgy toddler, an eager little boy full of questions.

"Look, Steve, I want you to stay home for the next few evenings and get caught up on your schoolwork," he said.

"Come on, Dad, get real! Most of these courses are so easy, I could do them in my sleep."

"I know you're a smart kid," Jon told him quietly. "But that doesn't mean you should be giving this any less than your best effort. I want you at home for a few nights."

Steven's eyes flashed. "What do you think I am, a little kid like Ari? You can't push me around anymore."

"You're living under my roof, and I still make the rules," Jon said.

"Then maybe I don't want to be under your damn roof!" Steven gripped the edge of the sink tensely as their eyes met in the mirror a second time.

Jon knew that it was dangerous to press the issue.

If his son was pushed too far, he might make good on his threats to walk out.

But he couldn't forget Camilla Pritchard's warning about Steven and his unsuitable friends....

To his relief, the boy was the first to look away. "All right," Steven muttered. "I'll do the bloody schoolwork if that's what you want."

"Good," Jon said quietly. "I'm glad to hear it. Hurry up and come down to breakfast, okay? You can catch a ride with us this morning if you like."

"I don't want to ride with you. I'll drive my own car." Steven lathered shaving cream on his face, looking sullen.

On impulse, Jon moved closer and dropped an arm around Steven's lean shoulders. "You know, you can always talk to me, son," he said. "If anything's bothering you, I'll be happy to listen."

A muscle jerked tensely in Steven's cheek but he said nothing, standing rigid and stubborn in his father's embrace. After a moment, Jon turned away and headed downstairs.

The rest of his family were already at the table, engaged in various pursuits while they ate.

Amy nibbled absently on a slice of toast, concentrating on a Tinkertoy model in front of her, adding little spokes and disks after intervals of deep thought. Beside her, Ari gulped cereal and made notations on a computer diagram of a dragonfly and a helicopter that he was showing to Enrique.

Enrique still looked pale and weak, but he was getting better every day. He'd been with them for two weeks. He now had a modest wardrobe of new clothes supplied by Jon, and was responding well to Margaret's nourishing meals.

But he was still painfully shy. Though he'd begun to establish a warm relationship with the twins, he seemed frightened of everybody else in the household, particularly Vanessa.

Jon's elder daughter sat a little removed from the others, reading an issue of *Vogue* propped next to her coffee mug. She was truly beautiful, with her glossy dark hair and delicate complexion, her slim figure set off by tight-fitting jeans and a black jersey top.

Jon looked at the girl's bent head and wondered what was happening to his two older children. How could he possibly reach them and start getting close to them again? Once upon a time it had been enough simply to love them.

But not anymore....

"Hi, Daddy." Amy beamed up at him. "I'm making a hydrogen molecule. Camilla said it'd be a good idea to use my Tinkertoys."

Jon kissed the twins and settled into his chair. "What does Dr. Pritchard know about hydrogen molecules? I thought her specialty was English, not chemistry."

"The model's just another kind of symbol," Ari said. "Camilla wants us to make a list of as many different symbols as we can find. Ordinary things that can stand for other things."

"So is a dragonfly a symbol for a helicopter?" Jon

smiled his thanks as Margaret set a couple of poached eggs in front of him.

The twins exchanged a thoughtful glance. "No," Ari said at last. "They're two things that are *like* each other, but one isn't a symbol of the other. That's not what a symbol is."

"I see. Van, could you pass me the salt, please?"

Vanessa pushed the saltshaker across the table without looking up.

"Enrique says that where he grew up, dragonflies can grow *this* big." Ari held up his hands, the forefingers about eight inches apart.

"That's a pretty big dragonfly," Jon said, smiling. "How are you feeling this morning, Enrique?"

"I'm fine, thank you." The boy cleared his throat and glanced nervously at Vanessa who was reading and paying no attention to him. He lowered his head again.

"All ready for our English class this morning?" Jon said.

"I think so. I finally have the assignments done, and I'm catching up on the reading I missed."

"Good." Jon glanced at his watch. "Do you want a ride to school, Van?"

"I can go with Steve."

"Steve might be a little late today," Jon said in a neutral tone. "You'd better come with us."

"Whatever." She shrugged, then closed her magazine, got up and wandered from the room while the others watched her.

ENRIQUE sat in the back seat with a twin on either side. Amy held a Barbie doll in one hand, frowning as she struggled to fit a pair of tiny plastic shoes on its feet.

Enrique found these little twins endlessly interesting and appealing. They were so smart, talking all the time about computer designs and molecules. But they also played with ordinary toys and involved themselves in all kinds of imaginative games, just like other kids their age.

He reached out to take the doll, showing Amy how to fit the shoes in place.

When his sister, Maria, was little, Enrique used to help her all the time with her toys and her schoolwork.

Maria had been such a pretty child, with her big dark eyes and shining ponytail. She looked like their mother, who'd worked with Enrique's father in a shabby school building at the edge of the jungle, trying to educate the local kids.

During the uprising, word had spread that the Valeros family was teaching political propaganda in the school. Soldiers stormed the building with their machine guns blazing, and Maria died along with her parents in the hail of bullets. Enrique stayed alive by crawling into the jungle and hiding for several days.

Later he made his way down the seacoast to Panama, traveling by night and hiding in the day. He talked himself onto a steamer bound northward up the west coast, laboring in the cramped galley to pay for his passage, and didn't breathe easily until he was

finally on Canadian soil. Every moment of that nightmare time, he kept expecting the monsters who'd
killed his family to find him and dispose of him, too,
because he was the only witness.

He still had nightmares about their slaughter and
his terrified flight. Sometimes it was almost more than
he could bear, looking into Amy's clear, trusting eyes
and thinking about his own little sister.

Maria had been just nine years old when she died.

"Thanks, Ricky," Amy whispered, smiling happily
when he handed the doll back.

On his other side, Ari was poring over a book about
judo. The little boy studied one of the diagrams, then
chopped the air experimentally as he made a dreadful,
threatening face.

Enrique chuckled and glanced at the two people in
the front seat.

Jon was driving. His eyes crinkled briefly into a
smile as he caught Enrique's glance in the mirror.
Enrique smiled back, feeling warmed and comforted.

He'd never met anybody as kind, strong and totally
competent as Jon Campbell. It felt safe to be near the
man, as if nothing could harm you when he was looking after you.

Still, it hadn't been easy for Enrique to accept this
kind of generosity. Jon had forced him to give up both
jobs for a while, arguing that Enrique would find himself in the hospital if he kept pushing so hard.

Enrique knew in his heart that his friend was right.
He was jeopardizing his precious education by keeping such a brutal schedule. Still, he didn't want to

live on another man's charity. As soon as he was strong enough, he had to find work again, get out of Jon's house and begin standing on his own two feet.

But when he recalled the grinding poverty of his life, the constant fatigue, the lack of study time, he could hardly bear to think about going back to his old room in that smelly basement.

Enrique glanced at Vanessa's glossy head, thinking wistfully about this girl and her older brother who'd lived all their lives with so much security. Neither of them had ever known a moment's hunger or fear in all their lives. They dwelt in a kind of luxury that was almost unimaginable for him.

And yet it seemed to him, amazingly, that the two young people weren't happy at all.

Steven was the nicer of the two, at least to Enrique, though he was hardly ever home and seemed tense and preoccupied when he occasionally showed up for meals.

Vanessa was so distant that Enrique was sure she resented his presence. He longed to be able to talk with her, to laugh and chat easily the way her friends did. But the mere sight of Jon's beautiful daughter made him feel tongue-tied and awkward, and she did nothing at all to ease his tension.

Jon stopped the car outside Vanessa's school. Enrique watched as she got out, lifted her backpack and strolled off into the milling crowd of students, giving her family a curt wave as she vanished.

"My turn to ride with Daddy!" Ari climbed out of the car and scrambled into the front seat next to his father, holding the judo book under his arm while Enrique and Amy exchanged a shy smile.

"Look, Ricky," she said. "Barbie's got her own little cell phone."

Enrique watched, fascinated, as Amy opened and closed the tiny plastic telephone. "Hey, that's really neat," he whispered. "I'll call her, okay?"

He made a soft ringing noise while Jon put the car in gear and headed toward the university. Amy beamed and held the phone to her doll's head.

"Hello, this is the store calling," Enrique said. "I have fifty dresses here for you. When can you come in to try them on?"

"Well, I have my scuba lesson at ten, and then I have to play my guitar in a rock concert, so I won't be able to make it until after lunch."

"After lunch!" Enrique exclaimed in his best department-store voice. "But after lunch we have seventy-five bathing suits for you to model."

Amy giggled in delight. "Okay. I'll have to make an appointment. Now, what time should I be there?" The little girl rummaged in her backpack for a pencil and notepad while Jon caught Enrique's eye in the mirror and grinned warmly.

They reached the campus and drove into one of the student parking lots, then walked across the lawn to the arts building where the twins scampered down the hall to their classroom.

Jon and Enrique went to their English class and found most of the students already assembled. Dr.

Pritchard was handing back essays, moving among the desks with brief comments.

She looked more beautiful than ever, tall and elegant in a long tan skirt, a white silk blouse and knitted vest. Enrique hadn't seen her for almost two weeks, and he was surprised all over again by her golden loveliness.

"Well, hello there." The professor greeted him with such warmth that he felt a little confused. "I'm very happy to see you back in class, Mr. Valeros. How are you feeling?"

He ducked his head shyly and gave her a folder crammed with papers. "Much better, thank you, ma'am. I have some assignments to hand in. I apologize that they are so late."

"Well, in this case I think we can make an allowance for tardiness. I'll try to mark these as soon as I can and get them back to you. Have you caught up with the reading?"

"Almost all of it, ma'am. And Jon gave me his lecture notes from the classes I missed."

The professor glanced at Jon, who stood quietly next to them. "Good morning, Mr. Campbell."

"Hello, Dr. Pritchard. Have you got my essay there, by any chance?"

She looked down and began to rummage through the pile of typed pages.

Enrique was certain he could see tension in her face, a sudden nervousness in the grip of her hands on the papers. For some reason, the English professor always seemed brusque and uncomfortable when she was with Jon, though Enrique couldn't fathom how anyone could dislike the man.

She handed over the essay and moved away to speak with another group of students. Jon and Enrique headed for their desks at the back of the room while Jon leafed eagerly through his paper.

"She didn't make a single comment," he said to Enrique at last, looking disappointed. "She just put the grade and nothing else."

"What was your grade?"

"She gave me an A." Jon settled in his desk and looked at the paper again, frowning thoughtfully. "It's the best grade she's ever given me. There must have been *something* she liked about this essay."

CAMILLA MOVED automatically through her lecture on characterization, more conscious than ever of the man at the back of the room.

She felt so brutally exposed with his eyes resting on her, and now that she'd read his essay and knew how vividly he recalled that long-ago encounter, she was terrified of what was going to happen next. It was all she could do to finish the lecture. At the conclusion, she answered a couple of questions and gave a writing assignment to the class, then hurried from the room, not even stopping at her office.

Instead, she left the building and walked swiftly across campus to her own apartment, letting herself into the familiar sanctuary with a sigh of relief.

Elton was napping on the back of the couch in a ray of sunlight. He stretched and yawned when she came in, then leaped down and padded across the room to rub against her legs.

Camilla scooped the cat gratefully into her arms and settled in one of the armchairs. Elton snuggled drowsily against her as she stroked him.

Maybe she should just come clean, tell the truth and let the rest of her life unfold from there. But she simply couldn't bear the anguish of having those dreadful memories revived and exposed. "I'd rather die, Elton," she whispered. "I believe I'd honestly rather die."

Somewhere along the way, in some secret part of herself, maybe she'd really started believing that she, Camilla Pritchard, had grown up in luxury and passed her childhood among the wealthy and privileged.

Or perhaps little Callie Pritchard, with her sad past and her shameful secrets, had simply been banished from existence for so many years that Camilla had really thought she was dead.

But she wasn't. Callie still lived in Jon Campbell's memory. And now the arrival of this man threatened to bring the whole careful structure of Camilla's life crashing down around her.

She got up abruptly, displacing Elton, who tumbled onto the chair and gazed up at her with startled reproof.

"I'm sorry, darling." Camilla bent to scratch the soft patch of skin behind his ears. "But there's something I have to do."

She crossed the room and went into the foyer, opened the door to her storage closet and pulled out a little wooden stool, climbing up to reach the upper shelves. Behind a row of winter boots, she found what she was looking for and dragged it out.

It was an old red duffel bag, faded almost pink by wear and sunlight. Camilla huddled on the wooden stool, her skirt falling around her as she cradled the bag in her arms.

All these years she'd kept it, the only physical remnant of her childhood.

The duffel bag had served her well in those lonely months and years after she'd run away from the motel. Camilla had used it while she stayed at various youth shelters, taken it to work with her change of clothes when she was laboring at two or three jobs to pay her way though school, and carried her books in it when she went to college.

Even after her life had finally changed so completely, she could never bring herself to get rid of the old duffel bag, partly because, after a few years, it was the only thing left from their brief time together.

And because he'd bought it for her.

But it wasn't safe to keep the bag any longer. Jon's children often came to her apartment for their research sessions. Maybe one of them would go looking for something in the storage closet, find the red bag and mention it to their father, and then he'd...

Camilla knew how paranoid she was being, but before she could change her mind, she left the apartment and ran down the hall to drop the faded duffel bag into a garbage chute.

After it was gone, Camilla stood for a moment gazing into the empty blackness of the chute. At last she turned away sadly, and trudged back to her apartment to wash her hands and prepare for her next class.

Only one term, she told herself.

If she could get through this term, Jon Campbell and his elder son would move on to other classes and she'd withdraw from the research program so she wouldn't have to work with the twins any longer. Her life would return to its quiet, safe path, and she'd never see any of them again.

She just had to find a way to get through the months ahead without ruining everything.

LATER THAT DAY, she picked up Ari and Amy from their classroom and brought them back to her office for their daily session. She was working this week on random selection, in which she showed the children a stimulus object along with a number of symbols and instructed them to pick the one that was the best match.

Then she asked the reasons for their choice and made note of their responses. She was trying to learn how the identification process functioned within their brains, and why they recognized some symbols while they discarded others.

The work was absorbing both to Camilla and to the children, who often made differing choices from among the available objects and then had lively arguments over the disparity.

"There's no right or wrong answers on these tests," Camilla said, intervening in one such dispute.

"It's all a matter of opinion. If Ari picks the grapefruit and Amy picks the beach ball, and you each had a good reason for your choice, then you're both right."

"But the beach ball's just stupid," Ari muttered. "It doesn't even have a peel."

"It does so!" Amy said indignantly. "The part you blow up is the peel. The rest is air."

Ari scowled in outrage and pounded his hand on the table. "That's not a *peel*, you dummy. That's the whole thing!"

"You're so fierce, Ari," Camilla told him gently. "You really need to learn the art of civilized intellectual discourse."

"What's that?" He cast her a curious glance.

"That's having an argument in a very polite way so nobody gets insulted." She ruffled his curly hair.

He looked up at her hopefully. "Can we go over to your place and see Elton and Madonna?"

Camilla glanced at her watch. "It's getting late, dear. Margaret will be coming along in half an hour to take you home. Besides," she added, "I think Madonna's probably not home yet. She went out exploring this morning."

"Why doesn't Elton go exploring?" Amy frowned over her Barbie doll.

"Because Elton's a stay-at-home kitty."

"Like you." Ari said. "You're a stay-at-home kitty, Camilla."

"I am?" she said in surprise.

"Sure. Daddy says you never go away for holidays

or anything. You just stay at home and work. You even live right at the same place where you teach.''

"Is that a bad thing?'' Camilla glanced cautiously at the freckled curve of Ari's cheek, wondering what this was leading up to.

"We think you should have a holiday this weekend,'' Amy said, looking up from her doll. "We want you to come with us to the ranch. Daddy thinks you should, too.''

Camilla felt a surge of alarm. "Now, why would I do that?'' she asked with forced casualness.

"Just to be sociable and make the kids happy,'' a voice said behind them.

Camilla whirled and found Jon Campbell standing in the open doorway of her office.

"Hi, Daddy,'' Ari said.

"Hi, son.'' Jon strolled across the room and folded his long body into one of the little chairs at the table next to Amy. "Am I interrupting anything?''

Camilla shook her head. "We're finished with our session. This is playtime.''

"Hi, pumpkin,'' Jon said to his daughter. "What's happening?''

"We did symbols again. Ari's mad because I picked the beach ball instead of the grapefruit. He says I'm a big stupid dummy.''

Jon reached out with mock fierceness to grasp Ari's foot. "Did you call your sister a big stupid dummy?''

Ari chuckled, trying to free his sneaker from his father's grip. "Camilla says I need to learn the art of civilized intellectual discourse.''

"A fine art, indeed. I think your teacher's right."
Jon settled back on the little chair and met Camilla's
eyes, smiling.

She was the first to turn away, and move behind
her desk to gather an armful of papers. "I guess since
you're here to pick up the children, we can—"

"I'm not really here to pick them up," Jon said
lazily. Ari went over and leaned against his father,
draping an arm around his neck. "I'm here to second
their invitation."

She looked up, startled. All three of them were
watching her intently from the little table.

"What invitation?" she asked, filing papers with
nervous energy.

"We want you to come to the ranch this weekend," Jon said. "We've all talked it over and decided
you could use a holiday."

"But it's...I have to work," she said helplessly.
"My classes...and there's my research project..."

"Your work won't suffer if you take a long weekend once in a while. It's Thanksgiving, remember?"
He waved his hand at the calendar, where the Canadian Thanksgiving was scheduled for the second
weekend in October. "This whole campus is going to
shut down for three days while everybody has a holiday. We believe that should include you."

Camilla began to put away the file folders in her
desk, trying to keep her face hidden from them while
her mind raced around in search of an escape.

"It works just right," Amy said, "because Daddy

can take six people in his plane and that's exactly how many are going.''

"Six people?" Camilla asked.

Amy counted on her fingers. "There's Daddy and me and Ari, and Ricky and Van and you. That's six."

"Doesn't Steven want to go? Or Margaret?"

"Steve never goes with us anymore," Ari said. "And Margaret's boyfriend is coming to visit her this weekend. They're going to drive over to the ranch in Eddie's truck so they'll have lots of time alone together."

"Who else did you say is going?" she asked helplessly.

"Ricky and Van." Any took out a plastic comb and began to tend her doll's long golden tresses.

Camilla looked at Jon.

"My daughter Vanessa," he explained. "And Enrique. It'll be his first trip to the ranch."

Their eyes locked while she continued to search for a way to escape. "Look, I appreciate your kindness," she began, "but I don't think I can possibly…"

Amy's green eyes filled silently with tears.

Camilla looked at the little girl in alarm. "Amy, darling, what's the matter?"

Amy got out of her chair and ran to hug her father, sobbing against his chest.

"She's disappointed," Jon said to Camilla, patting the child's back. "It's their birthday on Sunday, and they wanted you to be there. It was going to be a surprise."

"Oh, no…" Camilla looked from Amy's heaving

shoulders to Ari's downcast, troubled face. "All right," she said, feeling utterly helpless. "All right, I'll come to the ranch. When will you be leaving?"

Amy's tears vanished like a summer rainstorm. She darted across the room to hug Camilla, bubbling with plans. "Ari and I want you to see our ponies and our special pets and all our secret hiding places," she whispered. "We'll have so much fun!"

Camilla held the little girl and felt a treacherous stirring of anticipation. It really had been such a long time since she'd given herself a holiday, gone away and done something just for pleasure.

If only this holiday didn't have to be in the company of the one man she wanted desperately to avoid.

CHAPTER NINE

STEVEN CAMPBELL SAT in a corner booth at a shabby downtown restaurant, looking across the table at his friend Zeke who was making a pencil diagram on a table napkin.

"It's a piece of cake," Zeke whispered to the others at the table. "We knock off the liquor store at midnight, just when they're about to close. We run down the street with the cash, meet Steve who's waiting at the curb, jump into his car and take off. Two blocks away and we're home free."

Zeke had greasy brown hair in a ragged ponytail, and a big tattoo of a mermaid on the side of his neck. The mermaid was much admired by his friends because they all knew the neck was one of the most sensitive parts of the body to have a tattoo done, and carried the greatest risk of infection.

But that was Zeke's personality. If it was dangerous, he was interested. The boy had a wild, over-the-top kind of recklessness that appealed to Steven.

When he was with Zeke, he had a feeling of breathless risk, as if anything could happen. The danger was actually soothing, in a bizarre kind of way. It helped to ease the hard, aching knot of pain that Steven carried with him all the time.

"Why do we have to run a whole block?" Speedball asked plaintively. He was an overweight teenager with a round shaven head and a nose ring. His nickname was a result of his general laziness and resistance to any kind of physical exertion.

Zeke guffawed loudly and winked at Howie, who sat on the vinyl bench next to Steven.

Howie was the smallest of the group, a wiry redhaired boy who was actually a few months younger than Steven. But Howie had nerves of steel, and a streak of casual, mindless cruelty that Steven found deeply unsettling.

Howie was the kind of person who'd kill a cat or dog just for the fun of it, if he thought nobody was watching. And if he could inflict a lot of pain in the process, he'd probably be even happier.

Once or twice Steven had tried to talk to Zeke about his misgivings and his reluctance to have Howie in the group. But Zeke, who was their undisputed leader, scoffed at the objections.

"Howie's a pistol," he'd told Steven. "Howie can spit in a cop's face and not even blink. We need a guy like that. And it sure ain't *you,* Campbell," he'd added with calculated rudeness. "You're so polite it practically makes me sick. If you got any problems with Howie, you can just drop out."

Steven didn't want to drop out. He was committed to their plan, addicted to the thrill of what they were about to do. So he kept his worries to himself and went along with Zeke's leadership.

Now he studied the diagram on the napkin. "After you guys get to the car, where do I go?"

"Straight down Twelfth Avenue and onto Deerfoot Trail. We head for your place, zip right inside that old barn and lock the door. It'll be like we disappeared into thin air."

"But what if somebody gets a look at the car, even sees the license plate? What if the cops follow us out of town?"

Zeke waved his hand casually. "If we do this right, nobody's even gonna see the car. It'll be dark, and you'll be in the shadows! Why? Are you losing your nerve, rich boy?"

The others glowered at Steven, who shifted uncomfortably in the booth. "I've got as much nerve as any of you," he said coldly. "I want to get the details straight, that's all."

"You don't have to worry about the details." Howie jabbed him with a sharp elbow. "That's Zeke's job. You just have to drive the car, rich boy."

Steven ignored the comment. "I want you to promise me you're not going to keep the money, Zeke," he said. "Otherwise I won't get involved. I've already told you that."

Howie and Speedball exchanged a quick glance across the table, but Zeke gazed at Steven with guileless sincerity.

"Hey, what's your problem?" he said. "We been through this whole thing a hundred times. The money from our heist goes to the street kids. We just keep enough to cover our expenses, that's all."

"I want your word on it," Steven said stubbornly. "You guys have to promise we'll give the money away after we get it."

"You heard the man." Zeke looked at the other two. "Come on, give Stevie your word that we won't be keeping the money."

"The money goes to the street kids, so they can buy food and blankets," Speedball agreed solemnly. "Right, Howie?"

Howie looked down at the table, picking at a crack in the surface with a grimy fingernail. "Sure," he muttered. "We won't keep the money, Stevie. We'll be just like Robin Hood, stealing from the rich so we can give to the poor."

Steven nodded. He knew the guys were humoring him, but they'd given their word and Steven planned to hold them to it. He looked on their exploit as the beginning of a great experiment, a redistribution of wealth along the lines envisioned by Marx and Engels.

Steven slid out of the booth and stood up. "I gotta go," he said. "I'll see you guys later."

Zeke glanced over his shoulder, then leaned toward the others. "Two weeks," he murmured softly. "This whole thing's going down on the nineteenth. That's when they get their new shipment of liquor, so everybody except the cashier should be in the back unpacking crates. Don't forget, Stevie boy."

"I won't forget." Steven nodded at the group in the booth, liking the feeling of being included in their plans, right at the center of everything that was happening.

He walked jauntily out of the restaurant, climbed into his yellow Mustang and headed for the college in the waning daylight, planning to pick up a couple of books from the library.

As he drove, Steven grimaced at the irony of his situation.

He was a desperado, an outlaw involved in planning a daring heist to help his fellow man. And yet he was also playing the role of an obedient son, trotting out to get the books he needed so he could convince his father that he was keeping up with his schoolwork.

He gripped the wheel, frowning.

Steven didn't like to think very much about his father these days. It made him uncomfortable to picture those steady, measuring blue eyes, the lean strength of his father's body, the surprising gentleness of his hands.

Jon Campbell would never understand what his son was doing.

But that was because Jon had always been wealthy. He couldn't know how desperately the street kids suffered, or how much they needed help. People like the Campbell family passed their whole lives in a soft, disgusting cushion of luxury that kept them from understanding the real world.

Steven thought about his friends calling him "rich boy," as if he was just the same kind of person as his parents. Well, after the nineteenth, they'd know he was different.

He parked in the students' lot and wandered into the library. Listlessly he made his way among the reference stacks, picking out a couple of books he needed for his term papers, then searched for some of the novels that had been assigned in English class.

He paged through one of the books, frowning in concentration as he moved toward the end of the stack, and almost bumped into a woman standing next to him in the narrow aisle.

It was Dr. Pritchard, her arms full of books. "Hello, Mr. Campbell," she said.

"Hi," he muttered, looking nervously down at the floor.

She glanced at the book in his hands. "My goodness, you actually found a copy of *Vanity Fair*," she commented with a smile. "That must be the last one in the library."

Steven wanted desperately to be alone, but the professor was acting so pleasant that it would be churlish to move away without replying. He recalled Zeke's scornful comment that the "rich boy" couldn't be rude to save his life.

"I've already read the book," he said finally. "I just wanted to look up a couple of references."

"I see." Dr. Pritchard hesitated.

Steven was painfully conscious of how beautiful she was, with her slim, graceful body and the air of quiet elegance that he found appealing.

Not at all like his mother, whose dress and behavior was usually calculated to draw attention to herself....

"Well," he said, "I guess I'd better shove off. I've got a lot of homework to do tonight."

"Could you spare a few minutes, by any chance? I'd like you to join me in the student lounge for a cup of coffee."

He was speechless, astounded by her invitation. The icy Dr. Pritchard never socialized with students.

"If you don't mind," she added, putting a couple of her books back on the shelf, "there's something I'd like to talk with you about."

Steven wanted very much to refuse, but he was afraid of her. If Pritchard got annoyed and gave him a failing grade, he'd have to put up with all kinds of problems from his father. In spite of his anger and rebellion, Steven still hated that prospect.

The worst thing of all was when his father looked sad and disappointed in him. That really tore at his heart, made him almost want to cry. But of course he could never show that kind of emotion. He had to be tough or the pain would rise up and overwhelm him.

"Sure," he said. "I guess so."

She smiled politely and led the way to the check-out counter, offering a couple of novels to the clerk along with her well-worn library card, then waiting while Steven checked out his books.

He followed her to the lounge next door, wondering what she wanted to talk about. He'd written some pretty acceptable essays for his English class and received a good grade on his last test. She couldn't be upset about his schoolwork.

Maybe it was something involving the twins. They were always talking about the woman as if she were some kind of goddess. Or maybe it had to do with Enrique Valeros, who was living at their house now for reasons Steven couldn't entirely fathom.

While he pondered, she made her way to a table near the window where they could see the clean sweep of skyline and the pale glow of the sunset.

"Is this all right, Steven?"

"Sure," he muttered.

"I'll get us something to drink." She stood up and moved toward the counter. "Would you like a cappuccino or a soft drink?"

"Just plain coffee. Please," he added with automatic politeness.

"Cream or sugar?"

"Black, thanks."

She smiled at him, leaving Steven temporarily at a loss for words. In spite of her age, she really was a terrific-looking woman. Again he wondered what she wanted to talk about.

But when she sat down opposite him, carrying a small tray with two mugs of black coffee, she didn't seem in any hurry to discuss what was on her mind.

"I've had about a million cups of coffee in this place," she said with a wry smile. "It always tastes like a mixture of blackstrap molasses and river mud, but I can't resist the stuff."

Steven nodded, thinking once again about irony.

Half an hour earlier he'd been sitting across the table from Zeke and Speedball, who represented a stratum of society that Dr. Pritchard probably couldn't even imagine.

He thought about the campus rumors concerning this woman, how she'd grown up in a fabulously wealthy family and hobnobbed all her life with the rich and famous. No wonder she had such an elegant, confident manner.

In fact, Camilla Pritchard represented everything that Steven hated most. Power and privilege, brutal oppression of the lower class, mindless superiority based on position...

"You know, I have an interesting social engagement coming up this weekend." She sipped her coffee and set down the mug with a brief grimace.

Steven looked at her in surprise. As if this woman's social life had anything to do with him!

She smiled. "It seems I'm going to be visiting the ranch with your family."

His jaw dropped. "*Our* ranch? In Saskatchewan?"

"That's the one. The twins simply wouldn't allow me to refuse."

"They're pretty good at getting their own way." He peered into the depths of his coffee mug, shaken by this new development. "I guess it's their birthday, isn't it? I completely forgot about it until just now."

"Are you sure you don't want to go along with them for the weekend?" Dr. Pritchard asked, sounding hopeful. "I understand only six people can travel in the plane, but I'm certainly willing to give up my seat if you want to go."

He shook his head. "No, that's okay. I have plans this weekend. Besides, the kids are pretty crazy about you. If they think you're going and then you change your mind, there'll be hell to pay. Excuse me, ma'am," he added.

She smiled. "Yes, I guess you're right. There'd probably be hell to pay."

Dr. Pritchard sipped her coffee as she gazed out the window at the sunset. He shifted uneasily in his chair.

When she looked at him again, her blue eyes were mild and full of interest. "Are you enjoying college, Steven?"

He shrugged. "It's okay, I guess."

"You're a very capable student. Have you decided what area of study you're going to specialize in?"

What he really wanted was to drop out of school and take off, hitchhike around the world and find out how people actually lived. Maybe he'd join the Peace Corps and help people in some foreign country to dig wells and organize schools.

But Steven could hardly tell her that, especially when she was getting to be so cozy with his father and the rest of his family.

"I don't know for sure. Probably sociology," he said.

"So you're interested in the structure of society, are you?"

"Sort of. I'd like to find out more about how social

classes are determined, how the wealth is distributed, stuff like that.''

Steven wondered why he was telling her all this. He never confided in anybody for fear they'd laugh at him or use the information to embarrass him somehow.

But his professor wasn't laughing. She nodded thoughtfully and sipped her coffee again. ''I've gathered a bit of that from some of your written work. You have an interesting view of the world, and you express it very skillfully.''

He tried not to be warmed by her praise. She was probably just buttering him up because she wanted him to do something really lame, like applying for a scholarship or joining the debating team.

But her next words were so astounding that he could hardly believe his ears.

He gaped at her, feeling the color drain from his face. ''I'm not sure I…what did you say, ma'am?''

''I was asking you,'' she said calmly, ''how long you've known Zeke and Speedball.''

Steven fumbled for an answer, still too astonished to think clearly. ''How did you…''

She smiled, looking a little sad. ''Never mind how I know, Steven. I happen to have all kinds of sources for various bits of information. I assume you met them after you moved to the city this summer?''

''Yeah,'' he muttered. ''I went to a rock concert in the park one day and started talking with them. But how did you—''

"Do you know anything about them?" she interrupted, still regarding him with that calm blue gaze.

"Of course I do." He gripped his coffee mug tensely. "They're my friends."

"Did you know that both of them have been in trouble with the police a number of times, and that Zeke's still on probation for assaulting an elderly woman? Apparently, it was quite a brutal crime."

"How do you know all this?"

"As I told you, I have my sources," the professor told him quietly.

"Yeah, well, maybe your sources don't know what they're talking about." In his outrage, Steven forgot to be polite for once. "Guys like Zeke and Speedball always get a bad rap, just because people won't give them a chance. Everybody's down on them."

"In my experience, when everybody's down on a person, there's usually a good reason."

"Oh, sure!" he shouted, causing a few of the other students to look at them curiously.

Steven lowered his voice and leaned across the table.

"The reason is that they're poor and homeless and they've never had a chance, that's all. When I walk around downtown, everybody's so damn anxious to help me and smile at me, just because my dad's rich and I've never gone without anything in my whole life. But if Zeke looks sideways at somebody, they call the cops. It's not fair."

She was watching him with a calm, measuring glance. "So you believe Zeke's just a well-meaning boy who's been abused and misunderstood. Is that what you're telling me?"

"Yes. I bet if Zeke had half a chance, he'd be a good person. It's hard to care about other people when nobody cares about you."

"I see. Well, I'm afraid I have to disagree with you."

He stared at the woman, so angry that he forgot his usual caution. "Look, Dr. Pritchard, I'm not sure how you happen to know who Zeke is. But if you'll excuse me, I don't see how you could possibly understand anything about him."

"And why is that, Steven?" she asked.

"Because you're so..." He paused and groped for words. "You've never even been close to the kind of life those kids live on the street. You don't know what it's like to be oppressed and despised, and afraid for your own safety most of the time. If you'd ever experienced even a minute of it, I'll bet you wouldn't be so quick to judge."

She was silent, gazing out the window again. All he could see was her elegant profile, the clean, aristocratic line of her nose and chin.

"Dr. Pritchard," he ventured at last, feeling terrible.

"Yes, Steven?"

"I'm sorry if I was rude just now." He flushed. "I didn't mean to say all those things to you. I just...this stuff gets me really upset."

She smiled and patted his arm. "I admire somebody who gets aroused over moral issues. It shows real depth of character.''

"I wonder if..." He paused once more.

"Yes?" she prompted. "What are you wondering?"

"If you'd sort of...not say anything to my father about this."

"About what?"

"My friends. He gets all upset if he thinks I'm in bad company. He can be really dumb about some things."

"It's not dumb, Steven," she said quietly. "I also happen to believe you're in bad company, and it could be dangerous for you."

"But shouldn't it be my choice?" he asked. "I'm practically an adult. I think I should be allowed to choose my own friends."

She nodded slowly, considering. "Yes," she said at last. "I think you're probably right."

"Then you won't say anything to my father?" he asked eagerly. "Do you promise?"

"All right. But that doesn't mean I won't discuss the matter with you again, if I feel it's warranted."

Steven felt a brief surge of relief, then sagged in his chair. "I hope I can trust you," he muttered. "People break their promises, especially when they're dealing with kids."

"If you're talking about your father, I can't imagine him breaking a promise," the professor said. "He strikes me as a very honorable kind of person."

"Oh, my father's honorable, all right," Steven said

bitterly. "But my mother sure isn't. She lies all the time."

"Steven, I don't think…"

He didn't want to tell her more, but saying the words aloud had brought the pain surging back, hot and strong, and he couldn't stop himself.

"My mother's been lying to me ever since I was a kid. She says she'll come to visit and then doesn't turn up, or she promises to send a letter and then forgets. I learned when I was really young that you can't trust anybody when they give their word."

"Not even your father?"

"My father's different," Steven said in despair. "He's always *there*. I never even have to think about him. But my mother…"

"She's the one you crave," she said gently, "because you can't ever seem to grasp hold of her. Right?"

He looked away. "Not anymore. I don't care anymore. She can do whatever she wants. But it's kind of hard to…"

"Yes?" she asked when he paused. "What were you going to say, Steven?"

"Just that it's upsetting," he muttered, "to see her treating the twins the way she used to treat me and Vanessa. They're real smart but they're still just little kids, and they don't understand. They get hurt when she breaks her word."

The woman across the table sipped her coffee. Her sympathetic expression encouraged him to tell her more than he intended.

"My mother's a really selfish, immature person," he said. "But she can be nice, too. She laughs and tells jokes, and she's fun to be around. Sometimes it's like she actually cares about you, and you get all happy and warm and reach out to her again. But then something distracts her and she's gone, and you're left holding a handful of air. It really...it used to hurt me a lot."

Dr. Pritchard was silent a long time. Finally she touched his arm and leaned toward him. "Part of growing up is learning to understand people, and forgive them for not meeting our expectations," she said. "If your mother simply isn't capable of being the person you want her to be, it won't do any good to be angry with her."

"I didn't say I was angry," he muttered. "It just...hurts, that's all. Actually, it makes me hate everybody who's got money and lives the kind of selfish, careless life that she does."

"Does it make you hate yourself?" Dr. Pritchard asked.

Steven glanced up at her, startled. "What do you mean?"

"Sometimes when we're rejected and disappointed by the people closest to us, we tend to blame ourselves for it. We start thinking that we must be inadequate in some way because they don't love us. And those feelings can lead to all kinds of self-destructive behavior."

Her words were so surprisingly accurate that Steven was uncomfortable. He shifted in the chair and looked down at his coffee mug. "I don't feel like that," he lied. "Not a bit. Maybe my brother and sisters have problems with it sometimes, but I don't care how my mother treats me."

"That's good," she said. "Because you're a very valuable person, Steven, and your mother's behavior is her own problem, not yours. You have to forgive her, accept whatever she's able to give you and let the rest go. You can't allow the negative actions of others to affect your own behavior."

Steven sensed that in some obscure way she was still talking about his friends. Abruptly he got to his feet and gave her an awkward nod.

"Well, thanks a lot for the coffee," he muttered. "I have to go now."

He turned and made his escape, conscious of the way she sat in silence as he plunged out of the student lounge and headed downstairs to the parking lot.

CAMILLA SIPPED the last of the dreadful coffee and pushed her mug aside, still watching the doorway where the boy had disappeared.

He reminded her so much of Jon as a young man that it was unsettling to talk with him. And he shared a lot of personality traits with the boy she remembered—especially a generous spirit and a deep concern for the welfare of others.

But Steven seemed to lack Jon's sunny confidence, the balanced strength of character he'd displayed even in his youth.

She frowned, wondering about the woman Jon had married.

He'd obviously made a mistake in his choice of a mate. But she could understand how it happened. Jon had been the kind of person who could easily be drawn into a relationship with somebody he felt sympathy for, a woman he thought could be helped and transformed by a stable partner.

And then, like so many idealists before him, he'd learned when it was too late that nobody could ever transform another person. So his wife had remained self-indulgent and shallow, and her behavior had damaged the children in different ways.

Despite Camilla's first impression, the twins probably hadn't suffered quite so much because they'd never really known their mother. After all, the woman had left soon after their birth. Jon had been the only parent they were closely involved with. But the older children must have been deeply hurt that their mother showed so little interest in them.

Camilla wanted to forget about all of them. She longed to turn away from Jon Campbell and his children and run back into the comfortable, scholarly world she used to occupy, where she was safely locked away in a shell of cool detachment and nobody could touch her emotions.

Still, she couldn't forget Steven's troubled face, his look of edgy defiance when she talked to him about Zeke.

Something was going on there, and it worried her. Camilla wished she hadn't promised not to talk with

Jon about Steven's friends. But right or wrong, she'd given her word and the last thing the boy needed at this point was another woman breaking her promise to him.

Finally she gathered her armful of books and left the cafeteria, heading across the campus in the mellow autumn twilight.

She let herself into her apartment, where both cats were waiting by the door.

Madonna mewed loudly, demanding to be let out onto the balcony. Elton sat by the sliding glass door, looking on with wistful eyes as his friend's sleek gray body vanished into the depths of the poplar tree.

"You can go with her if you like," Camilla said. "Go on, Elton. Have some fun. Climb up on a fence and sing at the moon."

He put one of his paws on the metal track, then drew it back again and gave Camilla an eloquent, pleading glance.

She bent and scooped him into her arms. "I know just how you feel, darling," she whispered against his warm fur. "You don't have to go out there if you don't want to. You can stay home with me and be safe."

Safe.

Camilla carried the cat into the bedroom, brooding as she rested her chin on his head.

She'd been thinking about safety ever since the beginning of the school term when Jon Campbell had turned up so unexpectedly in her classroom and scared her half to death.

But she was also taking more and more risks, edging further out onto thin ice with every day that passed.

"I can't believe I'm doing all this, Elton. I'm falling in love with his kids, and now I've actually agreed to go to his ranch this weekend. What on earth is wrong with me?"

She tossed the cat onto the bed, where he curled up and watched with drowsy interest while Camilla opened her closet door.

"I don't have the slightest idea what to pack." She hauled down a couple of expensive tan-leather duffel bags from an upper shelf. "What exactly do you wear for a weekend jaunt with a man who terrifies you?"

CHAPTER TEN

MADONNA WAS SULKING. Camilla could see the faint glow of yellow eyes under the couch, her cat's favorite retreat when she felt ill-used.

Camilla knelt and peered into the shadows. "Come out and talk to me, sweetie," she coaxed. "Please don't be upset."

The only response was an indignant hiss and a rustling sound as Madonna retreated deeper into her cave. Elton sat nearby on top of Camilla's suitcase in a bright ray of morning sunlight, licking his front paws and rubbing them industriously across his whiskers.

Camilla sprawled on the rug, still addressing the space under the couch. "I can't possibly let you go out," she said earnestly. "I'm going away for three days, and you have to stay inside while I'm gone. Otherwise something terrible could happen to you and I'd never know."

Prolonged silence from under the couch.

"Mr. Armisch is coming up every evening to feed you and make sure you're all right," Camilla pleaded. "And Elton is here to keep you company."

Elton gave her a sympathetic glance and began to

groom his plump flanks, but there was no response from the darkness under the couch.

Camilla gave up and got to her feet, wandering back to her own room to look at herself nervously in the mirror. Elton jumped off the suitcase and padded along behind, settling in his accustomed spot in the middle of the bed while Camilla picked up a brush and toyed aimlessly with her hair.

"I know what you're thinking," she said to the cat, who regarded her with unwinking yellow eyes. "You think I'm crazy to be going away with him this weekend. Don't you, Elton?"

Elton yawned and sneezed.

"You think it's impossible that he hasn't recognized me by now, and he must be playing some kind of game. Don't you?"

The words hung uneasily in the air. Camilla felt her stomach tighten. She set the hairbrush on the dresser and stared intently at her reflection.

"Well, I've been wondering about that, too. But you know what, Elton? I was very young when he met me. Besides, lots of times I get visits from kids I taught less than ten years ago, and often they've changed so much I don't recognize them, even though they spent a whole term in one of my classes."

Elton kneaded the bedspread and stretched lazily, then rested his chin on his paws and watched her in thoughtful silence.

"In this case," Camilla went on, "it's been more than twenty years. I was smaller and thinner, my hair was a different color, my nose was all swollen and shaped differently, I still had those bruises around my eyes..."

She crossed the room and flopped onto the bed next to the cat.

"Now you're wondering why I had no trouble recognizing *him,* even after all those years, right?"

Elton blinked and yawned again.

"Well, it's different," Camilla said. "Jon was twenty-one, a grown man. In fact, he really hasn't changed very much. He's the same size, his hair's mostly the same color...he even dresses the same way. How could I not recognize him?"

Elton continued to gaze at her, then leaned over to lick her hand.

"Don't worry, sweetie," Camilla murmured, stroking his glossy back. "The man's not going to remember me. I'm safe, really I am. I'll just keep myself well away from him all weekend, and after this trip is over I'll figure out some way to separate from the whole family. Then I won't be in any—"

The front-door buzzer sounded, making her breath catch in her throat.

She climbed off the bed and ran to answer, waiting nervously for Jon to come upstairs. The doorbell rang and she let him in, then stood watching in silence as he looked around her apartment. The man seemed larger in this setting, and so handsome that she could hardly bear to look at him.

If she hadn't been so terrified, she would almost have enjoyed the irony. Of all the people in the world to be standing in her living room, admiring her plants and her little collection of Aztec pottery...

"This place is really nice," he said with a smile that made his eyes crinkle pleasantly. "Not exactly what I'd expected."

"What was it you expected?" she asked.

"I'm not sure. Something a little more conservative and understated, I guess."

"So you think I'm conservative?"

You idiot! Don't ask him things like that, she told herself furiously. *You've got to keep this relationship as impersonal as you can.*

"Well, I used to think that." He gave her a smile that made her feel a little dizzy as he crossed the room and stood near her to reach for the suitcase. "But now I'm not so sure."

She wanted to ask why, but this time caution prevailed. Instead, she stood back and watched while he lifted Elton gently from the suitcase and settled him in a nearby armchair.

"I thought there were two cats," Jon said, looking around.

"How did you know that?" she asked, startled and wary.

"The twins have been here a few times. They never stop talking about you."

Camilla relaxed. "Oh, that's right. They're very fond of the cats. Madonna is hiding under the couch. She gets really cranky when I...when I won't let her go outside."

"The kids also told me you like to wear blue jeans

and plaid shirts, but I wouldn't have believed it if I hadn't seen it.''

Camilla looked down at her faded denims and felt herself blushing. ''Professors are human beings, you know, Mr. Campbell.''

''Jon. My name is Jon.''

''I don't know if that's…''

He moved toward her, still carrying the suitcase, and held her arm gently with his free hand. ''Please, call me Jon.''

''Jon,'' she whispered, looking down at the floor to avoid his steady blue gaze. ''And I suppose…you and your family should probably call me Camilla. The twins already do.''

She was painfully conscious of the peaceful weekend morning, the lazy sun dappling the carpet, her drowsy cat and the warmth of Jon's hand on her bare arm.

Camilla felt languid and strange—almost lightheaded. Worst of all, her courage was beginning to desert her once again.

Oh, God, she thought with a shiver. I shouldn't be doing this. It's crazy to be going away with him. I should make up some excuse…

But before she could think of a way to extricate herself, they were heading out the door with her jacket and suitcase. They stopped briefly at the super's apartment for some last-minute instructions about the care of the cats. Then they were in his car and on their way.

The sunny morning was glorious—rich and mellow

with the scent of autumn, of dried grasses and warm sage and a hint of snow from the distant mountains.

A few minutes later, they were driving west across the city.

"Does this ever make you feel a little sad?" she asked, gazing out the window.

"What?" He glanced over at her, gripping the wheel casually, one arm resting on the back of the seat.

"Autumn." Camilla avoided his eyes. "There's always something a little melancholy about this time of year. It's so lovely that it brings a lump to my throat."

"I know what you mean. Sometimes beautiful fall weather makes me start brooding about lost opportunities," he said with rare seriousness. "Maybe because I'm getting conscious of how quickly my life is slipping by. I've always thought lost opportunities are the saddest things on earth. How about you?"

"'Of all sad words by tongue or pen,'" Camilla began, smiling.

He grinned back at her. "The saddest are, 'It might have been.' Right?"

"I suppose so." She settled in her seat, watching the trees and houses drift by as they headed out of the downtown core and toward the suburbs. "But your life seems very successful. It's hard to believe you've missed many opportunities."

He frowned thoughtfully as he maneuvered past a farm truck hauling a load of cattle. "I guess I'm thinking mostly of that experience I described in my last essay. It was probably the major lost opportunity of my life."

Camilla's heart began to pound, but she kept her voice carefully neutral. "I'm trying to remember the essay. I think it was something about a girl you met by chance when you were a young man?"

Jon nodded. "I tried so hard to find her after she disappeared. I've often wondered how my life would have turned out if I'd been successful."

"Perhaps you romanticized the whole thing," Camilla said, hoping he couldn't hear the way her heart was thudding gainst her jacket. "It's possible you might have found her again and learned that the two of you were totally incompatible, and caused yourself all kinds of heartache."

He gave her a quick smile. "So what are you saying, Camilla? You think dreams that don't come true are the best kind?"

"They're probably the safest," Camilla said after a moment. "You know what they say...be careful what you wish for, because you might get it."

"I suppose there's some truth in that, all right. But ever since, I haven't met anybody else I could talk with so easily about everything under the sun. It was a rare experience."

She stole a glance at him, but all she could see was his aquiline profile, strong and unrevealing against the blue sky beyond the window.

"Besides," he went on, "my dream girl could hardly have been more incompatible than the woman I eventually married, and that was a choice that's caused all kinds of pain for my whole family. So, in a way, I still look on the whole thing as a lost opportunity. Especially," he added quietly, "since life doesn't always give you a second chance."

He sounded so unhappy that Camilla longed to reach over and touch his arm, but she restrained herself. Instead, she looked around at the peaceful, rolling countryside they were passing through.

"It's nice out here," she said. "Look at all these beautiful acreages."

"Don't you ever go for drives in the country?"

"Not very often."

"So what do you do for pleasure, Camilla?"

"Well, I go for long walks on campus and play with my cats, and paint a little, and I read a lot..."

The words sounded so hollow in her ears that she was embarrassed.

What a contrast to this man's life, with his brood of children and his vast prairie ranch, his surprising return to college after a twenty-year absence, his airplane and lavish houses...

"Here we are," he announced. They pulled down a long approach road and into a yard where a light plane was sitting at the end of an airstrip. "Look, everybody's waiting for you, Camilla."

VANESSA STARED OUT the window of the plane, thinking how much she always loved this time of year and how desperately she missed the countryside around the ranch.

She would have been humiliated if anybody knew

what she was thinking, though. The whole family believed that all she cared about was clothes, makeup and boys. Vanessa liked it that way. She was terrified of showing her real feelings, and so skilled at creating a facade of brittle shallowness that it had become second nature.

She leaned forward to look down at a tightly bunched herd of cattle moving slowly along a country road. It was too far away to see details clearly, but she knew the herd would be followed by a couple of riders with their cotton bandannas pulled up over their mouths and noses to protect themselves from the choking clouds of dust.

Vanessa sighed and looked at Amy who was in the seat next to her, after losing a fierce battle with Ari over who would sit beside Camilla on the plane trip. Amy had unfastened her seat belt and was kneeling on the seat, also staring down at the cattle.

"Maybe that's Tom," she said, jumping up and down in excitement. "Hey, Ari, look at the cattle! Do you think Tom's riding down there?"

"Don't be stupid. It's not Tom," Vanessa said shortly. "The ranch is still a hundred miles away."

Amy glared at her sister for a moment, then returned to her study of the rolling landscape below the plane. Vanessa settled back in the seat and glanced at Camilla Pritchard's smooth blond head.

This slender woman was everything Vanessa wished she could be.

Camilla was elegant, quiet and intellectual, a self-possessed woman who knew exactly what she was

and where she was going. There was nothing shallow
or tawdry about her. Though she was dressed casually
for the weekend in jeans and a cotton shirt, she still
exuded an air of pure quality.

Vanessa always felt so cheap. Even her looks
seemed flashy and overdone, with black hair and blue
eyes and pale skin, as if nature was deliberately trying
to make her conspicuous.

Just like your mother, people had been saying to
her since she was a little girl, stroking her hair in
admiration. What a pretty little girl, Vanessa. You're
the image of your mother.

She gritted her teeth and rolled her head on the seat
back.

Vanessa was tormented by a constant fear that
she'd turn out to be the same kind of person as her
mother. How could you look so much like somebody
and not have inherited her personality, as well?

In Vanessa's opinion, there was no point in having
feelings and caring about others, being sensitive and
kind and considerate. Not if people thought you were
going to turn out just like your mother. No, it was
better to be coldly, deliberately selfish right from the
start. As soon as she reached adolescence, she'd begun to play the role.

By now she didn't really know how to be different.
In fact, Vanessa was growing increasingly convinced
that everyone had been right all along. She must be
cold and selfish like her mother or she wouldn't have
been able to fool everybody for all these years.

Involuntarily, she glanced at Enrique who sat up front with Jon.

This was the boy's first ride in the plane, and his first trip to the ranch. Vanessa could feel his excitement.

There were lots of times she could sense what Enrique was thinking. She knew that sometimes he was afraid, and often humiliated by the need to accept her father's generosity. He was lonely, too, yearning to reach out to her and Steven for friendship. And at the center of him was a dark well of sorrow that he needed to talk about. But the poor boy had no friends his own age to listen while he talked.

Vanessa felt sorry for him, and passionately admired his courage. She couldn't imagine being all alone in a strange, faraway country, making her own way without anybody's help.

But neither could she bring herself to approach the boy as a friend. If she did, she'd probably just wind up hurting Enrique even more, so it was best to stay away from him.

"There it is!" Ari shouted. "There's the ranch!"

"Buckle up, everybody," their father called over the roar of the engine. "We'll be going in for a landing pretty soon."

He gave some instructions to Enrique. Vanessa saw how the boy's shoulders lifted with pride as he handled a couple of the levers. She smiled in spite of herself, then sobered quickly and turned to help Amy who was struggling with her seat belt.

"Are you happy to see the ranch, Van?" the little girl whispered.

Vanessa gave a noncommittal shrug. "It's pretty boring out here. I'd rather be in the city doing some shopping."

"But it's our birthday on Sunday." Amy's face twisted with dismay. "Van, don't you want to be at our birthday party?"

"I'm here, aren't I?"

Camilla Pritchard turned and gave them a brief smile as she fastened her belt. Vanessa smiled back automatically, then looked out the window as the plane swooped in for a landing.

As soon as they were safely on the ground, Tom Beatch came shambling toward the plane, as skinny and bowlegged as ever. Vanessa looked at the old cowboy with a surge of pure affection. She'd known Tom all her life, and learned many important lessons at his feet.

But she held back and watched silently as Jon's foreman submitted to the onslaught of the twins, who ran forward and hurled themselves against him with shouts of joy.

Another couple of ranch hands appeared from the direction of the barn, called cheerful greetings and hauled luggage from the plane, carrying it off toward the big ranch house.

When Jon took Camilla's arm and drew her forward to make introductions, Vanessa saw how the woman tensed and her blue eyes widened in alarm.

The professor was scared, Vanessa thought in

amazement. In fact, she was practically as shy and timid as Enrique. Why would she be scared of them, when she'd traveled all over the world and met such classy people?

"And this is our friend Enrique," Jon said, touching the boy's arm. "He wants to learn how to ride horseback, Tom."

The old cowboy smiled at them from under the shaded brim of his Stetson. "Well, now, that's sure good, because we can always use a couple of extra hands around here. Matter of fact, we're all leaving in a few minutes to go up to the north pasture and gather the bulls. I reckon we can find a horse for you, Ricky."

Enrique ducked his head and smiled shyly.

"Have you got a horse for Camilla?" Ari asked. "We want her to come riding with us."

Again Vanessa saw the sudden tension in Camilla's shoulders.

"Oh, Ari," the professor said with an awkward laugh. "I've never been on a horse in my life. I think I'd better just go for a walk somewhere and let the rest of you do the riding."

Vanessa's jaw dropped. She stared at the woman in surprise. Camilla Pritchard was supposed to be an Olympic-class equestrienne, but now she was claiming she'd never been on a horse?

She would have liked to volunteer to go for a walk with Camilla. Vanessa loved wandering on the prairie, especially in the fall. And she longed to talk with this woman, explore the mysteries surrounding her and find out how she managed to remain so pleasantly quiet and self-contained.

But she couldn't bring herself to speak.

"How about you, Van?" her father asked. "Will you be riding with us?"

Enrique cast her a hopeful glance, then looked away quickly.

"Vanessa's a terrific horsewoman," Jon told Camilla. "She can ride like a champion."

"You bet she can," Tom echoed with a fond grin. "This little lady, she's one hell of a cowboy. Best I ever trained."

Even Camilla smiled at her with open admiration. Vanessa felt a surge of warmth and a longing to return their smiles. Instead, she forced herself to shake her head, keeping her face expressionless.

"Sorry, guys, but I think I'll just stay inside and watch TV," she said with the air of lofty boredom she'd been cultivating so long. "I don't want to get my hair all messy."

Enrique's face showed a flare of disappointment, quickly hidden.

"Didn't Steve come along with you?" Tom asked, peering toward the plane.

Jon shook his head. "Steve's busy with plans of his own. Seems like he's not all that interested in the ranch anymore. Or the family, for that matter."

"How about Margaret? We could sure use a few of her home-cooked meals."

Amy moved toward the old cowboy and slipped her hand into his, swinging it happily. "Margaret's driving out here with Eddie in his truck. They're bringing our birthday cake.''

Tom lifted the little girl into his arms. "Is that so?" he asked. "And which birthday is this? Now, let me see." He pretended to count on his callused fingers. "I bet you're...four years old."

"Four years old!" Ari scoffed. "We're going to be *eight*, Tom."

Vanessa saw her father and the English professor exchange a smiling glance, saw how her father's eyes kindled with warmth and how the woman looked away hastily, her cheeks pink.

Again she was astonished by what she'd observed. This whole thing was apparently something more than simply allowing the twins to bring along their favorite teacher for their birthday party.

Daddy's crazy about the woman, Vanessa thought. He's in love with her, but she doesn't feel the same way about him. She's probably just here because the kids insisted that she come....

"Come on, Van," Jon said. "Why don't you come riding with us? I plan to talk Camilla into getting on a horse, no matter what she says, so you'll be all alone in the house until Margaret and Eddie get here."

"I like being alone," Vanessa said languidly. "I'll see you at suppertime."

She walked away, conscious of the group watching her before they trooped off noisily toward the corrals to select their horses.

A COUPLE OF HOURS later, the little group of riders were following a herd of bulls as they lumbered and bellowed down a rutted trail toward the ranch.

Camilla shifted in the saddle and lifted her face to the sun, sighing with pleasure.

This was heaven, she thought. Pure heaven. She'd recovered from her initial nervousness at being on horseback and was enjoying the gentle, rocking motion of the old mare that Tom had selected for her. The afternoon was mellow and golden, and the air sparkled like champagne. A breeze touched her cheeks, fragrant with the scent of sage and sun-warmed earth. Lazy clouds of dust billowed from under the animals' hooves and drifted across the plain.

Off to her left she could hear the twins' lively chatter as they rode their ponies next to Tom and Enrique. The children were apparently telling Tom all about their new school, while he responded with news of the ranch.

On her other side, Jon spurred his horse and galloped ahead to turn a big Hereford bull back to the herd. The animal pawed the earth and faced him threateningly for a moment, then dropped his horns and fell into line with the rest of the bulls.

Camilla watched as Jon rode back toward her. The man was so handsome, looked so comfortable in the saddle with his hands low on the reins. He wore jeans, a denim shirt and an old baseball cap pulled over his eyes, shading his face.

He reined in beside her and smiled, his teeth flashing in the shadow of the cap. "You look great, Camilla. A born horsewoman."

She laughed and patted the sorrel mare's shaggy neck. "I think Tom found me the most placid horse on the whole ranch. She's so sweet and gentle, even a beginner can ride her. But I feel really embarrassed, bumping along here like a sack of potatoes."

His big bay gelding fell into step with the little mare. "You know," he said casually, "Vanessa told me a few weeks ago that she'd heard a rumor about you being a world-class horsewoman. In fact, you're supposed to have ridden in the Seoul Olympics."

Camilla gaped at him, astounded. She was familiar with most of the campus rumors about her background, but this was a new one.

"Me, riding in the Olympics? Jon, that's so ridiculous. I can't remember whether I ever rode a horse in a merry-go-round, let alone in an Olympic event."

"According to campus gossip, you also grew up in New England, dated one of the Kennedy boys and traveled around with the jet set."

Camilla felt her cheeks warming with chagrin and annoyance. "I honestly don't know where all these ridiculous stories come from," she said curtly. "There's absolutely no truth in any of them."

"So where did you grow up?"

You know where I grew up, she told him silently. You know the whole story. You're the only person I've ever told.

For a brief reckless moment she wondered how it would feel to tell him the truth, haul all her secrets out into the open and see what happened. But Camilla knew she was never going to do that. She'd spent too many years protecting herself from discovery to throw it all away now on a random impulse.

"My childhood was nothing special," she said briefly. "How about you? Have you lived here on the ranch all your life?"

He gave her a keen glance, but didn't protest the change of subject. "I was born here, and so were my father and grandfather. I've always loved this place."

"Well, I can certainly see why. Enrique looks like he's enjoying himself," she said, watching the dark-haired young man who rode his horse next to Tom. "You've done wonders for him."

"The poor kid, he just needs somebody who'll give him a chance. I like having him around. He's great with the twins."

"Has he told you anything about his life before he came to Canada?"

"A little. I know there's been some tragedy. It'll probably be good for him to talk about it, once he trusts us enough to tell the whole story. It's always good for people to talk about what's bothering them."

She brooded over his words, watching the little mare's ears twitching at flies as she plodded along the trail.

"What's the problem?" Jon asked quickly, reaching out to touch her arm. "Are you all right?"

"I'm fine." She forced herself to smile at him. "I was just thinking that I wish Steven had decided to come this weekend. I don't know how he can bear to miss out on all this."

Jon's face clouded. "He used to love the ranch, but

nowadays he's getting so distant. So's Vanessa, for that matter."

"She's really a beautiful girl," Camilla ventured.

"I know. She looks exactly like her mother. Unfortunately, she seems to share a lot of the same personality traits."

He sounded so bitter that Camilla glanced at him in concern. "Does that worry you?"

"It sure does. My ex-wife is so self-absorbed that she causes all kinds of misery to these kids without even realizing the harm she does. I hate to think Vanessa's going to turn out the same way."

Camilla thought about the girl's remarkable violet-blue eyes, her pale face and quiet, watchful air.

She didn't believe Vanessa Campbell was shallow. In fact, Camilla sensed depths of unhappiness in the girl that were almost as troubling as Steven's rebellion.

Privately, she resolved to have a talk with Vanessa if the chance arose, and see if she could find out what the teenager was thinking. But she was growing more nervous all the time about how involved she was becoming with Jon Campbell and his family.

"Look, Camilla."

She followed Jon's pointing finger and saw a coyote topping a rise just beyond the herd. He loped through the rippling grass, silent and graceful, and paused on the crest of the hill to look back at them, his feathery tail waving in the breeze.

"Oh," Camilla breathed, enchanted. "Oh, Jon, look at him. He's so wild and beautiful."

Jon watched her intently for a moment, then leaned over in his saddle and reached out to put his arm around her shoulders. She yielded to his embrace for a moment, shaken with memories and a flood of emotion.

With all her heart she wanted to cling to him, bury her face in his shirtfront and hold him tightly. She wanted to feel his arms around her, and his lips moving against hers.

Most of all she wanted to experience the closeness they'd shared more than twenty years ago in that shabby motel room. So many times in the intervening years she'd yearned for this man, ached to feel his touch again. Now, miraculously, he was holding her.

Maybe it was meant to be and she should stop fighting her emotions....

Appalled at her weakness, Camilla suddenly spurred her horse and bounced up the trail toward Tom and the children, leaving him behind.

CHAPTER ELEVEN

THE CLOCK in the front hall chimed softly, announcing midnight. The old house was wrapped in stillness. Jon lay in his big carved-oak bed, hands under his head as he stared at the ceiling.

He pictured Camilla just a few feet away, sleeping in one of the guest rooms. Jon couldn't seem to get her out of his mind, and the fact that she was so close to him in the darkness was almost unbearable.

It had been a long time since he'd wanted any woman so fiercely. He could hardly keep himself from getting out of bed, slipping down the hall to her room and gathering her into his arms.

He was constrained by the knowledge that the twins were asleep in their room across the hall, with Vanessa's next to them. And there was also something about Camilla Pritchard herself that kept him from pressing too hard. With any other woman, he would almost certainly have made his move by now.

But in spite of her beauty and intellect, Jon sensed a touching kind of shyness, almost a childlike air about the elegant college professor. Somehow, even though she was in her late thirties, she seemed like a woman who'd been protected from the harsh realities of life. There was an innocence in Camilla that was both charming and frustrating.

He tensed, suddenly alert. A muffled sound carried through the quiet, something different from the normal creaks and nighttime groans of the big old house.

Jon sat up, wondering if one of the children was having a nightmare. He detected cautious footsteps padding down the hall, and caught a brief glimpse through his partly open door of blond hair silvered by moonlight.

It was Camilla. The stairs protested softly as she began to descend, picking her way cautiously to keep from waking the household.

Jon climbed swiftly out of bed, pulled on his jeans and a pair of leather moccasins, grabbed a shirt and edged into the hallway.

He heard the front door open and close, and wondered for a crazy moment if she might be sleepwalking. But when he went out onto the veranda he saw her sitting in the porch swing, wrapped in a blanket as she gazed at the stars.

He crossed the wooden floor and stood next to her. She looked up at him, startled, her eyes wide and frightened in the moonlight. When she recognized him, she smiled awkwardly.

"Sorry, I couldn't sleep," she murmured. "Did I wake you?"

"Not at all. Matter of fact, I can't sleep, either. May I join you?"

She hesitated, then moved over to make room for him on the swing. "Do you want some of this blanket?'' she asked. ''It's kind of chilly out here tonight.''

''Sure, if you don't mind sharing.''

He watched as she unwrapped the blanket and spread it across their knees, then pulled it up under her chin and settled back in the swing again.

It was a cozy, pleasant feeling, sitting with her in the darkness and sharing the blanket. Jon enjoyed her closeness so much that he was almost afraid to speak for fear of breaking the spell.

''Can you name all the constellations?'' she asked, looking up at the dazzle of stars in the blackness above them.

''Most of them. When I was a little boy, I used to take a sleeping bag out on the prairie along with a flashlight and my astronomy textbook, trying to locate all of them.'' He looked down at her shadowed face. ''Did you ever do something like that?''

She turned away, avoiding his eyes. ''Not that I can recall.''

''And then when I was older,'' he went on, leaning back to gaze upward again, ''I had a motorcycle for a few years. I liked to ride around after midnight and look at the stars.''

For some reason, she seemed alarmed. He could feel her arm tense as she gripped the blanket tightly against her chest.

''You must have had a wonderful childhood,'' she said at last.

''It was pretty good, all right.'' He touched the floor with his foot to set the swing rocking gently. ''I wish my kids could grow up here the way I did, but there's no decent school in the district anymore.''

"I don't think it hurts them to live in the city during the winter," Camilla said. "The twins really need the mental stimulation. And this way, all four kids can have the best of both worlds."

He glanced at her delicate profile. "You're probably right," he said thoughtfully. "At least the twins seem a lot happier now than they did at first."

"Children adapt so quickly. Especially younger ones like Ari and Amy."

They rocked together in silence for a while, looking at the stars.

She seemed strangely vulnerable out here, and more mysterious than ever. It was all he could do to keep from putting his arms around her. He longed to learn all about the woman, to break through the barriers of cautious reserve and win her trust.

"Camilla," he began.

"Yes?"

"Why don't you tell me about your childhood? I don't even know where you grew up. I've heard all these wild rumors from other people, but nothing at all from you."

She drew the blanket snugly under her chin, huddling in its warmth. "I don't like to talk about myself," she said in a low voice.

"Why not? I'd like to know all about you. In a strange kind of way," he said when she didn't answer, "I feel as if I've known you for a long time. But I really don't know anything about you at all."

"There's not much to know. I'm a very ordinary kind of person."

"No jet-setting? No trips to Paris or fancy parties at the Kennedy compound?"

"Hardly," she said dryly. "I don't even go to the faculty parties on campus."

"So what do you do for fun? Any hobbies, or rare and interesting talents?"

"I've told you before. I just work on lesson plans and research projects, and look after my cats."

He chuckled. "Now, that sounds like a whole lot more excitement than most people could stand."

But she didn't smile in reply. When he stole a glance at her, she was looking at the stars again. The bleak look on her face touched his heart.

"Camilla," he whispered, putting his arms around her and drawing her close. "You've been looking sad all day. What's the matter?"

"Nothing," she murmured against his chest. "I'm all right."

He could feel her tension, but she didn't pull away. His arms tightened around her. She was slender and delicate in his embrace, and so desirable that his body shuddered with longing.

"I've never met anybody like you," he whispered against her hair. "There's something about you that just makes me crazy. I don't know what it is."

She shifted briefly in his arms, then nestled closer with a faint smile. "Look, that's no way to talk to your teacher."

He laughed, delighted that she was actually relaxed

enough to make a joke. "Why not?" he whispered. "Maybe it'll get me a better grade."

"You don't need help to get good grades. You're an excellent student."

He stroked her hair, then bent to kiss her cheek. "That's good to know," he said softly. "Is there anything else you want to teach me?"

"I doubt…" Her voice caught and she hid her face against his neck. "I doubt that you need much instruction. You seem like a pretty competent fellow."

He grinned. "I've always thought so, but nowadays I'm not so sure."

"Why not?"

"Because you're making me feel like a teenager again."

She was silent, resting warm and gentle in his arms. Jon stroked her face, then lifted it to kiss her eyelids, her cheeks and mouth.

The woman was so delicious. Her skin felt like silk, and her lips were warm and soft in the chill of the autumn night.

"Oh, Camilla," he whispered, kissing her again, feeling her mouth open in response. "You're so beautiful. I can't believe how beautiful you are."

His body surged with passion. He gathered her closer, kissing her hungrily, and began to run his hands over her body under the warm shelter of the blanket.

For a moment she yielded and pressed against him. He could hear the way her breathing quickened, and sensed the urgency of her response.

I knew it, he thought, exulting in her sweetness and fire. This woman has all kinds of passion. She's not cold at all.

Abruptly she pulled away and got to her feet, muttering something inaudible.

"Camilla," he said, grasping her arm. "What is it?"

"I'm not... Oh, God. I'm sorry, Jon, but I just can't do this. I can't..."

Then, before he could say anything, she was gone.

NEXT MORNING, Camilla woke from a troubled sleep and lay in bed watching rays of pale sunlight wash through the flowered chintz drapes. She rolled her head in confusion, wondering where she was.

At last her thoughts fell into place, along with that midnight scene on the veranda. She moaned softly and rolled over to bury her face in the pillow.

What must he think of her?

She'd come on this trip as a favor to his children, and then behaved with such shocking abandon, practically throwing herself into the man's arms.

Camilla remembered the feeling of that embrace, the hard strength of his body and the warmth of his kiss. She felt another surge of the hungry longing that had haunted her for so many years.

It had taken every ounce of strength she possessed to pull away from him last night and hurry back to her room. In another five minutes she'd probably have yielded completely and found herself waking up in his bed this morning.

"God help me," she whispered, sitting up and gazing at her pale face in the mirror above the oak dresser. "I *have* to keep my distance from that man."

She hurried into the adjoining bathroom, washed and dressed quickly, then opened the door and ventured into the hallway, wondering where the rest of the family was. The big house seemed unnaturally quiet in the crisp early light.

It was just after eight o'clock on Sunday morning, the day of the twins' birthday party. Maybe nobody was awake yet. Or maybe they'd all been up for hours and were outdoors by now.

She crept downstairs to the kitchen, where Vanessa sat alone at the big oak table with a cup of coffee.

"Hi," Camilla said. "Are we the only ones up this morning?"

The girl shook her head. "Daddy and the kids are outside helping Margaret gather the eggs. They've already had their breakfast. Margaret left some scrambled eggs and toast for you, and I made a fresh pot of coffee."

Camilla felt relieved that she wouldn't have to confront Jon right away. Maybe after a few cups of coffee, she'd feel stronger.

"I feel so lazy," she murmured, crossing the room to pour herself some coffee. "The rest of you must have been up for hours."

"Most people sleep late when they visit here," Vanessa said. "It's probably all the fresh air."

"I think you're right." Camilla smiled at the girl,

then sat down at the table across from her. "Do you like coming to the ranch?"

Vanessa shrugged. "It's okay, I guess. May I get you some eggs and toast?"

"That would be very nice, thank you." Camilla watched as the girl moved around the kitchen, filling a plate with scrambled eggs and toast. "You're really beautiful, Vanessa," she said impulsively. "You look so much like your father."

"My *father?*" Vanessa was so startled that she dropped her usual air of lofty boredom and looked at Camilla in astonishment. "You think so?"

"You have quite a few of his mannerisms. You hold your head the same way, and your mouth is shaped just like his. I suspect," Camilla added with deliberate casualness, "that you have a lot of tastes and attitudes in common with him, too."

"Well, he sure doesn't think so," Vanessa muttered bitterly. "Daddy thinks I'm just like my mother."

"Maybe he doesn't know enough about you to make a proper judgment," Camilla said. "Maybe you should talk to him and tell him what you're really like."

"What do you mean?" the girl asked, sitting down in the opposite chair.

Camilla swallowed a mouthful of scrambled eggs and took a bite of toast. "I've spent most of my life doing just what you're doing now, Vanessa. I've lived in a secret world and kept my real self hidden behind a wall where people could never see me. After that becomes a habit, you can't seem to do anything else, even if you want to.''

Camilla looked at her plate, hardly able to believe she was actually saying these things. The contact with Jon Campbell and his family seemed to make her say things she'd never dream of telling people otherwise.

The whole situation was getting more dangerous all the time. After this weekend, she definitely had to put an end to it. But in the meantime, she couldn't help feeling a wrench of sympathy for the beautiful, unhappy girl who sat across the table.

"What kind of secrets do you have?" Vanessa asked, then flushed in embarrassment. "Totally dumb question, right? If you could talk about them to a stranger like me, they wouldn't be secrets."

"That's the problem." Camilla toyed with her fork, using the tines to make neat crosshatched patterns in the tablecloth. "The things we can never bring ourselves to talk about are most often the things that control our lives."

"You mean, things that have really hurt us?" Vanessa asked in a low voice.

"Or frightened us," Camilla said. "The two usually go together in our minds. And they're so powerful we can't seem to get past them on our own."

The girl looked up again, wide-eyed. "But I can't believe you've ever been hurt or frightened in your whole life. You look so..."

"What?" Camilla asked when the teenager paused.

"So composed and elegant," Vanessa said, flushing again. "Like you grew up as a princess in some kind of royal family, and had every kind of privilege a person could dream of.''

''Believe me,'' Camilla said dryly, ''those looks are deceiving. Can you keep a secret, Vanessa? You won't tell this to anybody else?''

The girl nodded solemnly.

''Well,'' Camilla went on, ''there was a time when I was terribly hurt and frightened of my own shadow.''

''How old were you?'' Vanessa breathed, clearly fascinated.

''Just about the same age you are now. I was on my own with no idea what I was going to do or where I was going to go. I would probably never have found my way back to safety except that a kind person came along and helped me.''

''My God.'' Vanessa stared at her, lips parted in astonishment. ''And now you're so—'' She stopped abruptly, then looked down, running her fingers along the wooden handle of the spatula. ''Do you ever talk about any of it?'' she whispered. ''The bad things that happened to you, I mean?''

Camilla shook her head. ''I can't. I know enough about psychology to understand it would be healing for me to talk about it to somebody, but I can't seem to find the words. I've never spoken of it in any detail during all these years.''

''But your life is still a huge success. You're not lost anymore.''

''Whatever I've managed to achieve has been because I...'' Camilla paused and took a deep breath.

"I realized a long time ago that it was necessary to reach out somehow and get beyond my own misery. I decided to help people who were suffering the same way I had suffered. Now it's become a major part of my life."

"Helping people?"

"Yes." Camilla took another sip of coffee.

"But where?" Vanessa asked. "Do you mean, helping your students at the college?"

"No, it's something that has nothing to do with my work at school, just a chance to get involved and reach out to people who are going through terrible struggles. There's nothing I've done that's more meaningful."

Vanessa was silent a long time, looking down at the table. Her dark hair fell like a curtain to shield her face. "And that makes you feel better?" she asked. "It takes away some of the hurt?"

"Yes," Camilla said, touching the girl's hand. "It takes away the hurt."

Vanessa looked at her wistfully for a moment. Then her face set and she shook her head. "There's no point in my trying something like that," she said bitterly. "I'm so much like my mother, nobody would ever believe I wanted to help. They'd all think I was only pretending or making fun of them, and hate me for it."

"Maybe you should give them a chance," Camilla said. "Why don't you reach out a bit and see how people respond? They might surprise you."

"But don't you see?" Vanessa whispered, her face twisting with pain. "*I'm* afraid they may be right." Vanessa began to cry, lowering her head onto her folded arms. "I look so much like her," she said in a muffled voice. "And I act just like her, too. I'm as bad as she is."

"Oh, Vanessa." Camilla reached out to put her arms around the girl's heaving shoulders. "Vanessa, listen to me. People who are really, truly self-absorbed never give their selfishness a second thought. It doesn't even occur to them that they're doing anything wrong. Do you understand? The fact that you worry about being selfish is absolute proof that you're not."

"I never thought of it like that," Vanessa said. "So...if I were to...reach out to other kids who've been lonely and scared like me, where would I begin?"

"In your own home," Camilla said quietly. "That's always a good place to start."

"You mean, the twins? But they have so many people to help them. And Steve's really bitter about a lot of things that happened to us in our childhood. He's never going to accept any help from me. I don't know how I could..."

Vanessa looked up again at Camilla, who was watching her with a gentle smile.

"Enrique?" the girl asked. "Is that who you mean? I should try to help Enrique?"

"Well, I think there are some terrible things that

he definitely needs to talk about. And he doesn't seem able to confide in any of the rest of us.''

''But...'' Vanessa's delicate face turned scarlet with embarrassment. ''But Enrique must think I'm such a jerk. I've hardly said two words to him since he came to live with us.''

Camilla recalled the boy's expression whenever he looked at Vanessa. ''I don't believe he thinks you're a jerk,'' she said.

A noisy clatter mounted the back steps. Camilla heard the twins' high-pitched voices, followed by their father's quiet reply. The children burst through the door demanding Camilla admire their baskets of eggs.

She smiled and braced herself to respond with casual warmth, trying to avoid looking at Jon who stood quietly just inside the door, watching her.

ENRIQUE HAD NEVER witnessed anything like the twins' eighth birthday party. The whole dining room was decorated with balloons and streamers. There were dozens of guests in attendance and gifts were piled everywhere. All the ranch hands were at the party, and each had brought some small offering.

The cake was truly wonderful, designed to be a relief map of Alberta and Saskatchewan, showing mountains, plains and lakes, as well as the university at Calgary and the family's two homes.

''Eddie and I worked on that cake for three days,'' Margaret said, her broad freckled face glowing. ''Eddie's real good with maps.''

Caroline Kurtz, who ran the lunch counter in town, had also brought a mountain of food. She and Tom presided over a long table, serving up punch and salads, handing out stacks of sandwiches.

A rousing game of pin the tail on the donkey was in progress in one corner of the big room, supervised by Jon, who wrapped a kerchief around each cowboy's head in turn and spun them in dizzying circles. The booted young men lumbered toward the mural of a donkey hung on the wall, hands stiffly extended, holding a horsehair tail suspended from a long pin, while onlookers shouted helpful suggestions.

"Not there, Sammy, you're gonna hurt Caroline real bad! Hey, who put that rattlesnake inside the house? Sammy, if you run into that big china cabinet, Jon's gonna fire you for sure!"

Enrique sat alone in a corner, watching and smiling. Laughter swelled around him, making him feel happier than he had felt in months. The noisy fun reminded him of the festivals back in his village, when everybody laid aside their problems for a while and celebrated the joyful things in life.

But that was before the horrors began to rip his country apart, and wipe out all the people he'd known and loved.

"More cake, Enrique? How about some punch?"

He looked up, barely able to believe his eyes. Vanessa Campbell stood next to him holding a dish and a glass. She wore a long white cotton dress, delicately embroidered around her slim shoulders and hanging almost to her feet.

"You look like an angel," he said impulsively, then cringed in embarrassment.

What a ridiculous thing to say. Now her lip would curl in lofty contempt. She'd turn on her heel and walk away, convinced that he was a complete idiot.

But to his astonishment, none of those things happened. Instead, she settled in the chair next to him and put the cake and punch on a little table.

"I'm definitely not an angel, Enrique," she said dryly. "Come on. You have to eat some of this. I brought it all the way over here just for you, and almost got run down a couple of times by that cowboy in the blindfold."

Enrique took the dish of cake and began to eat obediently, though he was so dazed, he couldn't tell if the food in his mouth was chocolate or vanilla.

"Have you ever been to a birthday party like this?" Vanessa asked, leaning closer.

Again he felt bewildered. It was so unlike Vanessa to approach him and start a conversation without being prodded by her father. But she was looking at him with interest, even friendliness.

Enrique's shy, lonely heart was unable to resist. "A long time ago," he mumbled over the last of the cake. "Back in my village, we used to have parties like this. When my little sister—"

He stopped abruptly, his heart pounding.

Vanessa smiled. "Do you have a little sister, Enrique?"

"She died. Her name was Maria. She was...nine years old."

Vanessa touched his arm. "I'm sorry. What happened to her?"

"She was killed," he muttered. "Just before I left my country." Tears burned in his eyes. He brushed at them angrily, hating to have her see him like this.

But she was stroking his arm, touching his shoulder gently. "Do you think maybe you could tell me about it?" she whispered.

Enrique looked up at her, astounded. "You want to know about Maria?"

"Yes, I do," she said. "Let's go onto the veranda and get away from all this noise, and you can tell me the whole story."

"But I don't...I have never talked about it to anybody."

"Then it's probably about time you did, don't you think?"

He followed her, still feeling dazed, as she led the way through the busy kitchen and out onto the afternoon stillness of the big shady veranda, where she curled in the swing and indicated that he was to sit next to her.

Enrique settled himself timidly, overcome by her nearness and the way her white cotton skirt brushed his leg.

He was reluctant at first, but once he started talking, he couldn't stop himself. Vanessa listened while he told the whole story about his parents and their little school, the accusations against them and the terrifying day when soldiers came bursting out of the jungle with their guns blazing.

By the time he finished, both of them were crying.

"You must have been..." She paused, sniffling, and dug in her pocket for a couple of tissues, handing one to him. "You must have been so lonely and terrified, Enrique. How did you manage to keep yourself alive until you got to the seacoast?"

"A person does what he has to. Most of it is a blur by now."

"I feel so ashamed," she muttered at last. "After I listen to what you've been through, I realize I've never had a problem in my whole life that's even worth worrying about. I'm sorry for the way I've behaved, Enrique."

"But you have been very kind, Vanessa. I feel so much better now."

As he spoke, he realized in surprise that the words were true. Talking to her about those nightmares had somehow driven them away.

For the first time, he could think about Maria the way she used to be, laughing and pretty, instead of the horror of her lifeless small body in their yard after the massacre, lying next to his mother....

"Do you really?" she asked wistfully.

"Yes, very much. Thank you for listening."

She gave him a timid smile and patted his arm. "I know I'm not nearly as smart as you are," she said after an awkward silence. "But if there's anything I can ever help you with, like in your schoolwork, I mean, I'd be glad to try."

Enrique was fairly certain he'd died and gone to heaven, but he didn't care. If heaven was a place where Vanessa smiled and said kind things to him, then he fully intended to settle in and stay there forever.

WHEN JON AND CAMILLA left the ranch house and crossed the veranda, the two young people were still rocking together in the swing, laughing and talking with lively animation.

Jon looked over his shoulder at them in astonishment, then waved casually, took Camilla's arm and hustled her down the steps.

"There's definitely something magical about that swing," he whispered in her ear.

She smiled and pulled away, trying not to let herself be drawn close to him again. It was so dangerous to be with this man....

"Where did you say you're taking me?" she asked.

"Just over to the windmill. Tom's still busy helping Caroline, so we'll have to water the bulls."

She grimaced. "I'm not sure I want to be anywhere near those animals. They're so huge."

"Don't worry, sweetheart." He grinned at her, his eyes dancing. "I'll protect you."

Again she felt that treacherous flutter of warmth and looked away quickly as they walked toward a grove of cottonwood trees flaming with autumn colors. Jon led her down a path through the shady, rustling depths.

Beyond the trees a windmill rotated in the breeze, surrounded by a sturdy rail enclosure. The bulls jostled and bellowed around a row of big wooden troughs on the other side of the fence.

While Camilla watched from the base of the windmill, Jon climbed the fence and moved among the animals. He took the flowing water pipe from one of the troughs and transferred it to another, ducking aside hastily as a black Angus bull lowered his head, rumbled menacingly and took a few steps forward, glaring with fury.

When the pipe was in place, Jon sprinted for the fence and leaped it again, landing neatly beside her.

"I don't know how you can go in there," she said. "Aren't you afraid one of those bulls will kill you someday?"

"It's like anything else." He leaned against the fence with his arm draped over the top rail. "No real problem if you know what you're doing. I'm a lot more scared of some of the guys on those city streets than I am of any animal on my ranch."

Camilla thought of Zeke and Speedball, and Steven Campbell's handsome, rebellious face.

"I suppose you're right." She traced the sun-warmed wood of the fence with her fingertips. "Even rattlesnakes give you a fair warning before they strike."

"They sure do. And they won't hurt you unless they feel cornered. These bulls are the same way. Only human predators indulge in senseless violence."

Memories washed over her briefly, images of darkness and pain, the taste of blood and her own screams of terror. She bit her lip and looked down at the ground.

"Camilla?" he asked, sensitive as always to her change of mood. "What is it?"

She shook away the memories. "Nothing important. What time will we be leaving tomorrow to go home?"

"After Thanksgiving dinner. Why?" he asked, touching her shoulder. "Are you anxious to go home?"

She thought about the youth hostel and felt a brief tug of worry. This was the first weekend she'd missed in almost two years. She wondered how Marty was doing, if Chase was out of the hospital and staying sober, if there was any more news about what Zeke was planning....

"Not really," she said, forcing herself to smile at him. "Actually I love it here." She looked up at the rustling trees overhead, then across the pasture to the endless sweep of prairie beyond the ranch buildings. "There's something so peaceful about the landscape. It's very soothing."

He nodded in understanding and slipped an arm around her shoulders, standing next to her as they looked at the distant horizon.

"I know just what you mean. There's an ageless feeling about this place. I've often thought I wouldn't be surprised to see a family group of Blackfoot or Assiniboine come riding over the hill. They used to own this land, you know, and their spirit is still here.

When I was a boy, I used to believe I could actually see them when I was out on my horse.''

She gazed at the shimmering golden hills, enchanted by the image he described.

He tightened his arm around her shoulder. ''Your face is so expressive,'' he whispered. ''When you're thinking about something you like, your eyes light up and you look as young as Amy.''

''Jon...''

But it was too late. He was holding her now, his arms straining around her, and again she was lost.

She lifted her face for his kiss, feeling a delicious flood of excitement when his mouth closed over hers and his lips began to move softly.

I want you, she thought desperately. *I want you so much I can hardly bear it.*

He held her with one arm and continued to kiss her while his other hand stroked her body gently. He caressed her hips and waist, then reached under her shirt to cup her breasts.

She felt herself exploding with lust, a deep, hungry desire to be naked and close to this man, to feel his body moving inside hers.

''Camilla,'' he murmured against her mouth. ''I want you so much.''

''No,'' she whispered in panic, trying to draw away. ''Jon, you don't even know me.''

''But I want to.''

Birds trilled softly in the trees above them. Far away, they heard the melancholy cries of a flock of Canada geese heading south above the prairie. The sun dappled through the trees and the bulls bellowed and grunted as they crowded around the water trough.

Camilla found herself wandering in a misty world of dreams, a place of sweetness and joy where any kind of miracle seemed possible.

Really, there was nothing to keep her from giving herself to him. They could lie down on the grass in the shelter of these rustling trees and let their bodies unite. And the aching hunger she'd felt for twenty years would finally be appeased. All she had to do was yield.

"Jon," she said softly, reaching up to stroke his cheek, lost in passion. "Jon, I've always—"

"Daddy!" Ari shouted through the trees. "Daddy, where are you?"

They sprang apart hastily. Camilla tugged at her clothes and patted her hair, hurrying to compose herself while Ari trotted along the path and emerged into the clearing by the windmill.

"I didn't know where you were," he told his father reproachfully. "Why didn't you answer?"

Jon cast a rueful glance at Camilla. "I guess I didn't hear you, son. What's the problem?"

"It's time to open our presents now. Margaret said I should come and find you so Camilla could watch us."

"That was very thoughtful of Margaret," Jon said dryly. "Can you give us a few more minutes, Ari? I was just discussing something with Camilla."

"No!" the little boy shouted, clearly on the verge

of tears. "We've already been waiting a long time. I want to open my presents!"

"All right, dear," Camilla said, moving forward to take his hand. "Don't get upset. Your father and I will come with you."

She walked up the path with Ari while Jon followed behind them.

With every fiber of her being, Camilla was conscious of his nearness and of her own yearning. How could she have been so reckless, thinking even for a moment that the past didn't matter?

What a fool she was.

This time, she resolved with fierce determination, there'd be no more weakness. She intended to monitor her behavior rigidly from now on, watch herself every second until she was home again.

And after that, she wouldn't allow herself to be alone with this man ever again.

CHAPTER TWELVE

WHILE EVERYBODY ELSE was at the ranch, Steven spent Thanksgiving Day all alone, soothed by the emptiness of the house. Both his father and Margaret had expressed concern about leaving him alone on the holiday, but he didn't care a bit whether he ate turkey and cranberries for dinner. And he enjoyed the absence of his family.

Lately, they'd all been getting on his nerves. He couldn't stand the twins' lively chatter, their endless questions. And his father's thoughtful, measuring gaze was getting harder to endure all the time.

Especially in the light of what was going to happen next weekend....

He sprawled restlessly in a big leather armchair, watching the football games on television and trying to study. But it was impossible to concentrate on anything for very long.

When the sun began to drop below the mountains in a golden flare of splendor, he sat alone at the kitchen table to eat the meal Margaret had left for him. He must have microwaved it for too long because the stuffing tasted like cotton wool, and the turkey was as tough as cardboard.

Still, he ate all of his meal, taking a certain grim pleasure in the terrible food. It suited his mood.

After the meal, he drove into town to the area where Zeke had targeted the liquor store, and sat outside looking at the place.

Part of him recoiled at the thought of what they were about to do. Breaking the law and stealing all that money seemed so incredibly wild and dangerous. But along with his natural caution, all kinds of other impulses were at work inside Steven, as well, reckless urges that he couldn't seem to control.

He wanted the other guys to accept him and realize he genuinely cared about their plight, even though he'd grown up with so many privileges. He wasn't just another rich kid who didn't care. He believed that wealth should be distributed fairly. He knew his father would be horrified by Zeke's plan but it was time Jon realized that his son couldn't be pushed around and treated like a little kid anymore.

He grimaced and shifted his car into gear, moving down the street toward the place where he was supposed to wait on Saturday night. He parked in the shadowed area beneath the trees and glanced at his watch. It was only eight o'clock but already dark. In less than a week he'd be sitting here waiting for Zeke and Speedball to come rushing down the street with the cash.

As soon as they jumped into the car, he'd start up the engine and take off down that road and onto the freeway, heading for the farm. He couldn't afford to make any mistakes because there was almost certainly an alarm inside the liquor store. The police might even be after them before they hit the freeway.

Steven would have to drive fast and skillfully, and make sure he was familiar with every bit of the escape route.

He tensed, gripping the wheel as he pictured their wild ride.

At that moment, a patrol car drifted past and the officer behind the wheel glanced over at him casually. Steven's heart began to pound and sweat broke out on his forehead. He looked down hastily, pretending to rummage for something on the front seat as the other car's taillights vanished into the darkness.

When the patrolman was out of sight, Steven leaned back and expelled a long sigh of tension, his hands shaking. At last, feeling sick and miserable, he started the car and pulled onto the freeway.

What if the police officer had registered the make and color of his car, perhaps even made a note of the license plate?

He must have looked pretty suspicious, sitting there all alone and casing the street like a real amateur. Maybe the officer would remember this encounter next week after Zeke and Speedball knocked off the liquor store. He could look up the license-plate number in his notebook and track down the car.

Steven had a sudden desperate longing to be free of the whole thing, to be safe at home in his room, far away from all this danger.

But that wasn't possible any longer. He'd given his word to the guys. If he backed out now, they'd think he was just another spoiled rich kid, jerking them around for his own selfish pleasure.

All too well, Steven knew how it felt to have people break their word. His jaw tightened when he thought about his mother, who hadn't bothered to call this weekend even though it was a holiday.

Not that it was anything unusual for her, he told himself bitterly. Sometimes she even forgot to call at Christmastime.

He seemed to be the only one who was really troubled by her behavior. The other kids never gave it much thought, but Steven always waited, even though he knew it was hopeless. And he felt so hurt when she didn't bother to call or write for a long time, as if she was rejecting him all over again.

Steven didn't know what to do with his pain. It boiled inside him, seething and bubbling like a volcano. There were times when he felt as if he needed to explode somehow, blow into a thousand little pieces and destroy everything around him.

Let the police come looking for him, he thought grimly as he turned off the freeway and started down the road to the farm. What did it matter anyway?

Nothing mattered, except that he was committed to this plan and he intended to go through with it.

He parked his car and strode into the house, now ablaze with lights and activity. They were back, all of them. His father must already have taken Dr. Pritchard home, because she seemed to be absent. Everybody else was very much in evidence.

Steven, who was always sensitive to moods and

emotions, felt something different in the air tonight, a strange sense of heightened emotion. His father looked tense and unhappy, but the twins were more rambunctious than ever, yelling as they displayed their birthday gifts, demanding that somebody help them with a model engine they were trying to build.

Vanessa was utterly transformed. She sat curled in the leather armchair where Steven had spent most of the day, and seemed, amazingly, to be helping Enrique study for a psychology test.

Steven looked at her in astonishment, wondering what had happened to her. But she merely smiled and waved at him casually. "Hello, Steve."

"Hi, Van. How are you, Enrique?"

"I am fine, thanks." Enrique looked different, too. The miserable, haunted look he'd worn for so long was gone. He seemed as shy as ever, but happy and at peace.

"Enrique, pay attention," Vanessa said sternly. "I asked you to name three specific examples of behavior modification."

Enrique gave Steven a rueful smile, then turned back to answer her question.

"Hello, son." Jon passed though the room on the way to his office. "Did you have a nice weekend?"

"It was okay."

Margaret bustled in from the laundry room with an armful of sheets and towels. "Steven, did you have something to eat?" she asked.

"I ate Thanksgiving dinner in town," he said

curtly. "Thanks, Margaret," he added with forced politeness, feeling his father's eyes resting on him.

"Hey, Steve!" Ari shouted, waving a handful of colored building blocks. "Look what we got. It's a Lego set that makes little cars and stuff, and they have engines. Look, we get to build the engine! Can you help us? Daddy says he has to do some paperwork in his office, and we don't know how to install the pistons."

Steven cast a wistful glance at the bright clutter of toys.

It looked kind of neat, the little engine the twins were assembling for a race car they'd built. He felt a sudden longing to settle on the floor next to them and help with the engine. He wanted to forget all about getaway cars, dangerous bags of stolen money and police officers chasing him, and just be a part of his family again.

Amy glanced up at him with a shy, hopeful smile that tugged at his heart. Abruptly, before he could weaken and be drawn into their play, he turned on his heel and headed for the stairs.

"I don't have time," he said. "I need to finish a term paper."

He ran up the stairs two at a time, hurried into his room and closed the door gratefully behind him. But soon after he settled at his desk and got out some books, he heard a knock at the door.

"May I come in?" his father said as he opened the door.

Steven sighed and pulled the books closer, pretending to be reading. "Sure," he muttered. "Why not? Nobody ever gives me a chance to study."

"You've had all weekend to study," Jon said mildly, coming into the room and looking down at his son. "Are you okay, Steve?"

"I'm fine."

"We missed you at the ranch. All the cowboys asked about you."

Steven pictured the clean sweep of land, the horses and cattle grazing placidly under a warm prairie sun. "Was the weather nice?" he asked wistfully.

"It was beautiful. Everybody went riding on Saturday except for Vanessa. We brought the bulls in from the north pasture."

Steven looked up at his father. "Did Dr. Pritchard ride with you?"

Jon's face softened. "Yes, she did."

"She must have thought our horses were pretty ordinary after riding in the Olympics."

Jon sat down on the edge of the bed. "I don't think she ever rode in the Olympics. In fact, I doubt she's even been on a horse before this weekend."

Steven glanced at him, startled. "So where did all those stories come from?"

Jon shook his head. "The lady's a complete mystery to me. I don't know what to think."

"She's..." Steven paused, leafing idly through his book. "She seems really nice. I thought she'd be kind of a dragon, but she isn't."

"No," Jon said with a faraway look. "She's not

at all what I expected, either. You know, Steve, I keep thinking…''

''What?'' Steven asked.

''Nothing.'' His father got to his feet and dropped a hand onto Steven's shoulder. ''Are you sure you're all right? Nothing you want to talk about?''

''Nothing. I'm fine, Dad. I just need to get this work done.'' Steven gripped the book, conscious of his father's eyes resting on him.

Finally Jon turned and started toward the door. ''Okay, then, I'll see you tomorrow. Good night, Steve.''

Steven muttered something, then looked around in relief when he heard the door close.

At last he got up from his desk, flung himself onto the bed and lay staring moodily at the ceiling, tense with misery.

THE NEXT DAY was Tuesday, so Jon wasn't scheduled for Dr. Pritchard's creative-writing session. He delivered Enrique and the twins to their destinations on campus, went to a couple of his own classes in the morning and then strolled around enjoying the mellow autumn warmth of the campus. Mostly, though, he hoped to run into Camilla somewhere.

He found himself hungry to see her again, even though they'd been together all weekend. And the need wasn't only physical. He wanted to hear her voice, see her luminous smile, find out what she'd been doing and thinking since he last spoke with her. He wanted, quite simply, to walk and talk with her.

He was in love.

Jon sank onto a bench under a rustling golden cottonwood tree, picturing her face.

He wanted her walking at his side, in his life, sharing everything with him. He wanted to bring her into his home to spend time with his children.

And if he couldn't manage to win her love, he'd probably pass the rest of his life in a painful yearning for what might have been.

But what, exactly, was he going to do about these feelings? Camilla had made it painfully clear that she didn't want the relationship to go any further. A moment of physical closeness, a couple of stolen kisses prompted by the romance of a weekend in the country...that was all she was prepared to give.

She wouldn't even tell him who she was, or anything about her family or background. And, whoever she was, she'd certainly made it obvious that she wasn't the least bit interested in a weathered rancher with four kids and assorted other responsibilities.

But Jon Campbell wasn't a man who gave up easily on something he wanted. He lounged on the wooden bench for a while, frowning thoughtfully as he watched students passing by with their arms full of books.

It was time, he decided, to make a move. He needed to grasp hold of this quicksilver woman, demand her attention and make her talk to him. Somehow, he had to find a way to get close to her and penetrate all those mysteries she wanted to keep hidden. No man could endure this kind of frustration.

Finally he got up, grasped his load of books and went into the arts building, stopping first at the twins' classroom to see if perhaps Camilla had taken them for an afternoon session.

"Not today," Gwen told him, meeting him at the door with a laughing, yelling crowd of children. "We're just leaving for our field trip to the library. There's a puppet theater this afternoon."

Jon smiled down at his own children who stood in the midst of the excited group. Both Amy and Ari looked so happy that his heart warmed briefly.

"Thanks, Gwen," he said. "Maybe I'll try Dr. Pritchard in her office."

But the office door was locked, and the secretary shook her head when he inquired. "Dr. Pritchard's at a faculty meeting, Mr. Campbell. She said she'd be busy all day, and I should take messages."

Jon looked over at Camilla's closed door, then back at the secretary. Some of his fierce determination must have shown on his face, because she gave him a small, teasing smile.

"Honest truth, Mr. Campbell," she said. "The professor's not hiding in that room, so there's no point in battering the door down. I really wish I could help you, but I can't."

At last he nodded reluctantly, smiled back at her and left the building.

The October day was balmy and caressing, but for once its golden beauty was lost on Jon. He drove west toward home, drumming his fingers restlessly on the wheel as he struggled to decide what he should do about the feelings raging through him.

At the farmhouse he found Vanessa with a laundry basket, hanging damp bedsheets on a clothesline in the backyard. Jon paused by the gate and watched her in surprise.

"Hi, Daddy," she said casually through a mouthful of clothespins, her dark hair whipping in the breeze. "I'm helping Margaret. She's busy canning pickles this afternoon."

"Why aren't you in school?"

"We're hosting a visiting football team. No classes this afternoon."

"Didn't you want to stay at school and watch the game?"

She reached for another sheet. Jon moved over automatically and took the other end of the wet fabric, holding it clear of the grass while Vanessa fastened it in place.

"I wouldn't have minded watching the game," she said, taking another peg from her mouth, "but I wanted to come home and talk with Priscilla's dad."

"You mean George Rathburn, next door?"

Vanessa nodded. "Priscilla says he needs somebody to work in their stable for three or four hours a day, cleaning stalls and exercising horses. And he's willing to pay almost ten dollars an hour for somebody who's a good, reliable worker."

Jon's mind reeled. "You're... Van, are you telling me you plan to clean *stalls?*"

She looked at him in astonishment, then burst into laughter.

"Not *me,* Daddy. I thought this job would be totally perfect for Enrique. He wants to work and help pay his way, but it's so hard for him to have a job and try to look after himself in the city. This way, he could keep living here, work right next door and pay you a fair amount for his room and board. Mr. Rathburn already said he thinks it's's a good idea."

Jon considered, nodding thoughtfully. "He's right, it's a terrific idea, and just great for Enrique. Good for you, Van."

Her cheeks warmed at his praise and she began to rummage hastily in the laundry basket.

"Van," he said, moving closer, "what's happened? You seem so different."

She looked up, her eyes suddenly bright with tears. "Do you...do you love me, Daddy?" she asked in a trembling voice.

He stared at her, shocked by her words. "Sweetheart...of course I love you."

"You don't think..." She kicked nervously at a tuft of grass beneath the clothesline. "You don't think I'm too much like my mother? You're always saying how much I look like her."

His heart twisted with pain. "Oh, Van..."

"I was so afraid of turning out like her. I think there was a point when I made a decision to quit fighting and let it happen. I'd try to be as totally like her as I could, just so I wouldn't have to be afraid anymore. Like, it was inevitable, so I might as well go ahead and let it happen, you know?"

"I know, honey." Jon took her in his arms, holding her close. "And most of your unhappiness was my fault. It's not fair to evaluate people so lightly, and judge them by their looks. But I was hurt, too, with everything that happened to our family. I guess I was too wrapped up in my own problems to pay enough attention to the way you were feeling."

She burrowed against him, sniffling. "You mustn't blame yourself, Daddy," she murmured. "It's not your fault that she's such a selfish person. Besides, I was doing a pretty good job of being a prize witch. No wonder you all hated me."

"I never hated you, Van." He hugged her tighter, stroking her hair. "I just…worried about what the future might hold for you."

"Like when you first brought Enrique into the house and I…I looked at him and said he was… dirty," she choked, "and you were so disgusted with me."

Jon held her silently, remembering how appalled he'd been at his daughter's reaction.

"That wasn't what I was feeling at all," Vanessa whispered. "I was really sorry for him, and embarrassed because I had so much and he didn't have anything. But I couldn't say anything like that because it wouldn't have…"

She gulped and stopped talking, still nestled against his shirtfront. Jon stroked her hair tenderly, the way he'd often comforted her when she was a little girl.

"It wouldn't have been in character," he said. "Is that what you mean, honey? It wouldn't have suited this hard-boiled, selfish personality you were trying to project."

"Something like that," she muttered.

He looked over her head at a drift of cloud in the blue arch of prairie sky.

He should have been more sensitive and observant with this girl, more alert to her feelings....

"What made you change your mind?" he asked. "Why did you finally decide to come out of your shell and be yourself again?"

"Camilla talked to me."

He drew away, looking down at her questioningly.

Vanessa took a wad of tissue from the pocket of her jeans and wiped her eyes and cheeks, then gave him a misty smile. "Camilla told me people do all kinds of self-destructive things to deal with pain, and that there was a point in her past when she..."

"What?" Jon asked tensely when his daughter paused. "What did she say?"

Vanessa shook her head. "It's a secret. She told me some things about herself that I'm not supposed to tell anybody. We talked a long time on Sunday morning when everybody else was outside. I told her I was afraid of being like my mother, and she told me some things about what happened to her when she was growing up."

Jon gripped his daughter's arm. "What kind of things?"

"Daddy, I can't give away her secrets. I promised.

But she told me that the only way to heal the pain is to reach out. She says that's what she did. She decided that helping people would make her feel better, and it did."

"Helping people? How?"

"I don't know. She wouldn't tell me, but I suppose it's some kind of charity work. Anyway, I said I didn't know where to start reaching out, and Camilla said I could begin with my own home."

"Enrique?" Jon said.

Vanessa nodded. "I was afraid to talk to him at first," she murmured, looking down again. "Because I've been such a jerk. But he's...Enrique's really nice, Dad. And the terrible things that have happened to him and his family..." Tears filled her eyes and rolled down her cheeks again.

Jon lifted the girl's face and wiped her cheeks, then kissed her on the forehead.

"So you made friends with Enrique and now you've even found the perfect part-time job for him."

"It wasn't much. But from now on I'm going to try to help people as much as I can. I was thinking..." She blushed.

Jon looked down at her, bemused and enchanted by this beautiful daughter he'd never really met. "What were you thinking?"

"I'd like to put my name in for a volunteer job at the hospital. A candy striper, you know?"

He nodded, smiling.

"And I think I want to go into premed next year

and study to be a pediatrician. What do you think, Daddy?"

"I think," he said huskily, "that I'm so proud of you I can hardly stand it."

"Really, Daddy?"

"Absolutely." Jon gathered his daughter into his arms, holding her and patting her back while bed-sheets whipped on the clothesline and the autumn sun poured warmly onto their shoulders.

ON WEDNESDAY night Camilla went to the hostel early, preparing to serve a couple of long extra shifts to make up for her absence over the Thanksgiving weekend.

She took an armful of books and her ever-present folder of term papers to be marked, settled herself at the desk and got out a flask of coffee and some crack-ers, along with a couple of grocery sacks full of fruit. Then she went into the adjoining room to see what was happening.

Three boys in baggy jeans and ragged shirts sat along one wall, their feet splayed casually on the floor in filthy running shoes, their baseball caps turned backward on their heads. The boys seemed to be play-ing a game that involved tossing wads of paper at a bundle of clothes leaning against an opposite wall.

They exchanged guilty looks and stopped their game when Camilla entered the room.

"Hey, Queen," one of the boys called. "Long time no see."

"Hi, Zippy. Are you staying out of trouble?"

He shrugged and looked down at the floor, toying idly with the untied laces of his shoes.

Camilla regarded the boy for a moment. Then she knelt, put her hand under his chin and lifted his face, gazing directly into his eyes. He was about fifteen, with a thin, clever face and sensitive mouth. One of his eyes was swollen and surrounded by livid bruises.

"Oh, dear," she murmured, lightly touching the bruises. "When did this happen?"

He shrugged again, the expressive gesture that all the street kids used to express a variety of emotions. "A guy nailed me."

"Why?"

"He caught me stealing from his store."

"Why were you stealing, Zippy?"

"I was hungry. I went almost four days with nothin' to eat, and I got a little crazy."

"Zip got nailed for lifting a hunk of salami," one of the boys said. "He's the Baloney Bandit." The others rolled around on the floor, pounding their feet and shouting with laughter. Camilla ignored them.

"Why didn't you come here?" she asked. "We would have given you something to eat."

"Simon kicked me out for fighting. I was on the street all weekend."

"Oh, Zippy." Camilla sat back on her heels and looked at him sadly. "Have you eaten now?"

"Yeah. Simon let me come by for supper. My suspension's over now."

"Good. Come into the office later and you can

have some fruit if you're still hungry. I brought a lot of bananas and apples.''

Zippy's good eye brightened. He leaned closer to Camilla and jerked a thumb toward the ragged bundle on the opposite wall. ''You better check on that kid, Queen. She's in pretty bad shape.''

For the first time, Camilla realized that the bundle of clothes was another child. She crossed the room and knelt to peel away the ragged hood, revealing a mass of golden hair.

''Hi,'' she whispered to the child's bent head. ''What's your name?''

A face looked up at her, then vanished again. Camilla caught an impression of frightened brown eyes, pale skin and a drift of freckles across a dainty nose.

''Are you a girl?'' Camilla asked, taking a chance. With street kids, gender wasn't always easy to guess.

There was a brief, almost imperceptible nod.

''What's your name?''

The girl muttered something.

''Sorry?'' Camilla bent closer. ''I didn't hear you, dear.''

''Tracy.''

She settled next to the girl and put her arm around the thin shoulders.

''So what's happening, Tracy? I haven't seen you around before.''

More silence, but she could feel the child's body quivering in her embrace.

''How old are you?'' Camilla asked.

''I'm twelve,'' Tracy whispered.

Camilla felt a flood of weary hopelessness.

These kids were getting younger all the time. And the story was almost always the same...beatings, abuse, an intolerable home situation that forced children to run away and take their chance on the streets.

"Are you hungry?" Camilla asked.

Tracy nodded.

"Okay, come with me. I have some crackers and a lot of fruit in the office, and then maybe you can have a shower. You need to clean yourself up, dear, or you're going to get sick."

The little girl got to her feet obediently and faltered behind Camilla into the office. Marty was there, sitting with her feet propped up on the desk, strumming softly on Chase's guitar.

She looked clean and happy, wearing new jeans and sneakers and a bright red pullover, her dark hair freshly washed and braided.

"Marty!" Camilla said, bending to give her a hug. "I've been thinking about you all week. How's everything going?"

"Just great, Queenie. I'm working hard, even got a raise yesterday." Proudly, the girl displayed a pair of chapped, reddened hands. "And the boss's wife got me an interview for a job doing checkout at a grocery store. They pay really good."

"How's Chase?"

Marty's face clouded. "He gets out tomorrow. I'll know as soon as we're together if he's serious about staying sober." She looked down at the floor. "I'm scared, Queen," she muttered. "After a taste of the straight life, I don't want to go back to the streets."

While Camilla talked with the older girl, she opened one of the sacks and handed a couple of bananas to Tracy, who snatched them desperately, muttering her thanks.

"This is Tracy," Camilla told Marty. "She's new."

Marty wrinkled her nose and patted the child's arm. "You stink, honey," she said cheerfully. "You smell as bad as I did when I first came here. Come on," she added when Tracy finished eating her fruit. "I'll get you a towel and show you where the showers are. Maybe we can even find some clean clothes in the footlocker."

"Thanks, Marty." Camilla sat behind the desk again, giving the older girl a warning glance that meant "be gentle, she's really scared."

Marty nodded in understanding and led the ragged child from the room.

Camilla took out a pile of student assignments and began to work, but it was difficult to concentrate on essays. The image of that terrified little girl kept haunting her.

Many of these damaged waifs were far too small to survive on the streets, but unable to live in their own homes. And every one of them reminded her of herself as a child.

Camilla could hardly bear to imagine what might have happened to her if Jon Campbell hadn't encountered her on that desperate morning and given such gentle, loving assistance. If it had been anybody other than Jon who'd found her, Camilla's life might have taken a completely different turn.

She owed him everything....

"Poor kid," Marty said, coming back into the room. "She's in the shower now, and I found her some jeans and a sweater."

"Did she talk to you?"

"Not much. She's not ready to talk yet. Got some nasty bruises all over her body." Marty sank into the chair with a sigh of weariness and picked up the guitar again. "Somebody laid a whipping on her, that's for sure."

"Should I have a look at her? Does she need a doctor?"

Marty shook her head. "I think she needs a mommy and a daddy, but that's not going to happen. Don't worry, Queen. I'll stick around and keep an eye on her."

"Thanks, dear. So, you're enjoying your job?"

"I *love* it." Marty leaned forward with passionate intensity. "I love going to work every day and earning a paycheck, and buying the stuff I need without begging for it. God," she added moodily, falling back in the chair, "I hope Chase is going to stay clean."

"Marty..." Camilla hesitated, weighing her next words. "Your fate isn't in his hands, you know. If Chase doesn't want to go straight, you can still choose to keep your job and live in dignity."

"But I love him," the girl said simply. "If he can't

pull himself up, he's going to pull me down again. I know it.''

Camilla couldn't argue.

She was just beginning to understand the awesome power of love.

"Hey, Queen," Marty began, strumming idly on the guitar. "You remember how you were asking me about Zeke and Speedball?"

"Yes," Camilla said, suddenly tense. "Why? Have you heard something?"

"Sometimes they come to the pizza restaurant where I work. Zeke heard I was there, so he came back to the kitchen the other day and started bragging."

"About what?"

"This big score they're planning to make, using some rich kid as the patsy. The kid's driving his car for them. Howie's in on the deal, too."

"Howie!" Camilla exclaimed, horrified. "But that boy's a monster."

"That's for damn sure," Marty said grimly. "Howie's getting the guns for them."

"Oh, no," Camilla whispered, staring at the girl. "They're using *guns?*"

"Zeke says he doesn't want to take a chance on anything going wrong when he's got this perfect setup. He says he's going to be rich for the rest of his life."

Camilla leaned across the desk and gripped the girl's hand urgently. "Do you think you can find out when they're planning to do this? Please?"

"I'll try, Queen. I'll see if I can corner Zeke and get the little bastard talking again."

"Thanks." Camilla closed her eyes as Marty left the room. Suddenly the girl's words, "they're using a rich kid as a patsy," echoed in Camilla's head.

Oh God, Camilla thought. *They're going to use Steven Campbell.*

CHAPTER THIRTEEN

CAMILLA WOKE on Friday morning with a dark sense of foreboding. She stared at the ceiling, absently patting Madonna who had leaped onto the bed and was purring with noisy contentment.

"Oh, God," Camilla muttered when she remembered what Marty had told her. She frowned and moved restlessly under the covers, wondering what to do.

If Steven Campbell was really involved in a group planning an armed robbery, she had a definite responsibility to speak with his father about it.

But she'd given Steven her word. If she betrayed the boy now, he'd be more bitter than ever.

Madonna edged closer, meowing piteously.

"I know, I know. You're starving, but you'll just have to wait for a while. Maybe this is all a lot of childish bragging," Camilla told her cat, getting out of bed. "I can't believe Zeke would actually have the nerve to pull off something like this. And Speedball's far too lazy."

But she knew Zeke. Though cowardly, the boy was greedy and impulsive, capable of any wrongdoing that he thought he could get away with.

And if Howie was involved, the rumors were probably true.

"Tonight," she said firmly to Elton, who padded into the room and looked up at her with a hopeful expression. "Before I do anything about it, I'll see if I can track down a couple of those boys and force them to tell me what's going on."

She was relieved to have a plan, at least. But when she was in the steamy heat of her shower, other worries came back to haunt her.

She thought of Marty's fear that her love for Chase would drag her down again. Only somebody who'd actually lived that life could know what it meant to escape.

After all these years, Camilla still dreaded her own past with an obsessive, superstitious fear. She knew if she was going to recover her equilibrium, she had to restore a sense of peace and safety before she could tackle those personal demons. Being with Jon brought them crowding back too quickly.

So she had to terminate her research project with the twins. It was regrettable when the work was going so well, but she couldn't bear the emotional risks of being with them.

Finally, if the rumors about Zeke's plans turned out to be true, she'd find an opportunity to talk with Steven and try to convince him of the danger he was in. But there would be no more intimate, friendly contacts with Jon Campbell. Never again, she told herself firmly, rummaging in her closet for something to wear.

Her resolve lasted all morning, and continued when she entered her senior English class.

Jon sat quietly in his desk at the back of the room, watching her. His rugged face was so dear and familiar by now that Camilla felt she'd known him all her life.

In a way, she told herself, I guess I have. Almost all my life, anyway....

But there was also something new in his expression these days, a kind of hungry, meaningful intensity that told her he hadn't forgotten their embraces on the weekend. And he wasn't going to let her forget, either.

Her cheeks warmed slightly. She turned away and forced herself to address the class with her usual air of measured, pleasant calm.

"Good morning," she said. "I trust all of you are busy preparing for the midterm exam. We'll spend this morning going over a sample examination booklet so I can explain how I want the questions answered and how the marks will be distributed."

She handed out the booklets, smiling at Enrique as she passed his desk.

He looked utterly different from the ragged, weary boy who'd started this class more than a month ago. Now he was confident and relaxed, dressed like the other students in faded blue jeans and a cotton T-shirt.

Actually, Enrique Valeros was a very handsome young man, Camilla realized. He was also very intelligent and had a sweet personality. Vanessa Campbell might well be pleased one day that she'd chosen to befriend him.

She approached Jon's desk and gave him a booklet, painfully conscious of his hands on the desktop, his air of controlled power, his thoughtful gaze resting on her. He smiled up at her, blue eyes crinkling with warmth and humor.

She forced herself to look away. His smile faded to puzzled surprise as she moved toward the front of the room. While he continued to watch her, the rest of the students opened their booklets and prepared to take notes.

The hour droned on. When it was over, Camilla gathered her books and hurried from the room before Jon could approach her desk. Instead of going to her office, she escaped to the faculty lounge, poured herself a cup of coffee and settled in a corner to work until it was time to go downstairs and collect the twins for their daily session.

"I THOUGHT WE'D GO to my place today," she said as the children skipped along the hall beside her, chatting animatedly about their new motorized toys. "Is that all right?"

"Cool!" Ari shouted. "We get to see Madonna and Elton!"

Camilla's heart ached as she left the arts building with them. She watched while they raced ahead of her down the tree-lined walkway.

The thought of not seeing them anymore was so hard to bear. She loved these winsome, fascinating children with all her heart. Desperately, she tried to think of some way to maintain the relationship without endangering herself further. But her sorrow only made her see how deeply she was becoming entangled, and helped to strengthen her resolve.

This break had to be accomplished immediately, or she and the children were going to suffer even more when it finally happened.

"Let's not bother with the flash cards today," she said when they were inside her apartment. "Let's just play, all right? And later, there's something important I want to talk to you about."

Amy was already at the bookshelves, studying Camilla's collection of little porcelain cats. She was always very careful with the costly ornaments, lifting and handling them with gentle reverence.

"This is my very favorite," she told Camilla, holding out a dainty white Persian who licked his front paw with a look of detachment.

Camilla smiled. "He's beautiful, isn't he, dear? But I like the gray tabby, too."

"The one that looks like Elton?" Amy selected another figurine.

Ari lay on the floor and drummed his heels against the carpet. Elton curled nearby, purring contentedly. Madonna watched the little boy through bright slitted eyes and pounced on his feet whenever he moved.

"Look at her, Camilla," he said. "She's just like a lion in the jungle. See how she's watching me?"

"She has the very same hunting instincts," Camilla

said. "But she's playing with you now. She doesn't want to hurt you."

Amy left the row of china cats and came to lean against the chair, stroking Camilla's hair. "It's so pretty," she said. "Like real gold."

Camilla gathered the little girl into her lap and hugged her. "Your hair is pretty, too," she murmured, her heart breaking. "It's so nice and curly."

Seeing the attention his sister was getting, Ari came and stood close to them. "Daddy says you're a princess," he told Camilla gravely. "Are you?"

She swallowed hard. "No, dear, I'm not a princess. I'm a perfectly ordinary person." She lifted him, as well, and settled him on her other knee.

The children, always sensitive to her moods, both seemed to be aware of Camilla's tension. They cuddled against her and looked up at her quietly, their eyes wide and questioning.

"I have to tell you something," Camilla said to them. She paused, then steeled herself to continue. "It's about the tests we've been doing."

"Are we starting something different?" Ari bounced eagerly.

"No, we aren't. Actually, I've been thinking it's time for us to—"

The buzzer shrilled suddenly, announcing a visitor in the lobby.

Ari wriggled off Camilla's lap and ran to the intercom panel. He'd long since mastered the communication system but was still fascinated by it.

"Can I answer?" he asked.

"All right, dear."

The buzzer sounded again. Ari pulled down the switch. "Apartment 2E," he said in his deepest voice. "Who's down there?"

"It's Daddy. Let me in, Ari."

Camilla looked up in alarm while Ari signed off and activated the entry door.

But there was no escape. In a moment Jon's knock sounded, Ari opened the door and his father appeared in the foyer. Both children flung themselves on him with affectionate greetings, then returned to stand by Camilla's chair.

"No flash cards today?" Jon asked, addressing the children but gazing at Camilla with that same troubling look of grave intensity. She rubbed her arms nervously and busied herself straightening the collar on Amy's blouse.

"Not today. We're just playing," Ari said. "Camilla was going to tell us about something new we're doing next. Daddy, watch how Madonna jumps on my feet when I lie down on the floor."

Jon knelt and patted the two drowsy cats, then turned to Camilla again.

"If you're not in the middle of a test session, maybe we could all go out for ice cream. What do you think?"

"Oh, Jon, I'm not sure if..."

She searched frantically for an excuse, but the children were shouting with excitement and tugging at her.

"All right," she said in defeat. "Let me get my

sweater. Ari, you can put Madonna on the balcony if she wants to go out.''

Soon they were walking together down the leafy path, each of them holding a child's hand. The twins carried the conversation, peppering both adults with questions so the silence between them wasn't too obvious, though Jon frequently glanced at her with a quizzical expression.

They went into the cafeteria and selected their ice-cream cones, then strolled back outside. Jon and Camilla sat on a bench while the children raced up and down the path.

Jon leaned back, extending his legs comfortably, and squinted at the sky. ''Looks like a change in the weather,'' he commented. ''See how the clouds are massing all along the mountains? I wouldn't be surprised if we had a snowstorm before the weekend's over.''

Camilla shivered and hugged her arms. ''The summer's been so short,'' she murmured. ''I don't think I'm ready for winter.''

Melancholy washed over her in a suffocating wave. She could see her whole existence stretching ahead of her, like a bleak, cold winter that would never turn to spring.

But life was no different than it had always been, she told herself. Until this autumn, she'd been reasonably contented with her apartment and her two cats, her schedule of classes and research and the weekend work at the hostel.

Of course that was before Jon Campbell walked

back into her life and turned her world upside down....

"What's up?" he asked, glancing at her as he stretched his arm casually along the back of the bench, touching her shoulder.

She pulled away from him slightly. "What do you mean?"

"You seem a little sad today. Is there anything I can do to help?"

Camilla gripped her hands tightly in her lap and took a deep breath. "Jon..."

"Yes?"

"How's Steven? Have you been able to talk to him at all?"

"Not much. He's still pretty moody and withdrawn. Why do you ask?"

"I just wondered."

She'd do something about it right away, she promised herself again. As soon as possible she'd talk to the other kids and find out where Zeke was staying these days. Then she'd go and talk to the boy, see if she could get him to understand the utter foolishness of what he was planning.

Maybe it wasn't even true, Camilla thought with a faint surge of hope. Perhaps all Zeke's talk about this robbery was only more bravado....

"Camilla?" Jon said gently. "What is it?"

"Nothing." She shook herself and looked down at her hands. "I was about to have a talk with the twins when you arrived. I guess I'll have to tell them next week."

"Tell them what?"

"I'm terminating my research."

"Why?" he asked in surprise. "I thought everything was going really well."

"It's been fine. I just…"

"What?"

"I want to…sever this connection."

"Between you and me?" he asked, still watching her closely.

"Yes. I'm not comfortable with what's been happening, Jon."

"I see." He settled back, his face grim.

Camilla stole a glance at him, feeling wretched. "Please don't misunderstand," she ventured. "You're a…" She swallowed hard. "You're a very attractive man, and I'm fond of your children, too. I just don't feel ready to get involved in a relationship at this time. That's all."

"Oh, I understand well enough. If you don't want anything to do with me," he said quietly, "then I'll certainly leave you alone. But I wish you wouldn't abandon my kids."

"I'm not abandoning them!" she said, stung by the implication. "I'm merely…terminating a research project."

"Come on, Camilla. Both those kids love you, and you know it. How can you do this so easily?"

"Do what?"

"Allow people to fall in love with you, and then cut them adrift without a pang of regret," he said coldly.

Without a pang of regret.

She bit her lip, trying not to cry. If he knew the truth—how desperately unhappy she was right now, how afraid...

"You see," he continued in that same cold voice, "my children suffered in the past because of an unwise choice I made when I was young. I really hate to see it happening all over again."

He looked so miserable that her heart was torn with sympathy. She longed to nestle close to him, take him in her arms and kiss him, tell him how much she loved him.

If only life could be that simple.

"I'm sorry, Jon," she said. "But this is best for all of us, believe me."

He was silent a moment, his jaw clenched tightly. "Will you tell them?" He watched the children run and tumble through mounds of autumn leaves. "Or do you want me to do it?"

"I'll tell them. We'll have a final session next week, and I'll talk to them."

"Okay. That would be nice of you." He got up and turned to face her with an air of calm formality, though his face was still tense with pain. "Thanks for letting me know. I guess I'll see you in class on Monday, Dr. Pritchard."

"Jon..."

Camilla knew how fragile she was now. A word from him would break her resolve and send her flying into his arms, clutching him frantically. But he turned without speaking and started to walk away, his thick hair lifting and stirring in the cold north wind that blew across the campus.

"Goodbye, Jon," she whispered.

THAT EVENING Camilla arrived early at the hostel and started asking questions about Zeke and Speedball. But all she got in reply were blank looks and denials.

There was also no sign of Marty or little Tracy—the child who'd arrived earlier in the week. Finally Camilla left the young people in the shabby common room and settled in her office.

In the midst of her own problems, she'd also spent quite a lot of time worrying about Tracy. The girl was so young. Camilla wondered if she should have deviated from policy and reported Tracy to child-welfare authorities.

The hostel staff always tried to stay nonpartisan. They provided shelter without questions, and apart from a few basic rules, let the kids come and go as they pleased. The policy seemed rather heartless, but it was the only way they could maintain trust and credibility on the streets. If runaways knew they were at risk of being reported to the authorities, they'd stay away from the shelter and try to survive some other way, possibly putting themselves in danger.

Still, in a case like Tracy's, it was hard to think about a twelve-year-old child wandering around by herself.

Before long, Camilla realized she wasn't going to be able to concentrate on paperwork tonight. Troubling images kept haunting her...the faces of Jon

Campbell and his children, the memories of that long-ago motel room and of the sunny weekend she'd just spent at his ranch, the feeling of his embrace and his mouth moving on hers...

She pushed the papers aside, got up restlessly and went back to the other room where most of the kids were sleeping by now, curled on old mattresses under mounds of blankets.

Camilla moved quietly among them, bending to pull covers over thin shoulders, straightening a pillow here and there, carrying some extra blankets from the storeroom.

"Hey, Queen," a voice said softly as she was about to leave.

She paused, trying to see who was speaking.

"Yes?"

It was Zippy, lying still in the darkness as he watched her from the eye that wasn't bruised and swollen.

"Hello, Zippy." She moved toward him. "Is something the matter?"

He rolled his head on the pillow. "I can't sleep, that's all."

"And I can't work, so I'll stay here and talk to you for a while." She settled on the floor next to him, hugging her knees. "Are you still hungry?"

"Not anymore. Thanks for all that fruit."

"That's okay, Zippy."

"I got a real name, you know," he murmured shyly.

"What's your name?"

"It's Andrew. They used to call me Andy."

"Did you run away, Andy?"

"Yeah. I was living with my grandparents. My grandpa kept beating on me when he was drunk, so I took off."

She reached out and touched the boy's unkempt hair. "Is it hard for you?"

"It's pretty hard, living on the street. But I sure can't go back."

There was a brief silence while she sat near him. Rain began to fall outside, silvery and dense in the glow of the streetlamps, drumming against the windows and splattering onto the dirty sidewalk.

"I was real good in school before I ran away," the boy whispered. "I liked math and science."

"We can help you get back to school, Andy. Would you like that?"

"Maybe," he said cautiously. "If I could do it without going home."

"Why don't you stop by the office tomorrow and talk to me about it?"

"Are you coming in tomorrow?"

Camilla nodded. "I'll be in the office all afternoon."

"Okay. Hey, Queen..."

"Yes?"

"Do you have a family and all that? Do you have any kids?"

"No." Camilla stared into the darkness, listening to the soft breathing of sleeping children all around her and the distant rustle of the rain. "No, I'm just like you, Andy. I'm all alone."

SATURDAY AFTERNOON, Camilla parked downtown near the hostel and sprinted along wet streets, lowering her head into the wind, a woollen scarf drawn up around her collar. Inside the office she shook moisture from her coat, hung it on a shabby metal rack in the corner and wiped her briefcase, then settled at the desk to work throughout the afternoon.

Just after darkness began to fall, she was eating a sandwich at her desk when Marty came into the office. "Hey, Queen."

"Hi, Marty." Camilla put the sandwich down. "I'm so glad to see you."

"Nasty weather, isn't it? The kids will be piling in here tonight. You'd better make sure you've got lots of blankets."

Camilla looked at the girl thoughtfully. Marty's manner seemed deliberately casual but there was something different about her today, a tension and excitement that she couldn't hide.

"I have somebody who wants to say hello," Marty whispered, then went to the door and gestured.

A young man came in, looking shy and awkward. Camilla got up with a cry of delight and hurried around the desk to hug him.

"Chase!" she said. "How are you?"

He smiled ruefully and sprawled in one of the chairs. Marty sat next to him, reaching over to touch his arm protectively.

"Well, I'm a whole lot better than I was last week," he said. "Marty and I want to thank you for everything you did."

Camilla waved her hand in dismissal, examining him closely. Chase had a thin, sensitive face, a shock of ragged brown hair and an air of self-deprecating humor. His hands were beautiful, thin and finely shaped. They were also a lot steadier than they used to be, she realized.

"I'm staying sober, Queen," he assured her in response to her scrutiny. "I'm going to make it. *We're* going to make it," he corrected himself, glancing at Marty.

"I'm very glad to hear it," Camilla said quietly, returning to her own chair. "Have you started looking for a job?"

"The pizza restaurant hired me to wash dishes four hours a day," he said. "And I have a little gig at a club downtown, playing guitar in the evening. It's not much, but it's a lot better than being on the street."

"It's terrific," Camilla said warmly. "I'm so happy for you, Chase."

"I had my interview for the job at the grocery store," Marty said, her face shining. "I can start at the end of the month. Chase and I are renting a little basement suite a couple of blocks over. We moved in two days ago. And you know what, Queen? We even have our own bathroom," she added with touching pride.

Chase smiled at the girl tenderly and put his arm around her.

Camilla reminded herself that for each success story like this, there were a hundred disappointments. But on the rare occasions when a couple of them managed to beat the odds, it was worth every sacrifice she ever had to make.

"Marty," she said, "have you seen that little girl who came here the other night? I've been worried about her."

"Tracy? She's fine," Marty said cheerfully.

Camilla looked at the girl in confusion. "Where is she?"

"At her aunt's place in Banff."

"How did you find out about her aunt?" Camilla asked.

"We took Tracy home with us, bought her some clothes and got her talking yesterday," Marty said. "She told us about this nice Auntie Jean she hasn't seen for years. I called up there and the lady dropped everything and came right down to pick Tracy up."

"And you think they're going to be all right?"

"The aunt's a teacher, all on her own, says she'd love to have Tracy living with her. We're going up on the bus next weekend to visit," Chase said. "But we think it looks good."

"That's so nice of you," Camilla said warmly. "Both of you."

Chase smiled. "It's no trouble. She's a sweet little kid. And Marty told me..."

"I told Chase how you helped us," Marty said when he paused. "And how you said somebody helped *you* a long time ago. Chase and I decided we should pass it along. If everybody did that, there'd be no problems in the world, right?''

Camilla nodded through the tears that blurred her eyes. "You're exactly right," she murmured.

The two young people got up to leave. When they were almost at the door, Marty stopped and turned. "I almost forgot, Queen. You remember when we were talking about Zeke and Speedball?"

"Yes?" Camilla was suddenly tense.

"Well, Chase talked to Zeke yesterday."

"What did he say?" Camilla looked at the young musician.

"He was all hyped up," Chase said with a troubled frown. "He's got something planned, Queen."

"Is there any chance it's all just talk?"

"Not this time. I think he's going through with it. Howie got them a couple of guns and they're taking down a liquor store. Zeke says the bad weather's a big advantage for them, because they'll be able to get away easier. But he's crazy. Somebody's going to get hurt."

"The bad weather?" Camilla whispered in horror. "You mean, they're doing it right away?"

"Tonight," Chase said. "Zeke told me their hit was going down tonight, and by tomorrow he was going to be rich."

"Oh, God." She began gathering her papers, jamming them hastily into her briefcase.

"Queen?" Marty asked. "What's the matter?"

But Camilla was already shrugging into her coat. She ran out of the hostel and into the icy darkness where the rain was turning to wet snow.

CHAPTER FOURTEEN

SLEET POUNDED on the sides of the old stone barn and hissed around the open door, piling in slushy mounds at the end of the driveway. The sky was black, and the farmyard lay silent and deserted on this Saturday evening.

Steven sat in the darkened barn behind the wheel of his car, staring at the rough-hewn walls that enclosed him. He felt like a rat in a trap, even though the door stood open behind him and he was free to drive out of here whenever he wanted.

Too bad the sliding door wouldn't malfunction, he thought. The control button was on the outside of the building, so he'd be genuinely trapped until somebody came and found him. And by that time, it would be too late for what he was planning tonight.

Horrified at his own cowardice, he got out restlessly and prowled around his car, checking the tires, opening the hood to have another look at the engine. For at least the tenth time, he ventured toward the barn door, huddling in the chill, hands jammed deep into his pockets as he gazed at the storm.

With an anxious twinge of hope, he squinted up at the light in the sodden yard, trying to assess the strength of the wind and the amount of sleet that was falling. He wasn't scheduled to leave for half an hour yet. Maybe by then the weather would be so bad that he wouldn't be able to get into the city.

But that wasn't likely, and he knew it. Beyond their graveled farm approach, the roads into town were all hard-surfaced. And the storm, though windy and blustery, was hardly something you could call a blizzard. Steven had lived through enough real blizzards on their ranch in Saskatchewan to recognize that this was merely an autumn squall.

He stood in the entry to the barn and narrowed his eyes, watching the lights of the house as they glimmered through veils of sleet. Nobody was home but Margaret, and she was busy.

Eddie had left the day before, heading back to the oil rigs, and the housekeeper was drowning her sorrow in a great flurry of baking. At last count there'd been eleven pies lined up on the kitchen counter, along with masses of cookies and buns.

The rest of the family were in the city. Vanessa and Enrique were studying at the downtown library, while Jon had taken the twins to a musical at a local theater. They'd all planned to meet for dinner at a burger place.

Again Steven suffered that stab of wistfulness, the longing to be with his family again. He pictured them laughing together in the bright coziness of the restaurant, and felt lonely and excluded.

Even Vanessa, who'd always been so annoyingly

superior, was becoming a much nicer person these days. His father, though, seemed a lot quieter since their move to the city.

Something was making him unhappy....

This thought made Steven realize just how much he loved his father, which was absolutely the worst thing to be thinking right now.

Because after tonight, he and his father would never be able to have a warm relationship again. Jon Campbell would certainly despise his son for what he was about to do.

Steven's mouth settled into a desperate, stubborn line.

I don't care if he hates me. He doesn't understand anything. I'm doing this for the street kids, because somebody's got to start redistributing the wealth. And if my father can't understand that, I don't need him in my life.

Off in the distance a car came winding down the approach road to the farm, its headlights glistening faintly through the storm.

Steven ducked back inside the stone barn, rubbing his hands together to warm them. He ran another brief check on the car, then glanced at his watch again.

Time crawled by so slowly tonight that he felt like screaming.

He didn't want to leave too early and have to cruise the streets, since that would increase the opportunity for the car to be seen and remembered. But if he had to hang around the farm much longer, waiting and doing nothing, he was going to go out of his mind.

He took a cloth and rubbed the car furiously, polishing it to a high gloss. On a sudden inspiration he rushed outside, gathered a handful of mud from the damp ground and smeared it across the license plate, standing back to study the effect.

The mud obscured the letters and numbers quite effectively. He added another handful just to be sure, wiped and dried his chilled hands and checked his watch one more time.

Still fifteen minutes to go, but he couldn't wait any longer. He'd leave now and drive slowly, taking the long way around to his designated parking spot near the liquor store.

If he was this scared, how must Zeke and Speedball be feeling? They were the ones who actually had to do the holdup. But at least there'd be no guns or knives involved, and no possibility of anybody getting hurt. Zeke had given his word to Steven that they'd do the heist without weapons of any kind.

He took a deep breath, opened the car door and began to slide behind the wheel.

"Steven?" a voice called from the doorway. "Are you in here?"

He stiffened and looked around, then climbed reluctantly from the car, trying to figure out who was standing there. It appeared to be a woman, darkly silhouetted against the faint light in the yard, wearing a long hooded coat and boots.

The person stepped inside, dropping the hood and shaking moisture from it. Steven gaped in surprise when he saw a flash of blond hair and recognized Dr. Pritchard.

"Margaret told me you were over here working on your car," she said as casually as if they'd just met in the hallway at school. "It's a pretty terrible night, isn't it?"

"I...uh... If you came to see Dad and the kids," Steven floundered awkwardly, "they're all in town. They should be home soon."

"I know. Margaret told me." She shoved her hands deep in the pockets of her woollen coat and took a few steps toward him, "Actually, you're the one I wanted to talk with, Steven."

He had a wild urge to escape. It was so scary being alone with her in this isolated building.

"Sorry, I don't have much time right now," he muttered, reaching for the door handle. "I need to meet some friends in town. Would you like a ride back to the house, Dr. Pritchard?"

She was close to him now. In the glimmer of the outside light, he could see her halo of soft golden hair, the fine bone structure of her face.

"I don't think you should go to town tonight, Steven," she said.

He gripped the door handle and stared at her. "What are you talking about?"

"Did you know that Zeke and Speedball have

guns? Are you aware of what might happen if you get any more deeply involved in this?''

He swayed on his feet, thunderstruck, while his mind groped to understand.

Maybe this was a nightmare and he'd wake up soon and be safe in his bed.

''How do you—''

''Howie got a couple of guns for them. He's very good at that sort of thing. Steven, could we sit down, do you think?''

She gestured at a bench along the wall. He shook his head and refused to move, still gaping at the woman in stunned astonishment. Finally she sat down alone, gripping her hands tightly in her lap.

''They're vicious boys, and totally without conscience. But I don't believe you're like that,'' she said. ''I suppose they've told you all kinds of stories about how they'll use the money for a good purpose and how there'll be no violence under any circumstances. Is that right?''

He nodded, his mind still whirling crazily.

''But that's all it is, Steven. The things they're telling you are lies. These boys are using you. They want your car so they can get away safely, and apart from that, they don't care about you at all.''

''That's not true! They're my friends,'' he argued, afraid that he might be going to cry.

What she was saying was so awful, so unthinkable....

''No, Steven,'' she said sadly. ''There's no honor

among this particular pack of thieves. If they can find a way for you to take all the blame or lighten their own punishment, they'll betray you in an instant.''

"Who are you?" he whispered, moving closer so he could see her face in the dim light. "Are you… like, a cop or something?"

"Me?" She glanced up at him, startled. "I'm an English professor."

"I thought…" He looked away, kicking nervously at the floor. "I thought you might be working undercover or something, to know all this stuff. You must be spying on me."

"No, I'm not spying on you. But you're partly right. I do have some reliable sources of information, just like an undercover police officer."

There was a long silence while Steven tried to figure out his next move. She wasn't strong enough to hold him here. He could still get in his car and drive away to keep his appointment, and there'd be nothing she could do about it.

With sudden inspiration, he realized he could even close the door as he left, and lock Dr. Pritchard inside so she couldn't stop the robbery. She'd be trapped in the barn, helpless to get out.

But the damn woman knew everything. Somebody would find her eventually, and then she'd go to the cops and give all their names.

While he was debating, she watched him quietly, her beautiful face looking sad and drawn.

"Why are you involved in something like this, Steven?" she asked. "What's your motivation?"

He turned away, refusing to answer.

"You might as well tell me," she said. "I already know everything else. I just want to understand why you'd choose to involve yourself in an armed robbery when you have every privilege a boy could dream of."

"It's not an armed robbery!" he said. "There won't be any weapons involved. Zeke gave me his word, and I trust him."

"I see. But whether or not that's true, it will still be a holdup of a liquor store by two boys with long criminal records, and you'll be driving the getaway car for them. Why would you do that?"

"I want to share the money," he said after a long silence. "We're giving it to the street kids so they can buy food, coats and warm blankets before winter comes."

"You want to help the street kids?" she asked.

"Yeah, I do." He looked up bitterly. "Is that so hard to believe? There's a hell of a lot of homeless kids out there, you know, if you ever went downtown to see for yourself."

"I'm sure you're right. But there are other ways to help them."

"How? They don't need love and tenderness, or lectures about disease, or tickets to a free circus performance, if that's what you mean. They need *money*." He slammed the car door shut and leaned against it. "They need a share of what we've got, people like you and me. My damn family spends enough during one week to keep one of those kids in comfort for a year."

"So you've decided you're going to help redistribute the wealth."

"Yes." Steven set his jaw and stared at the wall above her head. "That's what I'm going to do."

"And you have no other motivation at all?" she asked gently.

"Like what?"

"Perhaps you're angry at the way life's treated you, and you need to lash out and hurt somebody in return. Maybe you want your mother to—"

"Don't talk about my mother!" he shouted. "What do you know about it, anyway? I'm sure *your* mother was a saint, and you grew up in luxury and never knew a minute of loneliness or worry about what was going to happen to you. That's why it's so disgusting when you go around judging other people!"

By now he was so furious that he didn't even know what he was saying. His hands shook and his whole body was gripped by chills, though anger burned hot and strong at the center of him. He wanted to choke the woman, kick her, do anything to shake her from the cold, superior way she analyzed and passed judgment on others.

Steven actually took a couple of steps toward her, his hands raised as if to strike her.

When she lifted her head and looked at him, he

stopped short in confusion. There were tears in her eyes. But the woman wasn't afraid of Steven. She seemed to be far away—scarcely aware of his presence.

She clenched her hands together and reached up with a tense motion to brush one of her coat sleeves across her eyes.

"My mother wasn't a saint," Dr. Pritchard said at last, her voice low and halting. "She was a drunk."

He paused in shock.

"My mother was a drunk," the professor said again. "She drank every night until she passed out. There was...usually a boyfriend with her, and I lived in fear of those men. When I was your age, my existence was squalid beyond anything you could possibly imagine."

"But I thought..." He watched her cautiously. "Everybody always says..."

"Nobody knows." She took a deep shuddering breath. "I've never talked about this, Steven. For the past twenty years I've kept it a secret."

There was something so wretched about her face and voice that Steven's fury ebbed rapidly. He sank onto the bench next to her, wondering if he should touch her hand or put his arm around her.

"We lived in a small prairie town," she said, "in a horrible old house trailer. It was so dirty and awful, I could never have any friends. Other parents didn't want their daughters associating with me, and I could hardly blame them. When I was a year or two younger than you," she went on in a flat, toneless voice, "one of my mother's boyfriends raped me while my mother was unconscious in the other room."

"My God," he whispered. It was so fantastic, listening to her. Could this possibly be his elegant, dignified professor? "What did you do?"

"I stabbed him in the chest with a hunting knife, took some of his money and ran away. I knew I could never go back so I wandered around for a couple of weeks, looking for a way to support myself and survive in the world."

"How old were you?"

"Seventeen."

"Where did you go?"

"I was heading for the city, planning to become a prostitute. I felt it didn't matter what I did, and I was terribly angry. I wanted to punish the whole world for what happened to me."

She looked up at him with a direct, searching gaze that made him flinch. But he couldn't turn away. Instead, he found himself being drawn into the depths of her eyes, mesmerized by the story she was telling.

"What happened?" he whispered.

"I was still on my way to the city, starving and sick because I hadn't eaten for several days. One morning I ran into a young man who was on a motorcycle trip. He'd camped in the ditch near me, sleeping in his little tent."

"Did he hurt you?"

She gave him another of those sad, faraway looks that tore at his heart. "No," she said. "He didn't hurt me. He saved my life."

"How?"

"By showing me more kindness than I'd ever known in my life. By making me understand that my life was valuable, after all, and it was possible to escape from the horrors and make something of myself. I can never, never repay that man."

"Did you stay with this guy?" he asked, his own desperate plans forgotten.

She shook her head. "Just for a couple of days. Then I had to leave him behind."

"Why?"

"Because I'd told him all about my past. I couldn't bear to be with anybody who knew the truth about me. And there was another reason. He'd been so kind to me. He deserved much more than I could give him."

"So you ran away again?"

"Yes, but this time it was different. I was determined to become the person he thought I could be. I went to the city and stayed at a homeless shelter for a while until I got a job and a room at an old boardinghouse. During the next few years, I worked my way through college, holding down two or three jobs at a time until I got my degree and was finally hired as a graduate assistant."

"And you've never told anybody this story?"

"Not a soul. After a while, because I never shared

any details about myself, people started making up stories. That suited me just fine. I let them do it, thinking myths would help to bury the reality of the past. But after a while the lies began to hurt even more. I really wished I could start over and be truthful.''

"But you couldn't?"

"I could never bear to tell anybody. I knew people would be repelled, and I guess I was afraid their reaction might bring all my memories back somehow."

Steven felt a hot flood of embarrassment. "I'm sorry, Dr. Pritchard. All that stuff I said, about how you couldn't know anything about street kids…it was way out of line."

She patted his knee. "Don't apologize, Steven. I know your heart's in the right place. But if you really want to help these kids, you've got to do it in constructive ways. You have to get yourself educated, find a job and give the street kids some of your time. What they need more than anything is people who care about them enough to get involved."

"That's how you know so much about Zeke and the other guys," he said with sudden understanding. "You work with those kids, don't you?"

"Every weekend. I've been doing volunteer work at one of the downtown hostels for more than five years."

Again he felt that deep wave of shame. "God, I'm sorry," he muttered. "I'm such a jerk."

She put her arm around him and hugged him. "You're certainly not a jerk. You're a fine, sensitive, compassionate young man. If I were your mother, Steven, I'd be so proud of you that I'd want everyone to know how terrific you are.''

Her words were unbelievably sweet to him, flowing over his wounded spirit like a healing balm. ''Really?'' he whispered.

''Really.''

They sat together in silence for a moment. Steven realized that the time for his appointment had come and gone, but he didn't care. Whatever was happening on that downtown street had nothing to do with him anymore. He felt free and unburdened, so relieved that he was almost light-headed.

''That guy,'' he said awkwardly, ''the one who... hurt you.''

''Yes?''

''Did you really kill him?''

She shook her head, staring at the glittering chrome on the car parked near them. ''I went back a few years ago, hoping to make some kind of peace with the past, but it wasn't possible. The trailer had vanished without a trace. I talked to a woman in the trailer park who didn't recognize me, and asked her about the people who used to live there.''

''Did she remember?''

''Oh, she remembered my mother, all right,'' the professor said grimly. ''And she certainly didn't have any kind words for her. Apparently, there was a house fire a couple of months after I left, while my mother and her boyfriend were sleeping, and both of them were killed. It was the same man. I probably didn't even hurt him all that badly, because the woman didn't say anything about a stabbing.''

"I can't believe you've never told anybody about all this. It must be so hard to…''

"To live a lie?'' she asked when Steven paused. "You're right, it's the hardest thing a person can do. And it's very self-destructive, because the hidden memories gain so much power they begin to destroy you. But still, I could never bring myself to talk about them. They were too horrible.''

"So why have you told me?''

"Because you're too fine a person to throw your life away,'' she said. "And because I still owe a debt of gratitude to that man who helped me.''

"So you think…'' He trailed off, searching for words. "You think by helping me, you'll be able to pay him back somehow?''

But she was no longer listening. She lifted her head and looked beyond him toward the door.

Steven followed her gaze and saw his father standing quietly in the shadows under the eaves of the barn, watching them.

She froze, terrified, wondering how much Jon had overheard. Did he know about the planned robbery, and Steven's involvement?

"Oh, no,'' he whispered in panic. "God, no.…''

His father took a few steps into the barn. The professor got to her feet and moved toward the open door, edging away from the man as if he might be about to strike her.

Steven also watched him in fear. Surprisingly, though, Jon didn't even seem to be aware of his son. Instead, he kept staring at the woman with such burning intensity that Steven found himself wondering why. Jon seemed to be gripped by some kind of powerful emotion, coupled with a strange look of wonder and joy.

"Callie?" he breathed, reaching for her. "Callie, is it you? Is it really you?"

She muttered something incoherent and began to run, stumbling out into the whirling snow. Jon started to follow her, then paused and glanced back at his son.

Steven could see the way his father struggled, looking first at the boy, then out at the darkness where the woman had vanished. Finally he drew himself together, shook his head and came into the barn.

Steven got to his feet and stood waiting for the anger and the terrible sadness he knew his father was going to express.

He stared down at his feet, aware that he deserved whatever happened. The silence between them lengthened, grew unbearable.

"How much did you hear?" he whispered at last, his voice husky.

"Pretty much all of it," Jon said calmly. "Look at me, son."

Steven forced himself to meet his father's eyes.

"I'm sorry, Dad," he murmured in anguish. "It was a crazy thing to get involved in. I know you're disappointed in me, and you probably hate me, but I want you to know I'm—"

"Oh, Steve." Jon's voice was rough with feeling. "Son, I love you so much."

Steven looked up in amazement. Despite the emotion, his father seemed utterly transformed. His strong tanned face was gentle with affection, the blue eyes clear and full of happiness.

"You love me?" Steven whispered. "You're not mad at me?"

For reply, Jon put out his arms. Steven moved into his father's embrace. For the first time in years the hard knot of pain loosened and fell away, replaced by soaring happiness and a sense of homecoming unlike anything he'd ever known.

THE STORM RAGED all night long, surprising everybody who'd dismissed it as a passing autumn squall. Snow began to fall more heavily after midnight, driven by a wind that howled across the prairie. Ice coated the power lines until they froze and snapped. And sculpted white drifts piled over highways and vacant lots.

When Camilla finally got home, weary after a two-hour struggle to keep her car on the road and see the fleeing patches of bare highway, her phone line seemed to be dead. She unplugged both telephones anyway.

She couldn't bear to hear Jon's voice tonight, and suffer through his attempts to be courteous now that he knew the truth.

Camilla groped her way through the darkened apartment, searching for candles. She put one in the kitchen and one on the bathroom counter where they created a mysterious secret world, like campfires in the center of a cave. Finally, feeling unbearably lonely, she took another candle and went looking for her cats.

Elton and Madonna huddled together in a warm ball in the middle of her bed. They stirred drowsily when she approached with the flickering candle.

"That looks...cozy," she said with a catch in her voice, gazing down at them. "I think I'll join you. But will it bother you if I cry all night?"

Madonna yawned, her whiskered face dim and secretive in the dusky glow of candlelight. Camilla fondled the silky ears, then hurried to bathe, take out her contact lenses and put on her nightgown.

She blew out the candles and climbed into bed, snuggling closer to the warmth of her cats. The apartment heating seemed to have failed, as well, so she was grateful to have Elton and Madonna. Under a mound of quilts with the cats piled on top of her, she lay and stared at the ceiling.

In truth, she felt like a turtle stripped of its protective hard shell. The revelation of her past had left her exposed, and so vulnerable that any ray of light or wayward breeze would probably destroy her.

On some level there was also relief, but she wasn't yet fully prepared to deal with that emotion. She only knew that the lies were all over. From now on she'd tell the truth to everybody, and let her life unfold from there.

If colleagues scorned her for having allowed the lies to go unchallenged all these years, or friends turned away...well, that was the price she'd have to pay.

At least she wouldn't have this dreadful weight on her soul all the time.

More important, she'd managed to prevent Steven Campbell from making a life-destroying mistake. Her debt to Jon was paid in full.

Camilla rolled over and buried her face in the pillow, trying not to cry.

But when she remembered his face as he stood there in the entry to the old barn, she was overcome with sadness. In the brief glimpse she'd had of him, he looked so shocked. Obviously Jon never had the slightest inkling that his English professor was actually the girl who'd shared that long-ago weekend.

What must he be thinking of her now? She writhed under the covers and moaned aloud.

All these weeks she'd played the role of dignified academic. She'd marked his essay without comment. She'd even visited his ranch and made friends with his family, recklessly believing he'd never find out the truth. But now he knew everything.

Misery welled up, too powerful to control. She gulped painfully, then began to sob.

Only now, in the depths of her humiliation, did she understand how deeply she loved Jon Campbell. For years he'd been part of a girlish fantasy, a scrap of memory, a daydream that warmed her barren life. But after meeting and talking with him again as an adult woman, drawing close to him and getting to know him, she loved him so much that her life without him would never be the same again.

She continued to cry, with deep, heartrending sobs that alarmed both cats. Sensing her need, they crept nearer and cuddled on the pillow by her face, purring raggedly.

Camilla hugged them and tried to stop crying, but the well of tears seemed bottomless. She wasn't just crying for herself. She was mourning all the wasted years, all the loneliness and sadness in the world, all the lost and wandering people who never found their mates....

At last, after what seemed like hours, she fell into a fitful, exhausted sleep. When she woke, she couldn't tell if it was day or night. The room was shrouded in a misty, surreal kind of half-light and none of the clocks worked properly.

She got up, pulled on a robe and stumbled to the window, where she was greeted by a remarkable sight.

Though the calendar said October, it might just as well have been January. Snow drifted over the roofs of cars and across the streets in an unbroken sea of white. Thin shrouds of fog wrapped around the buildings, making them look like spaceships drifting in a cold gray sky.

Most of the world was muffled in stillness, but a few people were out trying to shovel their cars from under drifts and make paths to their front doors. Camilla could see Mr. Armisch, the super, laboring below, clearing a patch of sidewalk in front of the building.

She looked around vaguely, wondering if the coffeepot would work or if the power was still off, and headed for the kitchen to find out.

Amazing, she thought bleakly, how these little things still mattered. Even though your heart was broken and your world had been torn apart....

A knock sounded at the door. Camilla looked up in alarm. Just one of the neighbors from down the hall, she told herself firmly. Somebody wondering if the power had been restored.

She pulled the robe more tightly around her and went to answer.

Jon Campbell stood in the entry, looking large and handsome, the shoulders of his leather jacket dusted with snow. He carried something soft and bulky in his arms, but Camilla was too shaken to register what it was.

She stared up at him, speechless.

"Mr. Armisch let me in," Jon said with a casual smile, entering the apartment and closing the door as he stamped snow from his boots, "after I bribed him by promising I'd come down later and help with the shoveling. I would have been here earlier, but they closed the roads at midnight and just opened them a couple of hours ago."

"How...how did you get here? All that snow..."

"I drove my Jeep. It's parked beyond the campus where the road crews have done some clearing. I had to hike the last few blocks, though."

"You didn't have to do this, Jon," she said. "Just because you know the truth, you didn't have to come all the way over here through these snowdrifts. I don't need..."

He ignored her, holding the paper-wrapped bundle in his arms as he examined her face. "Your eyes *are* gray," he said in triumph. "I knew they were."

"I've been wearing tinted contacts for years."

He grinned. "Well, this is much better. I prefer my gray-eyed girl."

His smile faded. He studied her so intently that she began to feel uncomfortable.

"Callie," he whispered at last, reaching out to touch her cheek. "Callie, sweetheart." His voice was husky, his eyes wet with tears.

She gazed at him in wonder, trying to understand what was happening.

"These are for you." He held out the package.

With shaking hands, she unwrapped the paper to reveal a massive bouquet of yellow roses, their amber hearts flashing like jewels in the depths of the glossy leaves.

"Jon…"

"Because you're a golden princess," he murmured, caressing her shoulders. "I wanted to pick you some wildflowers from the ditch, since that's what you really like, but all the ditches seem to be full of snow."

"Oh, Jon." She began to cry.

He took the flowers from her hands and placed them on the hall table. Then he gathered her hungrily into his arms, kissing her wet cheeks, her eyelids and neck and mouth.

"You don't know," he whispered, "how many times I've dreamed of this. I spent so long looking for you, then didn't recognize you when you were right in front of my eyes."

She nestled in his arms, hardly daring to believe what was happening.

She felt whole again, clean and unafraid, ready to face anything. And yet she felt strangely new and unformed, as if her life was just beginning and could take on any form. The squalor of her past, the lonely years of struggle, the weary burden of deceit were all gone. Now the joy and excitement made her tremble in his embrace.

"Callie," he murmured. "Are you all right, darling?"

"I'm fine." She leaned back in his arms to give

him a tearful, misty smile. "I'm just thinking how happy I am, and how terribly much I love you."

He kissed her again with seeking tenderness, then smiled at her. "You knew right from the start, didn't you? You recognized me the first time you saw me sitting in your class."

"That very instant."

"So why didn't you tell me?"

"I couldn't bear to have the past come back to life, or see you feeling sorry for me. At the time, my privacy seemed important," she told him. "Now, after everything that's happened, I'm amazed to find how little any of those things really mattered."

"And all that talk about not wanting anything to do with me," he asked, "and terminating the research project with the twins?"

"I was trying to protect myself. I was so afraid that if we spent any more time together, you were going to recognize me."

He hugged her again, whirling her around in boyish delight as he buried his face in the tousled fragrance of her hair.

"Jon," she murmured against his neck.

"Yes, sweetheart?"

"How's Steven?"

"He's fine. We had a long talk last night after you left, and I think I'm beginning to understand him better. You helped him so much, sweetheart. I owe you a huge debt of thanks."

"Then we're even."

"Like hell." His eyes danced. "I intend to spend a lifetime showing you just how grateful I am." He released her and bent to pat Elton, who rubbed against his legs, purring. "Hurry up and get dressed. Wear something really warm."

She looked at him in astonishment. "Why?"

"Because I promised the kids I'd bring you home with me for a sledding party this afternoon, and they're all waiting. I'll go down and shovel snow while you're getting ready."

Camilla smiled, her heart bursting with happiness. "You can't push me around like this," she teased. "I'm not seventeen anymore."

His face sobered briefly. "If I'd done a little more pushing when you were seventeen, we wouldn't have wasted twenty years of our lives. Come on, darling." He took her in his arms again. "We have to start making up for lost time."

The look on his face made her shiver with anticipation as a warm excitement whispered passionately through her body.

"Yes," she said softly, nestling contentedly into his embrace. "I think you're right. We can spend a lifetime, my darling, making up for lost time. And every second of it will be wonderful."

EVER HAD ONE OF THOSE DAYS?

TO DO:

- ☑ late for a super-important meeting, you discover the cat has eaten your panty hose

- ☑ while you work through lunch, the rest of the gang goes out and finds a one-hour, once-in-a-lifetime 90% off sale at the most exclusive store in town (Oh, and they also get to meet Brad Pitt who's filming a movie across the street.)

- ☑ you discover that your intimate phone call with your boyfriend was on company-wide intercom

- ☑ finally at the end of a long and exasperating day, you escape from it all with an entertaining, humorous and always romantic Love & Laughter book!

ENptY
LOVE & LAUGHTER™
EVERY DAY!

For a preview, turn the page....

Here's a sneak peek at
Colleen Collins's RIGHT CHEST, WRONG NAME
Available August 1997...

———————

"DARLING, YOU SOUND like a broken cappuccino machine," murmured Charlotte, her voice oozing disapproval.

Russell juggled the receiver while attempting to sit up in bed, but couldn't. If he *sounded* like a wreck over the phone, he could only imagine what he looked like.

"What mischief did you and your friends get into at your bachelor's party last night?" she continued.

She always had a way of saying "your friends" as though they were a pack of degenerate water buffalo. Professors deserved to be several notches higher up on the food chain, he thought. Which he would have said if his tongue wasn't swollen to twice its size.

"You didn't do anything...bad...did you, Russell?"

"Bad." His laugh came out like a bark.

"Bad as in *naughty*."

He heard her piqued tone but knew she'd never admit to such a base emotion as jealousy. Charlotte Maday, the woman he was to wed in a week, came from a family who bled blue. Exhibiting raw emotion was akin to burping in public.

After agreeing to be at her parents' pool party by noon, he untangled himself from the bedsheets and stumbled to the bathroom.

"Pool party," he reminded himself. He'd put on his best front and accommodate Char's request. Make the family rounds, exchange a few pleasantries, play the role she liked best: the erudite, cultured English literature professor. After fulfilling his duties, he'd slink into some lawn chair, preferably one in the shade, and nurse his hangover.

He tossed back a few aspirin and splashed cold water on his face. Grappling for a towel, he squinted into the mirror.

Then he jerked upright and stared at his reflection, blinking back drops of water. "Good Lord. They stuck me in a wind tunnel."

His hair, usually neatly parted and combed, sprang from his head as though he'd been struck by light-ning. "Can too many Wild Turkeys do that?" he asked himself as he stared with horror at his reflec-tion.

Something caught his eye in the mirror. Russell's gaze dropped.

"What in the—"

Over his pectoral muscle was a small patch of white. A bandage. Gingerly, he pulled it off.

Underneath, on his skin, was not a wound but a small, neat drawing.

"A red heart?" His voice cracked on the word *heart*. Something—a word?—was scrawled across it.

"Good Lord," he croaked. "I got a tattoo. A heart tattoo with the name Liz on it."

Not Charlotte. Liz!

HARLEQUIN SUPERROMANCE®

WOMEN WHO
Dare

*They take chances, make changes
and follow their hearts!*

WHERE THERE'S SMOKE... (#747)
by Laura Abbot

Jeri Monahan is a volunteer fire fighter in her Ozarks
hometown—and Dan Contini, former navy officer, is the
fire chief.

Jeri's a natural risk taker—and Dan's a protector, a man who
believes women shouldn't be exposed to physical danger.

Jeri's a woman who wants it all, including marriage—
and Dan's a divorced father embittered by his ex-wife's
unfaithfulness.

There are a lot of sparks between Jeri and Dan—and a lot of
problems, too. Can those sparks of attraction be fanned into a
steady fire?

Find out July 1997 wherever Harlequin books are sold.

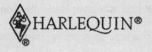

HARLEQUIN WOMEN KNOW ROMANCE WHEN THEY SEE IT.

And they'll see it on **ROMANCE CLASSICS**, the new 24-hour TV channel devoted to romantic movies and original programs like the special **Harlequin** Showcase of Authors & Stories.

The **Harlequin** Showcase of Authors & Stories introduces you to many of your favorite romance authors in a program developed exclusively for Harlequin readers.

Watch for the **Harlequin** Showcase of Authors & Stories series beginning in the summer of 1997.

If you're not receiving ROMANCE CLASSICS, call your local cable operator or satellite provider and ask for it today!

ROMANCE CLASSICS

Escape to the network of your dreams.

THE FRAUDULENT FIANCÉE

(#751)

by Muriel Jensen

*Amnesia. A marriage of convenience.
A secret baby.*

Find out what it's all about in August 1997.

Available wherever Harlequin books are sold.